NOWHERE is SOMEWHERE

MINDY HALL

BOOKSIDE Press

Copyright © 2023 by Mindy Hall

ISBN: 978-1-77883-174-4 (Paperback)

All rights reserved. No part of this publication may be reproduced, distributed, or transmitted in any form or by any means, including photocopying, recording, or other electronic or mechanical methods, without the prior written permission of the publisher, except in the case brief quotations embodied in critical reviews and other noncommercial uses permitted by copyright law.

The views expressed in this book are solely those of the author and do not necessarily reflect the views of the publisher, and the publisher hereby disclaims any responsibility for them.

BookSide Press
877-741-8091
www.booksidepress.com
orders@booksidepress.com

*Dedicated to the Rowe men:
Dean, the geologist, Dan, the landman
and Andy, for balance.*

Chapter 1

This was one time that best-laid plans had actually concluded the way they were intended. Louisa Daniel had been called upon to execute the will of her aunt in West Texas. How hard could that be? When John Utley, the attorney for her aunt, called and explained she was now needed to the do the job, he also told her that Aunt Atie had all her papers in order. Louisa would just need to go through them individually and sign an affidavit she had done so. How much effort could there be to going through a few papers? John Utley, and his father before him, had been Erato Ewell's attorney since the early thirties. They would be able to answer any questions she might have. Not only would she be helping her family, she also would have plenty of time to catch up on family doings. So, because Louisa would be going back to her roots, why not drag along another branch of the family tree to dig into the family dirt with her?

Louisa wasn't even sure Emily, her daughter, would entertain the idea of accompanying her the two thousand miles from California to Texas. Emily was one of those women who hadn't learned that nighttime is intended to rest and not as another work period for what she couldn't get done in the daytime. She might not allow herself to take the time to go with Mom visiting distant relatives. On the other hand, Emily hadn't seen said relatives since she attended Southern Methodist University in Dallas, and that was about twenty years ago. If she waited another twenty years to see these aunts and uncles, she'd be camped out in the local graveyard. Never hurts to ask.

"You want to go where?" Emily asked.

"It's not that I necessarily want to go; it's that Aunt Atie died, and I had promised your grandmother and Atie that I'd execute her will when the time came. It could be a week or more while I go through papers. But, I thought it might be fun for the two of us to have the time, and you could meet these relatives again. I know you're busy but thought I'd ask anyway. Want to come?"

"Possibly. The girls are off to swim camp, and David's busy installing that new computer system for that company. No one's going to miss me if I go. Byte might, but I bet if we get your Woofy over here, we could persuade David to dog sit."

That was easy. In one request Louisa garnered a comfortable traveling companion and a dog sitter for Woofy. Her caseload at Community Action Group was down, and her other social worker buddies would be able to pick up the slack. At Oakland International Airport, the wait in the security line had been relatively short, so she and Emily got through the scanners without any bells halting their progress. There were no loose ends left hanging to trip them up. What auspicious omens. What could possibly go wrong?

* * * *

Emily Kristich pressed her forehead hard against the window pane as the plane flew to Dallas from Oakland.

Louisa put her hand on her daughter's forearm and asked, "Are you okay, hon? Are you worried about David and the girls?"

Emily looked up, "What? Oh, sure, Mom. I'm fine. No, I'm not worried about them. Jojo and Lulie were so excited to get to swim camp, they won't even miss us. They've been looking forward to the summer just so they could go to camp. And, David is so busy with installing that new computer system, he won't miss me for awhile. In fact, it'll be easier for him when the girls and I aren't there. He won't have to keep anybody's schedule but his own. Byte might miss me; Woofy might miss you, but they'll be happy with David because he'll walk them every night. And, they'll have each other to play with.

"It just seems I've flown over so many cities, and I really don't know them. It would be nice if there were a way you could look out the window and learn their cultures and history through osmosis just by flying over them. Think how much you'd understand about the world that way."

"A veritable encyclopedia. But, where we're going probably isn't in the flight path of any plane. You'll have to learn about it the hard way. You'll have to meet the people and read some books. I bet they even have a little museum for the county."

Emily turned to her mother. "I like those little Texas towns. Those were nice people, those relatives of yours I met. And, the strangers, even they were nice."

"Hearts as big as the state of Texas, that would be those people. Doesn't matter if you're a relative or not; they're nice to everybody."

Louisa pushed her seat back and leaned against the headrest. "Those Texas people were always friendly. Shoot, Emily, it's not like the Bay Area where you have people coming out the wazoo. It can get lonely when your nearest neighbor is twenty miles away."

"Was Aunt Atie nice?" Emily asked thinking about the woman to whose funeral they were flying.

"Of the oldest sisters, she probably was the nicest, she and Aunt Terpie. Aunt Mel is super bitchwoman, and Aunts Clio and Callie, the twins, are just bitchwomen. My favorites were the younger sisters, Aunts Polly, Cora, and Lalie and, of course, Gramma Annie."

Louisa paused, and Emily braced herself because she knew her mother was going to launch into family trivia. She readied herself to enjoy the game that they had played repeatedly throughout her life.

"You do know how they got their names?"

"Yes, Mom. This is one of those stories we've heard a hundred times. It's good your Grandmother Briggs had nine daughters, so she could have a full set of Muses. How could she possibly know she would have nine daughters, so she could have nine Muses?"

"In those days, ranchers had to have large families. They just kept having kids. Guess if her first had been a boy, she could've done names of baseball players and had a team. Everybody worked the ranch, so the more people in your family, the more productive your ranch. She did it with daughters; those ladies are strong women."

"Your aunts' names are how I remembered the Muses for my Latin and Greek classes. I will now proceed to recite them.

"There is Calliope for epic poetry; there is Clio for history; there is Erato for lyric poetry; there is Euterpe for music; there is Melpomene for tragedy, Polyhymnia for sacred music, Terpsichore for dance, Thalia for comedy and Urania for astronomy. Of those Erato is now dead. How'd I do?"

"You get an 'A' on the exam."

Peanuts and soda pop in hand, Emily continued the conversation she and Louisa had been having, "So are you glad to go to your roots?"

"I think so. It's too bad Gramma Annie couldn't make the trip. I think she would have liked to see her sisters. Maybe when her hip heals, I can fly out with her another time. And, clearing out Aunt Atie's estate is going to be some work, but I think it will be nice to again see where I was born. A little melancholic nostalgia will be nice. The good ol' days and all that."

"I still can't believe your bitchy old aunt would make you executor She's got those thousand and one relatives out there."

"Those thousand and one relatives is the reason. She was bitchy, but she wasn't stupid. In fact, if she had been a modern day woman, she probably wouldn't be considered bitchy, just successful. How many other widows could take a forty-acre plot and expand it into a two thousand acre ranch? Especially in the thirties and forties. And, she was smart the way she did it."

"How do you mean?"

"She did it in checkerboards."

Emily gave her a questioning look, and Louisa proceeded to explain, "Whenever she got some profit from the sheep or cattle, and later, oil, she would buy a chunk of acreage on the corner of an acreage she already owned. That way, she saved the piece of land next to her acreage for when she could afford it. Very few people want land that is embedded in another person's ranch. So she bought land in squares that resembled a checkerboard and reserved the land she wanted for when she could afford it.

"She's the one who made sure her land was the first in that area that was drilled for oil. She had a time convincing someone to come and drill, but when she struck oil, she laughed about it all the way to the bank. She was a smart cookie.

"I think Gramma Annie was glad it is I who is executor and not she. In fact, I think Aunt Atie asked Gramma first, and she suggested me. Aren't mothers nice?" Louisa turned to Emily and asked with a wry smile.

Emily laughed at her chagrin and said, "Yes, mine is."

Alike more in stature than in looks, they were obviously mother and daughter. Louisa Daniel topped her daughter's height by a couple inches, but both had broad shoulders, square jaws and long limbed grace. Louisa had a leaner lipped smile than Emily, but years of being together had taught them similar mannerisms, so most people were unaware of their not replicating each other.

* * * *

When the plane landed at Dallas, the two women each slung purses on their shoulders, picked up their carry-ons and moved down the gangway. Out of deference to the rutted ranch roads they'd be traversing on Aunt Atie's spread, they had reserved a four-wheel drive which they picked up at the airport. Belongings stowed in the SUV, they located the airport hotel at which they stayed until they drove onto Interstate Twenty for West Texas early the next morning. Then it was off to the land where neighbors were more important than six-foot privacy fences. Emily and Louisa planned to drive to Big Spring and then cut south to Gold County where Aunt Lalie had promised they would leave the light on at Aunt Atie's ranch.

The dry, abrasive sand and wind of West Texas makes the green of East Texas and the central hill country look radiantly lush. One might think East Texas looks dry with its spotty green patches and sparse copses of trees, and it does. But, the further west one travels in Texas gives East Texas a new definition of botanical beauty. Sixteenth century Spaniards thought they had reached the land of gold when they trekked through the Texas desert. The sun braises the sand with a fiery heat until it glows a golden red haze. To intensify that golden haze, the heat rising from the ground sways in hula dance waves and adds a shimmer to the land that makes the ruddy golden mirage lustrous.

Imagine the elation of the explorers coming upon that land that shone its brilliant, hot gold and knowing their quest had been rewarded. Picture the demise of that elation as they tramped across hot, dusty, sandy nothing with no end in their sight, red dust that had no gold in it, only rusty iron mixed in the fine silt—silt that would blow into your mouth and nose so that every time your teeth connected all you could taste and feel was the fine grit of plain old red dirt. Little did those early explorers searching for the Seven Cities of Cibola realize the gold of Texas was not the land, but what was under it. And, that gold was black. Black and oily with a stinky sweet smell only a geologist could love.

There was white gold, too, in the form of soft fluffs of cotton yielded by sharp pointed bolls, sharp enough to tear fingers if handled incorrectly. And, sheep, their white fluffs of fur looking sunburned by the spray of fine gold silt that blew across the Texas desert. And, there was gold in the cattle herds that were able to freely roam the vast reaches of land that most people thought was useless. It took pioneers with nothing to lose to make Texas yield its golden treasures and make the land a state with everything to gain. They punched the land and coerced it to yield its oil and cotton and grazing for cattle and sheep. Knowing the wind and rain and dust could not be tamed, the pioneers made peace with the elements and cohabited with them. In turn, the elements molded the pioneers into a people who took nothing for granted and survived on their adaptability.

While Emily drove west, headed to the desert of America, Louisa looked at the land of her young life as they whizzed through the towns of Brock, Ranger, Putnam, Baird and Abilene. As they rolled westward, she watched tall, graceful, green elms give way to short, undernourished yellow-green mesquites, and yellow cat's claw vines yield space to gray tumbleweeds and spiky, yellowed grasses.

"Did you ever locate your friend?" Louisa's mellow voice edged out the music playing in the c.d. player.

Emily glanced quizzically at her mother. "My friend?"

"The one from college, your old roommate. I can't think of her name. Come on, Em. You roomed with her for two years. Honey hair, translucent skin. You know."

"Laurel."

"Right, Laurel Raines. Nice person. So, did you find her?"

"No, I've looked for that woman off and on for ten years. I called the university; I tried calling her mother; I've gone to the library looking at different cities' phone directories. I even tried those internet searches for missing people. It's like she's fallen off the face of the earth."

"Are you positive she moved to Dune County?"

There was a pause as Emily thought back to her life over twenty years ago to her first week of college in Dallas, Texas. Vacillating between excitement at finally being on her own and trepidation of the unknown, Emily had waited two days for her roommate to arrive. Their personalities were suitably different, but not diametrically so, so that they meshed well enough to enjoy rooming together the first two years of college. Very likely, they would have continued had Laurel not announced at the spring break of their sophomore year she was leaving school to go to Houston and find a career.

Emily exploded, "A *career*. You haven't finished undergraduate school. You don't even have one degree. How can you find a career?"

"You sound like my mother," Laurel had responded tartly. "I'm over eighteen. I can make this decision."

"But, you're too smart to not finish school."

"I have a wonderful opportunity I might never get again. I can always go back to school."

Famous last words: I can always go back to school. How easy it seems until time dons its wings and rockets by choking with life's other pursuits. As it was, Laurel's wonderful prospect was marriage; it wasn't a career climbing an opportunity ladder. And, the only reason to hearken off to Houston was for a wedding; the marriage played out in West Texas.

Emily met Dwayne Ed Twerms one time, and that was at Laurel's wedding. Laurel had called her three months after she left school requesting Emily to be her maid of honor at the nuptials which would be small enough to include only close family and a few friends.

"I'll name my child after you, if you come," cajoled Laurel.

"You know I'd come for you. I'll be glad to be there. Now tell me about Dwayne Ed."

"He's everything I've ever wanted. He's got those sturdy, rugged cowboy looks, is really polite and very attentive. He has a big ranch out west. You'll love him."

Emily didn't exactly love him when she met him. In fact, she didn't much like him. His good old country jokes were ribald to the point of being smut. He drank at breakfast, lunch and dinner, and, Emily suspected, in between meals. He hovered over Laurel, so Emily had very little chance to talk to the woman. But, Emily rationalized, he must be as excited about the wedding as Laurel was, and there really wasn't much time in any wedding chaos to have a long conversation.

"Hello," prompted Louisa bringing Emily out of her reverie.

"Sorry, Mom. I was thinking about Laurel."

"So I gathered."

"She sent pictures and letters after her twins were born—Dwayne Ed Jr. and Daphne Emily. Just like she promised, she named her baby after me. After about seven years, I never heard from her. I wrote, and some of the letters were returned with no forwarding address. I couldn't even locate her mother in New Jersey.

"I asked some sorority sisters, but they had heard from her less than I had. I can't find her. I tried again when you called me about coming out here, but her trail is certainly colder than when I tried five years ago. Maybe one of your relatives will know the family."

"Probably. Most likely, they're kin to her husband."

"I hadn't thought of that. You may be right. That means Laurel and I could be indirectly related. That's an interesting thought."

"Interesting," agreed Louisa.

Chapter 2

▼

At Sweetwater, Louisa took over the driving.

As they entered the Texas hill country, Louisa said, "Too bad it's not spring time. The bluebonnets are glorious, especially if they've had good rain the winter before."

"Prettier than California's?"

"By far. See that sky? Most nights just before sunset, the blue turns that violet color. That's what color those bluebonnets are. Looks like one continuous purple sea."

Making like a tourist and taking in the hills of Texas, Emily remarked, "I'm glad you're driving; you can probably find the ranch better than I could."

"I don't think there are but three main roads in the whole county."

"Yes, but they aren't the problem; it's those ranch roads that can be the neverending line to oblivion if you don't know them," countered Emily.

Louisa murmured assent as she climbed into the driver's seat, and after a few more hours of driving, she found Atie's ranch, Single Arrow, with little problem.

As Louisa stepped out of the Explorer to open the aluminum-slatted gate, Emily looked at the wooden sign over the gate, "That looks like a Cupid up there. Is that a Cupid, Mom?"

Louisa looked up. "Oh, I'd forgotten that. That's how Aunt Atie got the name, 'Single Arrow Ranch'. Her name, you see, is Erato, so she figured Eros who is the Greek form of Cupid would be the symbol for her ranch. We all know it only takes a single arrow from Cupid or Eros to fall in love. Pretty clever, don't you think?"

"I suppose so," said Emily doubtfully. "You need help with that gate?"

"Only if I step in the cattle guard and get stuck. Then you can yank me out. Stay there."

*   *   *   *

"Where have you been? You know it's past dinner. This isn't California where you people eat at 8:00. This is Texas where we eat on time. Do you hear, on time? Don't be late again. This is the only time I'm holding dinner for you. You hear?"

Louisa held out her arms to embrace the tall, dark haired string bean, but the woman walked past her. "Well, Aunt Mel, it's nice to see you after all these years, too. This is my daughter, Emily. You haven't seen her since she was a toddler. I don't think you saw her when she came out during college."

"She looks just like that no good husband of yours. I told you he was no good. I told your aunts he'd leave you, and, sure enough, I was right." Mel smiled triumphantly. "He left you just like I said he would. Him a Yankee and all. Your girl looked like him then, and she still does."

Aunt Mel came up to Emily's face and scrutinized her closely. Emily responded in kind by surveying the brown, wrinkled bark covering Mel's face.

"Shall I locate your glasses, Aunt Mel?" offered Louisa.

"Don't use 'em. They don't do any good. Threw 'em out. You hear?"

"I'm sorry we're here under such sad circumstances. Are your other sisters here?" asked Emily politely.

"Sad? Who's sad? You sad?"

"I, well sort of. Aunt Atie is dead; it's sad when loved ones die."

Not her. She was meaner'n any den of rattlers you could find. We got all those sisters. Losing one ain't gonna much matter, you hear?" Emily looked at her mother who rolled her eyes upward and said, "Come on, Em. Let's go see who's in the house. We'll get our stuff out later."

Mel followed them into the house. "Had to make a whole bunch of food for those vultures. Atie had no sooner'n gone off to Utley's, he's the undertaker, when the whole slew of 'em came over. Since I was here, they expected me to cook for 'em. It's like they've been here just feeding on Atie's food, just like a pack of buzzards. And, me cooking all that time."

"Why don't you go home? They can probably cook for themselves," Emily pointed out.

"And leave 'em here by themselves? Shoot, girl, I knew you were stupid. Soon as I saw you looked like your daddy, I just knew it. If I leave here, they'll steal everything. They'll take it. I've been waiting for your mama because she's the one who's s'pose to protect this place. These are *relatives*, girl. Everyone knows relatives steal when kinfolk die."

During her declamation on death and relatives, two smaller, softer versions of Mel came from the back of the house, pushed Mel aside and came over to Louisa.

"Louisa, we sure are happy to see you. It's been so many years." Each woman took a side of Louisa and gave her a hug in unison.

"This must be Emily. Welcome. We're sorry it couldn't be a happier time, but it sure is nice to have you here."

"Aunt Polly, Aunt Cora, I'm happy to see both of you," Louisa responded. She turned to Emily and said, "This is Aunt Polyhymnia and Aunt Terpsichore."

"But, don't you dare call us by those names. We never have figured out what our mother was doing naming us those names. Why, half the people we know can't even pronounce them. I believe no one but you, Louisa, remembers those are our names. Now, sugar," Aunt Polly said to Emily, "you call us Polly and Cora, never Polyhymnia and Terpsichore."

"I'm Emily."

"Of course, you are. You look just like your daddy. He was such a handsome man. We haven't seen you in years," Cora said as she and Polly took each of their arms and led them back to the kitchen. "Come and see who all is here."

They were led into a yellow, rectangular kitchen with a high ceiling. A wood-burning cook stove took up the east wall, two portly refrigerators occupied the west wall and a yellowed porcelain sink set in metal kitchen cabinets ran along the north wall. In the center of the room stood a dining table covered with a gold, floral oilcloth and surrounded by ten dark oak kitchen chairs.

"Do you recognize everybody, Louisa?" asked Polly as they went into the kitchen.

"Of course she doesn't," snapped Mel. "She never comes out to see us. How could she be bothered knowing who we are. Annie should be here, not them. Can't even come and see her own sisters. I bet she doesn't really have a broken hip. She's just too good for us. Always has been; that's why she left us and went to California. She and that no-good husband of hers. Hadn't hardly walked down the aisle, and they were on their way to California—just like Okies." Venom drenched the word, Okies.

"Let's see. Uncle Sam, Aunt Terp, Uncle Pete, Uncle Luke, Aunt Lalie. Where are Aunt Clio and Aunt Callie?"

"You know," said Aunt Lalie quietly, "they were busy with other arrangements."

"They didn't want to come. They know what you people from California are like. They know you'd have weird talk. Other arrangements, my foot," interrupted Mel.

Lalie's face reddened as she looked askance at Emily and Louisa.

"It's all right," Louisa went to Lalie and hugged her standing by the sink where she had been doing dishes. "We understand."

"I'm sorry, Louisa," she said gently.

"No problem and no offense taken. It's okay."

Louisa changed the subject, "And, all the kids? Are they around?"

"Kids? I can barely find enough in Atie's cupboards for this crew. What do you mean kids? Then they bring their kids. Atie wouldn't stand for all her stuff to be eaten. Just like locusts. That's what they are," Mel continued her tirade.

"So when's Atie going to use all this stuff?" asked Uncle Pete, eyes intent on stubbing out his cigarette in the remains of the food on his plate.

"See? That's just what I mean. None of 'em care a damn about Atie and her stuff. They're here just using it like it was theirs," Mel continued.

"But, you're here," interjected Uncle Luke.

"Luke Moss, that's right. I'm here. I'm protecting Atie's stuff until Louisa showed up. Atie would just die if she knew what was happening at her house."

"She is dead." A few of the table's inhabitants looked up at Lalie and smiled as she pointed out the obvious. Uncle Pete heaved his height out of his seat and said, "Damn right, and we got a funeral to go to tomorrow. Seeing as Atie had a lotta land and oil, Brother Johnson is going to preach a storm. He thinks there's a tithe on words—the more he preaches, the more money the family will dump in his church. Come on, Polly. Let's go."

As they went, everybody else took that as the wind down and followed Polly and Luke out of the kitchen, except Mel, of course, whose self-appointed duty was to act as steward for the dead Atie's belongings.

"Aunt Mel," Emily requested, "I'd like to call my husband. If you'll show me the phone, I'll use my calling card. Then I'll come out to help you in the kitchen."

"No, Emily, I'll help in the kitchen. You call David and find out how the girls are. Then we'll go to bed," replied Louisa.

"You promise you're gonna use that card?" asked the waspish Mel. "This is Atie's stuff, and you can't be wasting her money. Louisa, you tell your girl she can't be wasting Atie's money.

"Whyn't you have one of those phones you carry around? You're from California. All those people out there have those things. You're all gonna die of 'em; they're gonna eat away your brain." She cackled gleefully. "So where's yours?"

"I didn't bring it. I figured it'd be cheaper to use my calling card because Texas isn't in my calling area. I don't want to have to pay roaming charges."

Mel took a kerosene lamp off a shelf above the cook stove, lit it, took them into the entryway and pointed to a recess in the wall where a black dial phone sat. "There. There it is. Make it short." She set the lamp down on a table next to the phone and said, "We're running low on kerosene, so don't talk all night. There's barely enough in the lamps upstairs, so you might have to take this one when you go to bed."

The shiny gleam of the heavy, black phone had been grazed by small cracks in the finish over the last sixty years. The numbers that had once been prominent under the finger holes of the dial were wearing away, so they were barely discernable. Emily looked askance at the phone and asked, "Is it capable of making long distance phone calls?"

"'Course, it can," blustered Mel. "You think that only those modern phones can do anything. You'll never find a phone as good as that. Never breaks like those new contraptions. They break if they're dropped once. Atie never stood for that. She made her stuff last, so she wouldn't go spending money on junk. Now, that girl knew how to make money. And save, she knew how to save." She glared at Emily.

Emily picked up the receiver and said, "I don't need to worry about a workout. I can come and do weights with this thing. It must weigh ten pounds."

Listening to the conversation as she did the dishes, Louisa smiled. Mel muttered, "Ingrate."

* * * *

Emily completed her call with enough time to help Louisa dry the last of the dishes.

"Everything okay?"

"No problems. I even got to talk to David's live voice because he was home tonight. Said he had just enough energy to walk Byte and Woofy, and then they were going to sleep. The girls haven't called home since they arrived at camp, so all must be well for them."

Louisa laid the dishrag over the clean dishes and asked, "Mel, where should we sleep?"

"Go get your stuff and bring it upstairs. C'mere, I'll show you where to go," she said as though she were talking to misbehaving children. Emily and Louisa followed their aunt up wooden backstairs leading from the kitchen to the second floor. "There," Atie pointed to two side-by-side bedrooms off the room sized landing. "There's a bath at the end of the hall. You can use it after I get finished in the morning. I'm the first one up, so don't you come in until you hear me go downstairs. I got Atie's room, so you can decide for yourself which of those two rooms you want. Don't make me no never mind," she shot back as she stomped down the stairs.

As Louisa and Emily surveyed the large squares of rooms, Louisa asked, "Do you want a separate room, or shall we share? This one has two beds, the other has only one."

"Might as well share. At least, that way we each have a friendly face close by. With Mel, there might be safety in numbers."

There was no carpet on the wooden floor; there wasn't much varnish on the floor either. Purple wallpaper had faded to lavender, so the cabbage roses that once trailed up the wall were blurred into looking like water stains. Chenille bedspreads, their patterns made indistinct through years of use, covered the beds. Venetian blinds covered the three narrow windows.

Louisa reassured her daughter as she pulled the spread down to reveal patched, rough cotton sheets, "She's not so bad. She blows and goes, but she's harmless. No one listens to her anyway; she's got nothing worthwhile to say."

"She's a mean one," said Emily as she opened the armoire to put away clothes. "You say the others are just as mean?"

"Just the two older ones."

"Makes you really look forward to the next few days, doesn't it? If I had known I had her to look forward to, I might've changed my mind about coming. She doesn't add a whole lot to the vacation atmosphere."

"Then I'm happy you didn't know about her because I get to spend the time with you."

Emily smiled at her mother as she put her clothes in the armoire.

Chapter 3

A good funeral could be almost as good as a good college football game—lots of fellowship, entertainment and food. Anyone who had any dealings, remote or otherwise, with Erato Ewell would be part of the three counties' worth of spectators at her funeral the next day.

Henry Wade wouldn't be there, though. Even if he had known Atie Ewell just a little bit, he wouldn't be one of the spectators at her final farewell. He wouldn't be there to exchange stories about eccentric Atie Ewell. He wouldn't be around to witness the final rite of dying. He was too busy dying himself.

Ever since he returned from the veteran's hospital, this former all-state, high school football player had embarked on a lethargic, torturous death. His instrument of demise was alcohol. If he could force feed himself with enough liquor, he could forget his participation in the Gulf War, and he could forget the high hopes he and his family held for him before he left San Domingo after high school.

When Veterans' Administration decided they could babysit him no longer and discharged him into the unpredictability of life, he had attempted to define that uncertainty and become productively stable. But there were too many nightmares and flashbacks lodged in his unconscious. No matter how gloriously war was whitewashed to be, war was war. He never should have volunteered to fight. Every time he'd close the trunk of remembered horrors, one would seep through to his consciousness and cause him to forget his present; he could only remember his past, and he could never build a future. He should have used the scholarship he was offered after high school, but it was easier to think he would be of more help to his family in the military. His mother needed the money he could send her. There's never a guarantee a good football player is going to make it to the pros. From high school football to the pros is a grand quantitative leap, like winning the lottery itself. It had proven to be a good thing, the military. He got his college degree and was headed up the officer ranks. If only he hadn't volunteered to fight in the Gulf. Then, the decision had been so clear; now, it was as muddy as his life had become. No matter what you hear, fighting on the ground can kill you in more ways than bullets.

It wasn't that it was easier to go back home. People remembered him when he was psychologically whole, and they weren't comfortable enough with his fragmented personality to look him in the eyes when they passed him on his hometown streets. That's if they even recognized him minus fifty pounds of bulk, multiple lines carved into his face, and confident stride replaced by listless shuffling.

It wasn't easier to go back home, but it was the path of least resistance. His mother's will had left him a shack in the shantytown of San Domingo, and there was a bar in the part of San Domingo that resides in Gold County. It was just as easy to let his life ebb away in the bar as in the shack, and since they were close enough to each other, San Domingo served his purpose.

So, the night before Atie's funeral, he sat soaking up alcohol in the bar until the proprietor, as he did almost every night, escorted him to the sidewalk fronting his establishment. There Henry Wade could collapse into the gutter until someone kicked him back onto the curb, or he could find his way home.

Chapter 4

There are three kinds of law of the land. There's ordered, procedural law spelled out in volumes of tomes on lawyers' bookshelves. There's vigilante law carried out in spur of the moment interpretations. And, there's biblical law pummeled out of pulpits with thermal intensity. In the old west, vigilante law and biblical law went hand in hand. What order cowboy justice couldn't keep, biblical law could and vice versa. Each could be as torturous as the other.

Brother Johnson was making sure biblical law was doing its work at Sister Erato's funeral. He couldn't let the opportunity pass to remind three counties' worth of denizens of the compensation of sin. God would forgive him for stinting his sermon, but the attendees would not because they might not get their full value of entertainment for a day given over to a funeral.

He started his invective out with a soft pace, slowly, tediously skittering from *Bible* passage to *Bible* passage until his baritone reverberated in a low growl. The low growl became a clear toned shout as he increased the crescendo of his delivery punctuated with graphic descriptions of the wages of sin. Just as the listener squirmed with the pain he knew Atie was surely enduring and flapped his fan from Utley's Funeral Home at double time, Brother Johnson paused and intoned a generous, "But—brothers and sisters, Sister Erato Ewell was a woman who knew the ills of sin and armed herself with the good book so she would not fall into the path of," and here he sang out on a clear note, "eeeevil."

A collective audible sigh of relief from his listeners was as rewarding for Brother Johnson as a standing ovation with several encores was for the actors of a play. It also, unfortunately, gave him renewed energy to carry out his sermon another half hour.

A few hymns, including two uncut renditions of "Amazing Grace", wrapped up the funeral.

Emily sat quietly next to her mother for a few moments.

"You coming, Em?" asked Louisa as she got up to join the throng moving up to Atie's open casket.

"Yes, I'm just so worn out. That is the longest funeral oration I have ever heard. I think I need a nap."

"No can do. We've only just begun. You now have six hundred relatives to meet after we say goodbye to Aunt Atie," Louisa said as she put her hand out to help Emily out of the pew.

Utley, the undertaker, had done a creditable job on Aunt Atie. Not having seen her great-aunt for many years, Emily was able to recognize her from family pictures. Not too much make up, hair not restyled into something she had never worn, Aunt Atie looked suitably preserved.

"Just like the wax museum," muttered Emily to her mother. "In this heat, it'll be amazing if she doesn't look like a candlestick at the end of a long meal."

"There's been an Utley as long as I can remember. That funeral home has seen more dead bodies than you or I have seen live bodies, I bet. If they can't fix her, so she doesn't melt, I don't know who can. Now, come on, it's reunion time."

* * * *

Louisa hadn't been kidding when she said six hundred relatives. When they arrived at the Single Arrow, most of the six hundred were milling around long banquet tables pregnant with bowls, dishes and trays of the best food from every kitchen in the tricounty area. Most of the attendees had divulged themselves of tears and sorrow and had come to enjoy the revelry of a good party. Only the black, navy and purple garb still worn by the partiers indicated they had been to a funeral.

Children tagged other children and screamed at their cousins and friends in the trees. Some of the older people stood near the few pecan trees at the verge of the gathering comforting each other, but most of the people milled around greeting one another. Louisa and Emily were part of the milling group when they came into the vicinity of Ty Barnes and his wife, Magnolia May, the only celebrity produced by Gold County, Texas. Ty had such sharp and craggy features that he would only be described as ruggedly handsome. She was one of the clique of North Texas State University beauties who had joined the ranks of finalists in the Miss America pageants. And, a beauty she was—blonde hair, blue eyes and a smile as inviting as Andrew Jackson's inauguration. Standing beside her tall ash brown haired husband and holding a two-year-old blonde girl created a picture of the ideal American family.

She accosted Emily and Louisa with a drawled out, "Well, hello, you must be the California Briggs. We are so happy to have you. I have been dying to meet y'all."

Before either Louisa or Emily could return the greeting, Magnolia May said, "This is my husband, Ty, and my name is Maggie. My boys will be here as soon as Ty finds them. I want them to meet y'all."

On cue, six boys, all dressed in western style shirts, bolo ties and cowboy hats lined up in chronological order. Mama started in, "Now, this is our oldest son, Dallas."

Dallas turned to Emily and Louisa and tipped his hat with a polite, "Ma'am."

"This is Houston." Houston tipped his hat in the same polite gesture.

"This is Waco." Waco did likewise as did sons Austin, Galveston and Worth.

"And this, this is our baby…" started Maggie.

"No, wait. Let me guess," interrupted Emily. "I bet I know the name."

Maggie was surprised, but she stopped the introduction as she and Ty stared at her.

"How about…" Emily started as she looked around. There was a small crowd developing around the group.

She began again, "How about—Odessa?"

Maggie laughed and said, "How did y'all know that? Someone told you, didn't they?"

When Emily shook her head, Maggie's laughter tinkled in the air as she said, "No, truly, someone had to tell you."

Emily said, "There aren't many Texas towns that could be used for a girl's name. It almost had to be that—that or Corpus Christi. How'd you decide to use those names?"

"Ty is named after Tyler, Texas, so we thought we'd continue the tradition. We even visited those towns to spawn them. That way, we can carry a little of Texas wherever we go."

Louisa and Emily were quiet as they assimilated the logistics of the Barnes' family planning, and the pause was long enough for another group to move into Ty and Maggie's conversational circle.

"This county has got the strangest way of naming their children," murmured Emily to Louisa.

"I can tell you're impressed."

"Or something."

"But, Em, look around. What do you see?"

Emily looked around beyond the irrigated patch of land on which the house and the gathering were standing. Heat glazed, sandy flatland, broken only by shrubs baked into grotesque twists by the sun, stretched to the line of blue sky.

Louisa repeated her question, "So, what do you see?"

"Brown. I see brown."

"Exactly!" Louisa beamed at Emily's quick perception of the point she was making.

"So what does that have to do with these strange naming customs?"

"Color, Emily, color. Those names are colorful, and they bring color to this land. That's what makes this part of the country interesting—how they make color."

Chapter 5

▼

As they passed through the crowd, Emily's head snapped back when she heard Maggie spew, "Why, Dwayne Ed and Dwayne Jr., we haven't see y'all in an age. Where y'all been?"

The man, shorter than Ty and about twice Ty's girth, was facing Ty and Maggie, so Louisa and Emily were unable to observe Dwayne Ed, but they could see his accompanying son.

"That kid has enough leather on him to cover three head of cattle," commented Louisa.

His father's height, the sixteen year old wore leather cowboy boots, leather pants, leather chaps, leather wide brimmed hat and carried a leather coat.

"Chaps? Why would someone wear chaps to a funeral?" wondered Louisa out loud.

"He rode his horse?" guessed Emily. "I hope that leather covers up the smell of sweat because he's got to be blazing. Do you suppose that's our man—Laurel's husband?"

"Don't know. Does the kid look like Laurel? And where's his sister? Didn't you say he had a twin?"

"I can't much tell what he looks like from here, and, yes, he had a sister. Remember, they gave her my name?" Emily strained to look without appearing to stare.

"Let's go see if Maggie will introduce us." Louisa grabbed her daughter's elbow and hauled her back into the circle.

Maggie didn't have the chance to introduce the women to Dwayne Ed because Dwayne Ed had led Ty to the pecan tree at the farthest piece of property where the sandy expanse had not encroached. While Louisa stayed behind and watched the two men as they bent heads together in intense discussion, Emily approached Maggie and nodded in the direction of the young man, "I wonder if you could introduce us."

"Why, sure, darlin'. Dwayne Twerms Jr., this is Emily Kristich, the one from California. Emily, Dwayne Ed Jr., he came all the way from Dune County," smiled Maggie expansively.

The boy looked up and gave her a sullen smirk as he said, "Hello."

"I wanted to meet you because I think I know your mother, Laurel."

"What mother? I don't have a mother."

Maggie stepped between them and said placatingly, "Of course, you don't, darlin'. There's been a terrible misunderstanding. It's okay; you can relax."

She turned to Emily and steered her out of young Dwayne Ed's hearing. "Now, sugar, you didn't know, but that young man has suffered a tragedy. His mama ran away, and we must never, never say anything about it. Now, darlin', there's just no way you could know.

"But, never, never say a word to his daddy. He just comes unglued. He has suffered so much. It like to broke his heart when his Laurel left. We can't ever talk about it, understand? Never, never."

"Maggie, Laurel was a good friend of mine. I want to know what happened. I wasn't even sure she lived here until I heard Dwayne Ed's name."

"Well now, honey, she doesn't live here, never has. She lived in my county, Dune County. That's south of here. She was a good friend of mine, too, and I don't know what happened either. Neither does Maria Elena Easter, but, honey, she's gone, just gone. It's like she just fell off the face of the earth. But," she implored, "don't say a word to that boy's daddy. Shh, here they come now."

As Ty and Dwayne Ed approached Emily, Maggie ran interference and said as quickly as her drawl could be shortened, "Dwayne Ed, meet

Emily Kristich. Her mama is the daughter of Annie Briggs, Atie's sister. We are so happy she is here."

Emily looked Dwayne Ed in his glinting, black eyes surrounded by fleshy, cracked clay leather. The color of his thin lips had leached into the rest of his brown face, but lack of laugh lines embedded around his mouth indicated he didn't use his lips to smile anyway. A bulbous nose, hair in need of a shaping and a grease stain on the wide lapel of his polyester suit completed his look of dissipated waste.

Dwayne Ed held out his pudgy hand with the diamond ring grafted in the bloated flesh of his last digit and said with one corner of his mouth raised in salute, "Glad to meet you. Y'all met my boy?" He jerked his head in the direction of Dwayne Ed Jr.

Emily responded, "I have, and I think..." before Maggie said, "I'm so happy we've had this opportunity, aren't you, Dwayne Ed? You have to meet her mama. Maybe we can all have dinner sometime. Come on, Ty, let's find the boys."

As Ty and Maggie went to locate their brood, a muscular, shorthaired man accompanied by a preteen aged girl approached them. Ty tipped his hat. "Howdy, Jonas, Ruthie."

Maggie halted long enough to exclaim, "Why, Ruthie, how's your mama? Is she feeling okay? I need to get by and see her. You tell her I'll be over one of these days, okay, darlin'?"

Ruthie was chock full of potential. Someday, her height would elongate her overstocked flesh; her face would widen to accommodate her nose; her arms and legs would proportion themselves to her body, and her adult skin would eradicate the pocks and pits of adolescence. There was a someday in Ruthie's future when she would laughingly bewail her 'tween age looks, but right now she wallowed in insecurity. In answer to Maggie's concern about her mother, she reached for the sleeve of the man next to her, looked down and said imperceptibly, "She's here, ma'am."

"What'd you say, sugar?" asked Maggie loudly.

Ruthie grabbed another handful of Jonas' sleeve and, still looking at the ground, repeated more loudly, "She's here, Mrs. Barnes. She's right behind us."

Maggie looked behind the two of them to see a woman shuffle slowly behind her husband and daughter. Maggie rushed to the woman, swooped her in her arms and said, "Ruth, darlin', I'm so happy to see y'all. Just how in the world have you been? I worry about you so much."

Not looking up when Maggie hugged her, the woman let out a gasp as Maggie crunched her in her embrace.

Ruth looked at her hesitantly and replied, "Oh, it's you, Maggie. I, I'm fine, I think." Her eyes nervously flicked from the back of Jonas' head to Dwayne Ed's head. She said again quietly, "Yes, I, it's okay." She smiled automatically although she didn't appear to understand why she smiled.

Maggie, happy to divert Emily's attention from Dwayne Ed, turned to Jonas and Ruth with, "Now you can meet the California Briggs. This is Emily, and her mama is Louisa. She's just coming up behind us. Come on, Louisa, meet Jonas, Ruth and Ruthie. Ruthie is Jonas and Ruth's daughter. Ruth is one of my oldest friends, aren't you, darlin'."

Ruth smiled her tentative smile. She was a bit taller than Jonas, but her shuffling walk seemed to shorten her height. Her darting eyes and tongue which peeked out the side of her mouth belied any strength the bone structure of her face made her appear to have. An unkempt look washed her. Her blue flowered cotton dress fit unstylishly loosely; a strand of oily hair escaped her ponytail, and the low heels of her scuffed shoes were well worn.

"And, Jonas and Ty and Dwayne Ed have been friends since they were little boys. The sheriff, too. Have you met the sheriff?" Maggie, craning her neck in a semicircle looked for the sheriff.

Turning to Ty, she asked, "Have you seen Bonham here, honey? I don't see him anywhere."

Reticent Ty shook his head.

"Well, come on, maybe we can find him when we find the boys." She guided him along. Turning to the group she smiled and said, "It's been so nice meeting y'all."

Dwayne Ed turned to Jonas. "You got the truck?" Jonas nodded.

He then turned to his son. "Ready?"

He responded petulantly, "Yeah."

Dwayne Ed turned to the boy and cuffed him on the side of the head. "What'd you say, boy?"

The boy closed his eyes and swallowed. "Sir. I meant yes, sir. Sir."

"That's better. Girlie," Dwayne Ed barked at Ruthie, "you get in the back seat with Junior. You two will go to the movies. We'll drop you off now.

"Come on, let's go."

And, they did.

After standing by themselves in silence for a few minutes, Emily turned to Louisa. "Where were you? I think you might have missed the most entertainment this afternoon has to offer—even more entertaining than Brother Johnson."

"Talking to some cousins. I also bumped into Clio and Callie, but I don't think I'm going to introduce you to them. If Mel is rude, Callie and Clio are hopeless. What I wanted to do is follow Ty and Dwayne Ed, but the cousins found me first. What happened?"

Emily summarized for her mother the introduction of Dwayne Ed and his entourage.

"So, that's your man?" concluded Louisa.

"Guess so."

"Does the kid look like Laurel?"

"I couldn't much tell. Same color hair, I think, under that hat, but he kept his face down sulking most of the time, so I couldn't see it."

"How're you going to find out where Laurel is if you can't talk about her?"

"I think I'll go to the Twerms Ranch. If I can talk to Dwayne Ed about Laurel without Junior being around, maybe he'll tell me what happened. I wonder if she took Daphne with her."

"Is Daphne the other child?"

"Yes. There's another possibility. Maggie Barnes said someone named Maria Elena was a friend of hers. Maria Elena…I can't remember the last name. Isle or something."

"Easter," supplied Louisa.

"That was awhile ago," Emily said absentmindedly.

"Not the holiday. Easter is her last name. You're thinking Easter Island, that's why you said 'Isle'. Her name is Maria Elena Easter, and her husband is Hugh."

"That's right. How'd you know that?"

"I met them. They're over there, and it looks like they're getting ready to leave."

"Come on, Mom. Let's go find them." Emily grabbed her mother and hustled off in the direction of the Easters.

* * * *

Catching up with the Easters just as Maria Elena was sliding her legs into the front passenger seat of a Cadillac, Emily panted at her, "Mrs. Easter, my name is Emily Kristich, and I'm a friend of Laurel, only I haven't been able to find her, and Maggie said you were her friend, too, and I think you know what happened to her. Can you tell me?"

Puzzled confusion clouded the olive skinned face of Maria Elena as she tried to understand what Emily was heaving at her, "Laurel? Do you know Laurel? Where is she? She's been gone so long. Can you tell me where she is?"

Hugh Easter stepped out of the car and demanded, "Who are you?"

Emily began, "I just told you…"

Louisa interrupted and said, "We met earlier; this is my daughter. She's an old friend of Laurel Twerms and has never been able to find her. She heard your wife was a friend of hers and wanted her help in locating Laurel. That's all."

Geniality washed over Hugh Easter with Louisa's explanation while Maria Elena said, "I didn't understand. I thought you knew her now and had some information. We really can't talk about it here, but you could come and see me. If that is too hard to do, I could meet you in town, in San Domingo, if you want. I'll tell you what I know, but not here. Not with Dwayne Ed around. Dwayne Ed would be quite nasty if he found out we were talking about Laurel. I can see you tomorrow."

"That's fine. Where do you live?"

Hugh tipped his hat back, a smile cracked the redtoned walnut of his skin as he gave directions, "Well, ma'am, it's not hard to find. Take that road that goes by the Single Arrow south and follow that until you get to Easter County. There's only one sign telling you're in our county, so watch carefully, but there's only one main road, so you can't get lost. The first house you see on the left is ours. Now, if you come to a clump of houses, you've gone too far. Those're the houses of the ranch workers and their families."

"Is tomorrow afternoon okay? I can be there tomorrow afternoon."

"Then come and stay for dinner, and we can talk about Laurel," invited Maria Elena. Turning to Louisa she said, "Both of you. We could make an evening of it. But, not here, we can't talk here about Laurel."

Waving goodbye to the Easters, Louisa said to Emily, "Laurel must've gone off on a toot. If no one will talk about her, she must have screwed up badly."

"Maybe. It doesn't make sense though. Except for running off to marry Dwayne Ed, she was always focused and stable."

"That could be the problem, Em."

Chapter 6

With each punch of the potatoes she was mashing, Mel started a new sentence, "I don't know why you all had to stay. Atie's gone. The funeral's over. Everyone else went home. Why I have to cook for you, I don't know. You all should be at your own homes, you hear?"

No one standing around the two tables brought in from the funeral listened. The women were setting plates and silverware out while the men were setting up chairs they were bringing in from the outside. Children were bringing in the leftover food that would make up the Briggs' family dinner that night. Violet clouds were hovering in the west waiting to pound the desert with a nighttime display of wind driven rain and crackling lightning. The impending storm had cooled the day's heat outside, but it was still warm in the house.

Dabbing her face with a dishtowel, Cora said, "Atie could have done us all a favor and put in air conditioning."

"She saved her money. Didn't spend it like you folks do. All your fancy do-dads. Who needs 'em. We didn't have 'em as kids, why should we now? You're all soft. Just wait 'til Louisa gets hold of that will. Then you all will see what saving money can do for you, you hear?" Mel said with a self-satisfied smirk.

"All that money sure has helped Atie," said Luke. "We probably should have cashed it in and lined her coffin with greenbacks instead of satin."

Mel let out an indignant snort while the rest of the gathering chuckled.

"Uncle Luke," Emily interjected into the efficient hum of readying dinner for many, "do you know where the Twerms ranch is?"

The hum died as if an audio wire had been snipped, and all eyes turned to Emily.

"The Twerms ranch, you mean Dwayne Ed's place? What's a young gal like you want with him? He's a mean son of a bitch. Pardon me, ladies," Luke said to no one in particular.

"I believe he's the husband of a friend I had in college. I want to know what's happened to her."

"You mean you knew that young thing he brought home? What was her name?" asked Uncle Pete.

"Laurel," some uncle chimed in from the back of the group.

"None of us really know where she is. She just upped and ran off one day. I imagine she had enough of him," continued Pete.

"The ranch. Where's the ranch? Will someone tell me where the ranch is?"

Sam rubbed his jaw with his hand as he explained. "His south border is my north border over there in Dune County. When it rains, I got a creek running on my side of the border, and he's always giving me fits over it. Claims it's his, and I diverted the path of water. I got the survey to prove it's mine and always has been my family's since before statehood. I don't know that you should go there."

"You mean all this time you knew Laurel, and I didn't know you knew her?" Disappointment plastered Emily's face. "I didn't even know my relatives knew her." She sat in the nearest chair, hands hanging in her lap, shoulders slumped.

"Sorry, honey," said Aunt Cora trying to comfort her grandniece. "We didn't know her well. They didn't get out much, only when Dwayne Ed was scamming or something. When they did go out, they stayed with the younger people, but even they weren't keen on having much to do with Dwayne Ed. You really don't want to go out there."

"Let her go. He won't hurt her. He'll be so surprised someone's stupid enough to come on his land, he'll forget to get his shotgun," Mel shot back.

"They're right, honey," Aunt Polly said gently. "Dwayne Ed is rotten to the core. Don't go. Maybe Maggie Barnes can tell you what happened to your friend."

"Or Maria Elena Easter. She and Laurel were good friends," put in Aunt Cora.

"I know. Maggie won't talk about it, and Mom and I will see the Easters for dinner tomorrow." To Aunt Mel, Emily said, "So you don't have to cook for us tomorrow night."

"Maybe not for you, but some of these other buzzards will be here," muttered Mel as she stared at her family.

"I just thought her husband would talk to me."

Luke closed the discussion. "Take it from me, he won't. He doesn't give the time of day to a stranger without expecting something in return."

The group's mute agreement accompanied Lalie's entreaty of "Please, don't go."

* * * *

"What're your plans tomorrow, Mom?" Emily asked that night as they readied for bed.

"Either tomorrow or the next day, I have to go to San Domingo and talk to the Atie's lawyer." As she realized what her daughter was planning she asked, "Do you think after all the relatives said you're still going to the Twerms ranch?"

When Emily nodded her head, her mother pointed out the obvious, "You heard what the uncles said. They asked you not to go."

"So do you want to go with me?"

With an exasperated sigh, Louisa said, "Yes. With two of us, it'll be safer."

"Do you know where Uncle Sam's ranch is?"

"I think so."

"Then we just have to find his north border. If it rains tonight, then that creek will be running, and it will help us locate the Twerms ranch."

"Maybe."

*   *   *   *

The lightning of the storm that night provided an eerie strobe for Emily's dream. As she passed by Atie's coffin, she looked down and saw Laurel instead. Laurel started to slowly rise out of the casket when Dwayne Ed, who had been standing at the head of Laurel's box, cuffed her on the side of the head, so she fell back into the coffin. Dwayne Ed Jr. looked down sullenly while Mel repeated waspishly, "Buzzard, buzzard, buzzard." There was the presence of a girl about the age of Dwayne Ed, Jr. who wove in and out of the dream, but Emily couldn't determine who it was. Laurel started to get up again, but, in the chaotic order of dreams, Maggie Barnes appeared and said, "Don't say anything; don't say anything." Laurel sat back in the coffin.

Chapter 7

Sometimes Dwayne Ed Jr. could convince his father he needed to go to the library to do a school project. Being summer time with school out of session, it was harder to convince Daddy he needed to get to the library, but he still thought of plausible excuses. The English department at San Domingo High had issued a reading list of books it considered advisable for its students to have read before they graduated from the San Domingo Unified School District. It didn't matter that in the years he had possession of the list, he had already read the books, sometimes two times. Dwayne Ed Jr. still used the list as his summer excuse to get to the library. Daddy and Jonas were always checking to make sure he was doing just what they wanted him to do, be just what they wanted him to be and act just like they wanted him to act. They did it with him, and they did it with Ruthie. The library was one of the few places Junior could go and escape the suffocating vigilance of Jonas and Dwayne Ed Sr. Neither one of them gave any relevance to a library. For them it was a repository of dust and gibberish, nothing worth wasting their time. Dwayne Ed Jr. was allowed to go only to complete his high school graduation and get out of school as quickly as he could. Dwayne Ed Sr. had big plans for his boy when he was no longer required by the state to go to school.

It was harder for Ruthie to get away from her father. Sometimes the fathers arranged outings for Junior and Ruthie with the idea they would always be together. Ruthie and Junior were never quite sure what they were to do on these outings, so they had, over the years, spent the time talking and analyzing their lives. They had analyzed their lives with a maturity unavailable to many twice their ages, and, as a result, become friends who could rely on each other.

Jonas dropped Junior at the intersection near the library and told him he'd be back in one hour to pick him up at that spot.

"Don't be late," warned Jonas.

"No, sir, I won't."

Junior's bronze skin was impervious to the scorching of the hot sun as he hiked the two blocks to the Hugh and Irene Easter Memorial Library. He walked into the library, shivered momentarily as his body adjusted to the air conditioned frigidity of the interior and looked, as he often did, at the long spans of shelves which held the multi-colored rectangles.

Taking a deep sigh, he wondered, as he often did, if he read all these books, would he be better able to understand the confusion of his confused life that his confusing parents had created?

Chapter 8

City dwellers can't look on a map of rural areas and pinpoint an exact destination the way they can in a city. Lack of street signs and landmarks makes it difficult to find one's way in the country. As hard as she tried, Louisa made several wrong turns down rutted cattle trails and loosely defined roads before she and Emily could determine the north border of Uncle Sam's ranch. Fortunately, one of those wrong turns afforded them access to Uncle Sam and Aunt Terp's ranch house with its inevitable pump jack and oil storage tanks in the front yard. Vehicles were so scarce on the ranch roads the women could hardly drive by without giving regards to their relatives. Both women took it to be a good omen for their mission when neither aunt nor uncle was at home. The other good omen was crossing a stream newly formed by the previous night's rain thereby yielding the south border of the Twerms ranch.

"You think that's it?" Emily asked.

"Could be. Look across there. You see that dark blob on the horizon, looks kind of square? Bet that's Dwayne Ed's house."

"How do we get there?"

"Let's cross the stream and follow that road. When we think we're close, we'll try the roads until we hit the right one. It may take all morning, you know. Texas distance is longer than any I know. That flat land makes you think you are driving the road of eternity. Let's try it."

The four-wheel dribbled its passengers along the pocked road with a modicum of comfort. Each road they tried in the attempt to locate the one leading to Dwayne Ed's house was less civilized than the one they had taken from Sam and Atie's house.

"Is this trip really worth it?" asked Louisa with clenched teeth as she drove surrounded by a haze of dust kicked up by the car.

"Don't know," agreed Emily in a voice marking the ups and downs of the road bumps. She hung onto the armrest to steady her jostling body. "I would have thought that rain would keep the dust down."

"Only until the sun comes out and nukes the sand so any moisture the sand could hold is gone in a flash."

After turning down three questionable roads, the two-storied box house looming before them was a surprise to the women in the car. Whereas, most of the houses on the ranches had been built of as much sand colored brick as could be used thereby preventing the need for frequent paint jobs as the wind abraded the finish, the Twerms house was built of wood. Paint was not an issue because no one had bothered to paint the house for a number of years. Gray weathered wood was striated by broken lines of a yellowed white coating. The porch had softened with age, so it bowed at the middle. Slats were placed across the risers of the former steps. Some of the windows still had working shutters used as more of a hope than an actual barrier against the ravages of the dust storms. Freckles of blue paint dotted some of the shutters, and most of the second story windows displayed fastened ones.

There were some outbuildings, a small barn with the roof lying in two of the stables, a chicken coop appropriated for storage of rusting iron farm equipment, a couple sheds and two unused, one presumed, outhouses. None of those appeared to have ever been painted, and all would have made better firewood than storage. Parked to the right side of the porch was a new pick-up with a cab designed for two bench seats instead of the usual one. A gun rack mounted in the back window held a couple shotguns and a rifle.

Oil pumping units could be spotted with the naked eye, one in the front yard and one beyond the outbuildings. If there had ever been a cultivated patch of green, sand and lack of care had obliterated any evidence of it. Tumbleweeds scooted across the land dodging rocks and dead limbs like bumper cars. With the exception of an occasional whine of wind, the rhythmic groan of the orange nosed pump jack was the only sound in the dead silence.

"Sure looks inviting" commented Louisa. "You sure you don't want to turn around and go back?"

Emily hesitated before she said, "I'm sure. We've tried too hard to find this place, and I've waited too long to find out what happened to Laurel to stop now."

"Then let's go together," said Louisa as she stepped out of the car, her booted foot sending a couple horned toads hurtling themselves toward the nearest rock. At the moment they stepped gingerly on the porch to avoid the holes in the rotten wood, they heard the shrill yelp of a dog.

Thinking a car had hit it, both heads jerked in the direction of the sound, but there wasn't a highway in the observable area.

"Maybe around back," suggested Louisa.

"That dog is hurt," responded Emily.

Immobilized by what they were afraid they might see, they stood on the sagging porch until they heard the crunch of footsteps around the corner of the house. At the same time, the front door creaked open to reveal a hallway darkened by shuttered windows and a layer of dirt. Ruthie peeked around the edge of the door and said, "Yes?"

"Is Mr. Twerms here, Ruthie? We'd like to see him."

In a soft voice, the young girl held the screen door open, asked them to come in and told them she would find him. Emily and Louisa stepped into the wooden hallway worn white with years of feet trodding over it. Coming from the bright sun to dank darkness, the women's eyes were blanked into non-seeing, and their nostrils stiffened at the combined odor of old cooking grease, dust, and dirty toilets.

"Wait here. I'll find him," said Ruthie shyly as she escaped to the back area of the house.

At her exit, the screen door was yanked open behind the ladies by Dwayne Ed with a cattle prod in his hand.

"Who're you?" he snarled.

"We met you at our aunt's funeral yesterday. I'm Emily Kristich, and this is my mother, Louisa Daniel. We'd like to talk to you because I think I was in your wedding to Laurel Raines."

A slow leer spread across his face. "I thought you looked familiar, girlie. Now, I remember. Laurel had to have you come to Houston, but I didn't want her to. That life was over for her; she was coming to my life."

"We wondered if you could tell us what happened to her."

Cattle prod in hand, he gesticulated emotionally. As he spoke, he jabbed the air with the prod.

"How the hell do I know? She's gone, just run off leaving me and the boy here. Stupid bitch. Probably ran off with some salesman. Leaving me and the boy here; she was shit for a mother."

"But, your daughter. You have a twin daughter…"

"Get outta here. I haven't got a daughter. Just me and the boy. Get the hell outta here. Don't ever come trespassing on my property again, goddamned nosy bitches."

"But, Laurel wrote me and said she had named the daughter after me. Her middle name is Emily."

He shoved the cattle prod at Emily repeatedly. At the last poke in the air with the prod, he touched Emily's chest and sent a bolt of electricity through it. Her eyes bulged out of her head, her arms pushed out from her body, and her face was dumbfounded. As though an invisible hand shoved her backward, she fell roughly on her backside to the rotting wood of the porch.

"Oh!" shouted Louisa as she pushed Dwayne Ed aside and tried to help Emily. "You son of a bitch. You hurt my daughter. You can't do that. I'm going to report you to the sheriff."

She knelt by Emily, who was taking deep breaths as though she'd been under water too long, and asked, "Are you all right? We've got to get you to a doctor."

"You don't need a goddamned doctor, but you do need to get off my goddamned property," warned Dwayne Ed as he sliced the air with the prod. "If you don't get off it now, I'll use this thing on both of you. Move it!"

At that moment, Jonas appeared behind Dwayne Ed and said, "Ladies, let me escort you to your car. Mr. Twerms is upset."

He helped Emily to her feet, took the crooks of both ladies' arms and led them to their car.

Louisa said, "I'm going to report him. Did you see what he did? He can't endanger someone that way."

"This is his ranch, ma'am. You were trespassing. I don't think you'll get much sympathy from the sheriff."

"But, he can't do that."

As Jonas seated Emily on the passenger side of the car she asked, "Do you know about Laurel? Can you tell me anything about her daughter?"

"No, Ma'am. I can't."

"But, you do know something, don't you?" Louisa continued the questioning.

He paused and said, "Her mama lives in San Domingo now. Try her." Then, he opened the car door for Louisa and made sure she was seated and had started the car.

"Don't come here again."

He disappeared before Emily or Louisa had a chance to ask where to look for Mrs. Raines.

*   *   *   *

"Are you all right?" asked Louisa, the anxious mother.

"I think so. I feel like I'm shivering inside my body. I can't stop this tingling. It's like a little earthquake in my body with lots of aftershocks. This is horrible."

"We need to find a doctor."

"No, I don't want that. I'm not burned anywhere. If that dog is still living, I'm sure I'll be fine. They do that to cows all the time."

"They're a bigger mass than you, plus they have a one inch thick hide covered with hair. You don't. I'd feel better if we could find a doctor."

"No, it's better now. I'm going to be fine."

As they drove across the Gold County line, a sheriff's car began tailing them.

"You going to pull over?" asked Emily.

"I'm not speeding, and this is a rental car, so everything should be working. He's probably just going back to San Domingo." Louisa answered just as the siren on the police cruiser started, and the lights flashed.

"Apparently not," was Emily's dry comment.

Louisa sidled her car onto the shoulder of the road where they could see in the rearview mirror a sheriff talk into a radio receiver, take his hat off the front seat and slowly exit the car. Muscular arms attached to a broad chest made the man of medium height appear formidable. Dark glasses and shade provided by the brim of his hat gave the ladies no inkling to his facial features as he sauntered to their four-wheel drive.

Touching the brim of his hat, he said, "Afternoon, ladies. Where y'all headed on such a hot day?"

Louisa began, "We're going back home to the Single Arrow Ranch. Atie Ewell was my aunt, and I'm seeing to her estate."

"You Atie's kin? Wondered if I'd get to meet you," he grinned. "So you're Louisa Daniel. This must be your daughter, huh? Sorry I couldn't get to the ranch after the funeral, but I was real busy that day. That was a powerful sermon Brother Johnson hung on us, huh?"

"It was," agreed Louisa. "Sheriff, since you know us, might we know your name? And, why you stopped us?"

"Why, sure, ma'am. I'm Bonham McIntire, Sheriff of Gold County."

"You must be related to Ty Barnes," Emily said sarcastically.

A polite, "How's that?" was the Sheriff's response.

"If you're named after a Texas city, you must come from that family."

"No ma'am," he chuckled, again, politely. "I was named for the one and only, James B. Bonham, hero of the Alamo. My Daddy knew every nook and cranny of the Alamo, and all his boys were named for Alamo fighters. But, Ty and I have known each other all our lives, so we could almost be brothers.

"Now, I stopped you because I got a complaint from the sheriff at Dune County. Seems there's a couple of ladies, kind of like yourselves, pestering one of the ranch owners over there. Now, ladies, we have an unwritten rule here where we help our fellow law officers, so I'm giving you a real friendly warning to not trespass on the Twerms ranch. It's not safe."

Emily' tone was biting as she said, "You have nothing better to do than wait for us to warn us off property in another county?"

"Yes, ma'am, I run a tight county, so I have time to help out another sheriff. I know everything's that going on here. Don't forget that." Again touching the brim of his hat, he smiled slightly and said, "Afternoon, Miss Louisa and Miss Emily."

"No, you wait right there," Louisa demanded. "Are you telling me you help enforce the law in Dune County?"

"If I can."

"Then just let me tell you what happened." Louisa related the story of Emily and the cattle prod to the Sheriff.

"What am I suppose to do?" asked the Sheriff, again politely.

"Well, I want you to arrest that person. He can't do that to people."

"Well, ma'am, that's his property. You weren't supposed to be on it."

"But, he deliberately hurt my daughter."

"Yes, ma'am, he did."

"Well, if you have jurisdiction in Dune County, you need to keep the peace."

"No, you don't understand. I don't have jurisdiction. I just help out which is what I'm doing by warning you to stay away from the Twerms ranch."

"Then I'll go talk to the sheriff of Dune County."

"Yes'm, you could, but…"

"But, what?"

"It won't do much good."

"Why not?"

"The sheriff is a cousin of Dwayne Ed."

"Oh, for crying out loud. Are you saying we have no recourse in this god forsaken piece of sand?"

"Yes'm, I believe you understand what I'm saying. Maybe you should go home, now."

"This is ridiculous. That's not justice. If you're saying we can't get any fair treatment, you're violating our civil rights. You can't run a county that way."

"Now, that's where you're wrong. I can run the county any way I see fit to enforce the law. That's why I've been elected over and over and over."

"But, that's not right."

"Maybe not in your eyes, but that's the way it's done here."

After the Sheriff had driven off with a wave and a smile, Emily said, "I think we just met the law of the land."

"Son of a bitch. I bet he doesn't do spit in this county. Let's go back to the ranch and change to get out to the Easter ranch. We've got another long drive ahead of us."

Chapter 9

Hugh and Maria Elena greeted their guests at the door of their sprawling adobe ranch home. The hosts brought them through ornately carved doors that stood ten feet high into a terra cotta tiled entryway. Louisa and Emily observed wrought iron and glass furniture mixed in with the heavy antique Spanish pieces. Soft teal greens and pinks made the house already cooled by thick, stone walls seem cooler. They were led to a porch at the back of the house that was deep and wide enough to ward off any harsh wind and sun where a barbecue big enough to roast a whole cow was blazing.

White Adirondack porch chairs had been set around a table decked out in teal, pink and beige pottery. Nancy, the Easters' cook, was at the massive wet bar concocting the dressing for a Caesar salad large enough to feed the Texas A&M football team. Hugh walked over to the wet bar to pick up a tray of glasses and a pitcher of Sangria and brought it back to the table to offer his guests. Pecan trees had been strategically planted to allow protection of the house from the intense sunlight except where the rectangular pool lay. Verdant green grass surrounded the area where the house sat.

"I haven't seen this much grass since we left Dallas/Ft. Worth," said Emily.

Diminutive Maria Elena's full brown eyes widened at the compliment, and she said in her soft, sweet voice, "Hugh built this house for me when we got married. He knew I liked to grow things, so he had a deep water well dug for me. He has so many oil wells, he was afraid he couldn't find water before he hit oil. But, the geologists were able to locate a site for water. It was actually a hole being drilled for oil that flowed fresh water, so it became a dry hole."

"There's an oxymoron there, you know," smiled Emily.

Maria Elena giggled as she explained, "A dry hole is an oil well that has no show of oil. Even if there is water in it, and oil is being looked for, it is a dry hole. Hugh happened upon an artesian reservoir which is about as valuable out here as oil wells. That reservoir lets Hugh do some farming on the ranch and send the products back to the big cities. So, there's also an irony here. About three hundred feet below us is a river that flows to the Davis Mountains, and we sit on the sand of an old, dried-up ocean. After the geologists found the reservoir, Hugh told me I was his good luck because he never would have looked for water except that I wanted to grow things."

"Tell us how you knew Laurel," Maria Elena asked Emily.

Emily explained her story while Hugh kept their glasses of sangria filled. "I was still in graduate school when she quit corresponding, and I never realized how closely Laurel had been living to my mother's relatives. In fact, I didn't realize it until Mom said something just before we came out here. Then I started to look for her again, but I had thrown out her address."

Hugh said, "We were surprised when Dwayne Ed brought a wife home. No one around here would marry him. For that reason, we figured she had to be a gold digger because he has so much money. We were surprised by how nice she was. She was surprised by how different Dwayne Ed was at home. It was a pathetic situation to watch; he just ate her up and threw out the pieces."

"So where did she go?" Louisa asked.

Maria Elena replied softly, her brown eyes full of concern, "We don't know. There was an incident here one night about ten years ago. We thought it would be nice to have a formal dinner with our old friends. We put out the good service, silver, china and crystal. Dwayne Ed was in one of his moods, and he had been drinking. Just like always, he came over here and filled up his flask with Hugh's liquor. Said Hugh couldn't pick a wife, but he could pick booze. He thought my being *Latina* was beneath Hugh."

Hugh reached a protective arm around his wife and continued, "He tipped a plate all over Nancy, our housekeeper, as she was serving him. Told her to clean up the mess because she was just a servant, and he was helping her keep her job. They left because of that, and we never saw Laurel again. That must have been the last straw for her."

Maria Elena took up the story. "She was in tears when she left. I can still see her that night. Let's see, she wore a black satin, long skirt with a white, silk sweater. She was a beautiful woman, that honey blonde hair done up on the top of her head with little wisps all over. She looked just like a Victorian heroine. She was as long-suffering, tragic and burdened as any Victorian heroine could be."

Maria Elena discreetly dabbed her eyes. "I still miss her. She was a kind woman; she never complained. She never gave up on her children, her friends, even her husband. So nice to everyone."

"Didn't anyone look for her?" interjected Louisa.

"Oh, sure. All the sheriffs in the near counties rode posses looking for her. Dwayne Ed claimed he had a private detective looking for her. I don't think he really wanted an investigation though. It was easier for him not to think about her. Bonham McIntire even tried to get the FBI in on the search, but we couldn't say it was a kidnapping or any actual crime. She just disappeared, and so it was treated as a missing person's case. Back then, you had to wait the three days for reports of missing persons to shake any law enforcement loose," Hugh explained.

"I would have thought she would have taken Junior and Daphne though. They were her life," Maria Elena added. "That's why I don't think she ran away. She loved them too much to leave them."

"Do you know Daphne?" asked an excited Emily. "Where is she? We've only met Dwayne Jr."

"Don't you know?" asked Hugh. "Tell her the story, honey."

"It was so sad. When the twins were very young toddlers, they got sick. Little Dwayne was okay, but Daphne ended up with meningitis. She recovered, but she was deaf as a result of the high fever.

"Dwayne Ed blamed Laurel for the deafness and the fact *her* daughter was retarded. He wouldn't listen to the experts tell him how well she could do, that deafness wouldn't exclude her from the world. Said no daughter of his would talk funny like she was stupid. Daphne was the apple of his eye, but after she got sick, he neglected her. The little girl got so frustrated because she couldn't make her needs known that she would throw these terrible tantrums. One day, she was having a tantrum, and her daddy threw her across the room."

Hugh picked up the story. "Laurel brought the children over here and told us what had happened. I got Sheriff McIntire from Gold County, he's a close boyhood friend of Dwayne Ed and me, and went over and talked to him. We finally got him to agree to send the little girl to the school for the deaf. It took some fast talking, believe you me."

"So we never talk about Laurel, and we never talk about Daphne. That's one of the reasons I asked you here," said Maria Elena. "We can talk about her in private, not out in the town."

"So," prodded Louisa, "what do you really think happened to her?"

Maria Elena looked at her husband with permission to pronounce their judgment.

Hugh hesitated and said quietly, "We think she might be dead. Not taking the children with her makes us feel that way."

"Dead as in an accident, or dead as in deliberately killed?" summarized Louisa.

Hugh spread his hands out and smiled ruefully. "Is there much of a difference now? Accident or murder, which is what you're asking, she's gone, most likely dead."

During the ensuing pause, Nancy started to serve the salad she had created. Dinner conversation included the life and times of Gold, Dune and Easter counties with a little California spice tossed throughout. As they exclaimed over Nancy's Jeff Davis pie, known to the rest of America as butter chess pie, Louisa asked, "Who's the sheriff of Easter County. I bet he's related to you, isn't he, Hugh."

"No, this guy doesn't come out of his office much. He even has Bonham McIntire in the next county enforce some of the law here, kind of by proxy. He was elected not long ago. Too bad, the other guy was related to me, and he did a good job. But, when you got the name Easter in a county named Easter, sometimes folks just want a change. I imagine next election we'll get back in."

"Jonas said Mrs. Raines lived in San Domingo. Is that true?" Emily asked.

"Yes, it's true, she's a spunky little lady. Moved out here from the North, New Jersey or New Hampshire or something, when she figured out Laurel wasn't doing well. When Laurel disappeared, she used all her money to try to find her. The money ran out before she could locate her. Lives over in Shanty Town in San Domingo. Still feisty, though. She's organizing the neighborhood to clean it up. Sure needs it, too."

"One last thing," said Emily on their way out the door. "What school is Daphne at?"

"Best one in the state," said Maria Elena. "Easter School for the Deaf in San Domingo."

As they walked to their car, Louisa said to Emily, "Guess you'll want to join me tomorrow when I go to San Domingo to see Atie's attorney."

"Yeah, guess so."

Chapter 10
▼

Henry Wade tripped as he walked up the sandy path to his ill-defined house. As he fell to the ground, his dark clothes and dark skin blended into the dark night making him barely perceptible. He lay facedown breathing in the sand until enough of it clogged his air passages that he had to turn his head allowing the clean night air to slap his face. It was enough to force him out of the sand to slowly balance on his feet and into the door of his house. As he reached for the handle of the screen door, he cut his hand on a piece of metal screen that had been pushed out of the doorframe. He stopped to look at it while it bled, licked the blood off and spit the salty warmth onto the sand surrounding the house. Inside he went to the kitchen sink, ran water over his hand and scooped some up to splash his face.

Again, he thought. *He did it to me again. I've told him never. I never want to talk about it. He wants to go through those games like I was still playing football. Those days are over; they're gone. They're gone just as surely as the Gulf sand choked the life out of Henry Wade. He can't keep talking about them.*

Henry Wade stumbled back to the shoebox sized living area, sat on the blanket covered springs of the one chair in the room and looked around. He saw the sway backed sofa, the wooden slats of the walls and the one luxury of the room, a small color television set. He ran his hand over his face as he thought about the bartender when he mentioned Cindy.

"Whatever happened to that little gal you dated in high school?" he had asked.

The mention of her name was enough to startle Henry out of his stupor.

"Cindy?" Henry asked Toast. "You mean Cindy? She's not here, is she?"

"Don't know. That's what I'm asking you."

"I saw her the night before I left for the Gulf. Haven't seen her since. Never see her around here."

"Ladies like that don't go walking around town the hours you're out, Henry."

"No, guess not. Guess I wouldn't see her."

Henry left after that. The thought of Cindy made a void in his belly, as if he could put his hand through his body and he'd feel nothing.

Cindy.

God, how he missed Cindy!

Chapter 11

▼

Situated in the southeast corner of Gold County but creeping into its neighboring Dune and Easter Counties, San Domingo is the county seat of Gold County. It's a small city big enough for the needs of its region. It has all the amenities of modern American civilization including several fast food places, a WalMart, a Target, a couple strip malls and even a few traffic jams, particularly on Saturday when the ranchers came in for supplies. The town has also retained and capitalized on its early Texas charm particularly in the downtown area which is comprised of a courthouse square, a wooden sidewalk skirting the shops along the square and angled parking lots with meters that allow parking all day for a quarter, three hours for a dime and one hour for a nickel. The courthouse itself was built in a style best determined to be Southwest Romanesque, square buildings with small windows built of buff colored brick and a few pillars supporting porticos at each side. The area around it was landscaped with native Texas plantings, pecan trees and oil pumping units. Across from one of those pumping units lay the office of Atie's attorney.

As Emily and Louisa drove around the square, Louisa said, "The attorney said there would be a sign in the window that said, J. Utley and Son, Attorneys at Law."

Emily said dryly, "I can only guess what the 'J' stands for. Something colorful, I'm sure."

"Right," said her mother who was scanning all the shop and office windows. "It's a very unusual name. It stands for John. And, get this, the young Utley is named John, Jr. Strange, don't you think? And, the cousin who is the undertaker is named Robert. And, the cousin who is the coroner and doctor is named William. We're going to see the son. I'm not sure John Senior is still practicing. You can hardly die in this town without an Utley taking care of your affairs."

"So much for your theory of naming patterns."

"There it is. Right on the corner. Why don't you just drop me off here?"

Emily dropped Louisa across from the courthouse at the office of Atie's attorney and headed southwest to Shanty Town. "Since Easter county lies on the western edge of the green hill country of Texas, the part of that county that is within the bounds of San Domingo became the living area of the societal privileged. Conversely, the area of San Domingo situated in Dune County which lies in the middle of Texas desert became the less desirable area of town to inhabit. Shantytowns are to the rural south what tenement buildings are to the big citied north. They are shameful excuses for packaging people into a semblance of shelter. Emily drove across the railroad tracks, the line of demarcation between the good and bad sides of town, into a section of skewed houses with corrugated iron roofs that had corners as dogeared as those of a well worn book. Most of the houses teetered on foundations that consisted of piles of cement blocks. If there was a porch on a house, it did not require steps as it had sagged to ground level allowing access to a one to three room shack.

As Emily wandered streets, most of which were unmarked, she saw children, skin muddied by the hot sun, playing among the off centered houses. A few of the younger children were watched by mothers too disgusted with the futility of existence to be anything but exhausted. Because many of the streets were unmarked, Emily had to stop to ask these women where Laurel's mother's house was. A brief explanation of directions sent her further into the maze of shanties until she located another live body from whom to obtain further directions.

A young black woman came out of one of the houses near where Emily supposed Laurel's mother lived.

"What you looking for?" she said suspiciously.

"Someone told me Mrs. Raines lived near here. Is this the house?"

Her eyes lightened. "Miz Raines, you mean Phoebe? That be her house right there. If she don't answer the door, check round back. She's a Yankee and thinks she can grow a garden here." She chortled at the possibility of anything green gracing the dry, crusty sand.

While discussing directions on how to find Laurel's mother, the women looked up to see a sheriff's patrol car slowly edge down the narrow streets. The young woman eyed its progress carefully.

"That looks like the sheriff from Gold County," remarked Emily.

"Yes'm, it is. He be dropping off Henry Wade. Sheriff McIntire is good that way."

"What way?"

"Oh, you know, when Henry drinks too much, Sheriff brings him on home. If it's too late at night, he'll lock him up in jail and bring him home the next day. Poor old Henry, just drinking his life away."

"Why doesn't he drink here?"

"Because there ain't no bars here on account of this being a dry county. You can only drink in Gold County, don't you know that?"

"No, I guess I didn't. What's a dry county?"

"Means we can't have no booze sold anywhere. That's one of the reasons San Domingo grew so much in Gold County and didn't grow here. People like poor old Henry go spend any money they got in Gold County."

"Oh, I see. Well, thanks for your help."

"Glad to do it. Tell Phoebe hi for me."

Before Emily could ask for whom she was to say hi to Phoebe, the young lady had gone. Emily turned to a house with an asphalt roof, instead of a corrugated iron one, and yellow paint on the boards instead of bare wood. The green shutters that had been placed on the windows and the multi-colored zinnias in the gardens on either side of the porch gave the house a jaunty air and decreased the dilapidation of the neighborhood.

There was no answer to her tapping of the doorknocker, so she followed the young woman's instructions and went around the house to the back yard. There she opened a steel gate framing pig wire and stepped around the back of the house to see Phoebe hauling a rolling clothes basket as she hung sheets on a clothesline to dry. They caught the hot wind and billowed in the air, sails on non-existent boats.

A young man dressed in jeans and a polo shirt laughed and said as he raised a maul high in the air, "Watch this, Gramma, I'll get it in one blow."

"Sure you will, Eddie."

The maul came down on its target and with a groaning crack, a log reluctantly split into two halves. As he positioned one of the halves to split into a smaller log, Emily called out, "Mrs. Raines?"

Phoebe Raines, her dry, blonde hair shooting out of her baseball cap in wavy wings, looked up blankly, stared at Emily and then smiled, "Well, Emily Daniel, where have you been all these years? I haven't seen you since Laurel's wedding. How come you're out in this neck of the woods? This is about the furthest into the middle of nowhere that I know of."

Emily advanced towards the rounded lady wearing blue and white patterned pants cut off the knees with an orange plaid sleeveless shirt. "My mother has relatives in Gold County, and she's the executor of the estate of one of them, so we came out together. We stumbled on the fact that we were pretty close to Laurel's home. I can't find her, but a few people told me you were here."

As she came into closer proximity of Phoebe, she saw the teenaged Eddie draw closer to her. His look of concern was appeased when Phoebe put her arm around Emily's waist and explained, "Eddie, this is one of your mother's oldest friends from college, Emily Daniel. Emily, meet Eddie, my favorite grandson."

"Hello, Eddie, I believe we've met before. Emily Kristich. I was at the funeral…"

"I know. I remember." It wasn't said with sullenness; it was said as an invitation to pursue the conversation already started.

The young man allowed Emily to appraise him, and she saw that he was, most surely, his mother's son from the honey blond hair to the slender body build. His mother was reflected in his smile that came quickly in this relaxed atmosphere. To his grandmother he explained, "I met Mrs. Kristich at Atie Ewell's funeral. Remember, I told you Dwayne Ed was making me go. Only Mrs. Barnes wouldn't let her talk to me. Everyone's so scared of Dwayne Ed." The last statement was pegged with bitterness.

"I know, honey. Why don't you go in and get us some drinks, something cold. Bring me a Corona. I got Dr. Pepper for you this week at the store. Get Emily whatever she wants, and we'll sit on the porch and talk."

"Be glad to. What'll it be, Mrs. Kristich?"

"Dr. Pepper."

"If you don't mind, we'll sit on the porch here. We got us a little bit of cool left in the morning. I mean, it probably doesn't seem cool to you, but, believe you me, it's going to be hotter 'n hell in about two hours, and that house'll be like a little oven."

"By the way, one of your neighbor ladies told me to tell you hello, but I never found out her name," Emily said as she headed toward Phoebe's porch.

"That's probably Stacy. Got a lotta promise, that girl. I'm trying to get her in some extension courses from University of Texas, so she can get out of this hellhole. She's too smart to spend a whole life here.

"Come over here, honey, and tell me about Laurel. Have you seen her?"

Surprised at the question, Emily said, "Why, no. I can't find her, and no one will talk much about her. Mom and I went to the Twerms Ranch…"

"You went to the ranch? I won't even go to the ranch. One time Dwayne Ed chased after me shooting bullets at my feet; another time he kept after me with his truck. And, all that was when Laurel was alive. No telling what he'd do now. I don't even know if he knows I'm still here."

"What do you mean 'when Laurel was alive'?"

The eyes of Phoebe Raines became glassy. In a silent invitation to sit, she pointed to an old kitchen chair. Phoebe Raines sat in another chair and said, "Well, now, honey, Laurel loved those two kids of hers. She was so bent on protecting them from their father, she never would've left them. She figured as long as she took his hatred, he wouldn't be cruel to them. Then when he threw Daphne that day, she got Hugh Easter to persuade him to pay to send the little girl to the deaf school. Laurel knew she'd be safe there.

"That's how I know she's dead. Took all my money for a detective to find her, and he couldn't. And, I know he was the best money could buy because I paid another detective to check him. That guy couldn't find hide nor hair of my Laurel. So I know she's dead."

"But, there would have been some notification of her death. Someone would have found her and identified her."

"No, honey, not if Dwayne Ed had anything to do with it."

"Are you saying he killed her?"

"I'd stake my life on it, my money, too, if I had any left. Now, I don't say anything to Eddie. I make like his mother's still alive, so you do the same when he comes out, okay?"

Emily nodded. "Why do you call him Eddie? I thought his name was Dwayne Ed."

"I hate his son of a bitch father so much, and I don't want to be reminded Eddie is a part of him. That's Laurel's boy, and he's a good kid. I know he is. When he comes, we just talk and talk. He's a good kid." She screwed up her eyes in vehement corroboration of her statement.

"He's so different when he's not with you. If you'd seen him at that funeral..."

"I know, I know. I know what you're going to say. I got friends who keep me informed about my grandchildren. I won't say who they are because I don't want them on the bad side of that bastard, Dwayne Ed. But, I know everything that goes on in my grandkids' lives."

"Daphne? Do you know where Daphne is?"

Phoebe laughed as though she heard a tremendously funny joke. "Daphne? I go see Daphne all the time. She's just a little ways from downtown. The school is right here in town; that's the reason I stay here. I get to see Daphne all I want because her father has written her off. Sometimes, Eddie can sneak over here, and we have a good time, but I don't get to see him as much as I want.

"Here he comes. Now act like his mother isn't dead, okay? Okay?"

Again Emily agreed.

"Could I go meet Daphne? Would the school let me see her?"

Phoebe mulled over Emily's request and said, "Tell you what. Next time you're coming to town, call me. I'll meet you there, and we can see her together. I know sign language, so I can explain to her who you are and why you're important. Okay?"

"Sounds good. I'll do that."

Eddie came out of Phoebe's house with a tray of drinks and asked, "Who're you talking about?"

"Your sister. Emily wants to meet her, and we were working out a plan to do that."

Eddie smiled gently at the mention of his sister, "She's a nice person, you know. Pretty, too." A new thought obviously struck him, "You're the person who gave her her second name. You're that Emily."

The realization demolished any misgivings Eddie may have had about Emily although he made his next request timidly. "Would you tell me about my mother? Tell me about how you knew her?"

So, Emily talked until the sun overhead shortened the shadow of the house to a mere few inches, and the heat squelched any cool air that might refresh their lungs.

Eddie got up with a start. "I gotta go, Gramma. Dwayne Ed will be furious if I'm late. He thinks I'm at the library. Did you get a couple books for me?"

"They're inside, love, on the table. Give me a hug, and come when you can."

"I'll take you home, if you wish," Emily offered Eddie.

"No, ma'am, that's not safe. But, I'll take a ride into town. I'll keep my head down in the car and get out at an intersection that doesn't have much going on. That way, no one can tell my father I was with you. He's real annoyed at your coming to the ranch. He and Jonas talk about it all the time."

"If that's the way you want it. Come on, then. I'll drive you into town.

Chapter 12

▼

"Did you find her?" asked Louisa as she settled into the passenger's seat.

"Yes. She's the same as she was twenty years ago, practical and down to earth. Guess who else was there?"

"Dwayne Ed?" Louisa said caustically.

"No, but you're close. It was his son."

"You mean that twerp we met at the funeral? The one decked out in all the leather?"

"Yes, but he wasn't twerpy. In fact, he seemed to be a pretty neat kid. His grandma appears to be his point of stability. She swears he's a good kid."

"I don't know many grandmothers who won't swear that about their grandchildren. Maybe she doesn't know him well."

"She knows him, and, I have to agree, he was impressive."

"So, does that make you feel better about his father?"

Emily paused before she said, "No, it makes me feel worse. How long can a kid hang on before an influence like his father brainwashes him? How much hatred can grandma's love eradicate? I bet there's no way on this earth anyone could bust that dad apart from that son."

"Short of murder, you're probably right."

"So what's Mrs. Raines say about Laurel? Does she know where she is? Did Laurel keep in contact with her?"

Another pause and Emily said, "She said she's dead."

Louisa stared at the profile of her daughter as she reiterated her conversation with Phoebe Raines.

"I bet that's killing her every day she's alive. Her only daughter, her only child, killed by her child's own husband. And, there's nothing she can do about it. If the law enforcement in Dune County is the same as it is in Gold County, nothing's going to touch Dwayne Ed Twerms."

They had stopped at a Burger King on their way out of town.

Bags of burgers warming their hands, they were just about to sit down when they heard, "Howdy, ladies."

Standing behind them was Sheriff McIntire, this time with his hat in his hand and sunglasses in his pocket. Louisa shielded her annoyance better than Emily and said, "Howdy yourself, Sheriff. Isn't this off your beaten path?"

"Yes, ma'am." His eyes crinkled in mockery. "We're back in Gold County. Only two little corners of San Domingo hang into the other counties. I kind of keep a look out for the other sheriffs though. You know, we have an unwrit…"

"…an unwritten law that you help each other out," mimicked Emily. "Was that why you were dropping that fellow off in Shanty Town?"

"Why, yes ma'am." Sheriff McIntire feigned surprise. "I didn't know if you knew I was there or not. But, Miss Emily, I sure knew you were there, and I knew your Mama here was at the courthouse. Now, ladies, I hope you're not trying to bother Dwayne Ed or any of our fine, upstanding taxpayers in these counties. We don't take kindly to harassment, ladies."

"So did you do anything about Dwayne Ed?" asked Louisa.

"Now, ladies, I already told you. I have no authority in another county."

"Except when convenient for you."

"That's how I run the county."

"I would think the people in your county would be interested to know just what you do to run it."

"They voted me in."

"If I lived here, I'd mount a campaign so fast and furious to get you recalled, you wouldn't have time to get into the next county, where your so-called fellow officers could take you in."

"But, you don't live here."

"You need to take a few courses in public relations."

"Now, now, ladies, don't get your backs up."

As he left the restaurant, he placed his beige hat on his curly head of hair and took the sunglasses out of his pocket to shield his eyes. He turned and gave the two women a half smile and a tip of his hat.

"Let's go eat in the car," Emily said.

*   *   *   *

After a pause to display the contents of the now cold wrappings, Louisa complained, "That guy could be a real pain if he protects the county that way. We're only visitors, think what it must be like to live here. He has such a sure fire way of bringing out the worst mood in me."

"He and Aunt Mel. I'll be glad when she goes to her own home. I wonder when it will be. She appears to think she has squatter's rights."

When Louisa didn't answer, Emily asked, "Does she?"

"What? Have squatter's rights?"

At Emily's nod, Louisa started to hedge, "I'm not really sure; I don't really know."

"But, Mom, you were just at the attorney's office. You saw the will. Does she or doesn't she belong there? I know your social worker professionalism makes it hard to give out information that you think is confidential, but just where do you think I'm going to tell anything you say to me?"

On a drawn out "Well", Louisa summarized the issue of the wills. "It seems there was to be an even split to all Atie's sisters, but, about a year before she died, Atie wrote a codicil to the will and had Mel taken out of the split."

Louisa forestalled Emily's next question. "The attorney doesn't know why. He doesn't know if it was a personality difference or an event. It doesn't make sense to me that it would be personality because Mel's always been mean. It seems something must have happened. Here's something else, Em. Polly and Cora were the witnesses to the codicil. That means they've known for a long time what was going to happen to the family."

"Bet that's why they were so happy to see you. It also tells you why you're the executor and not one of the aunts."

Louisa sighed, "I had such hopes that this was going to be a paper shuffle formality. Now, I'm getting this inkling that Aunt Atie isn't going to go for a mere shuffle; she wants a whole dance."

"Lucky you," laughed Emily.

Louisa just grimaced.

* * * *

Approaching the house at the Single Arrow, they heard high pitched screeching. Emily stomped on the emergency brake in the haste of the women to get out of the car and determine what the fracas was. They ran into the house to find Mel, her straight, black hair flying in clumps about her face, holding on to the edge of a cabinet which housed a sewing machine complete with straight, zigzag, and reverse stitches. Grasping the other end of the cabinet was a taller, broader version of Mel, her gray, short hair plastered to her face with the sweat of exertion.

"It's mine!" yelled Mel.

"No, it's not, you snake in the grass. It's mine," screamed the gray haired woman.

"She promised it to me, you vulture."

"No, she promised it to me, you scheming traitor."

"Let go before I call the sheriff."

"If you call the sheriff, you have to let go, and then I'm taking what's mine home," shouted the woman triumphantly. She gave a yank and pulled hard enough that Mel almost yielded her grip on the sewing machine.

Not to be overcome by the infallible logic of her opponent, Mel tried again, "You always took what belonged to me. This time I'm going to get what's rightfully mine." Beads of sweat congealed together to make rivulets of water run down her cheeks in her struggle.

"That's because I deserved it. Mama always said I had to take care of all of you, so I deserved it."

"Well, Mama wanted me to have that stuff. Now, Atie would want me to have whatever I want. I've been taking care of her place ever since she died."

"That's not my problem. You're just here to make sure you get all the good stuff. If I know you, you've hauled it off already and have it stashed at your place." The woman gave the cabinet another yank almost strong enough to force Mel to yield her edge of the machine.

"That's a bald faced lie, you hear? You're always accusing me, you bitch." Mel shoved the cabinet into the other woman's stomach forcing her to wheeze convulsively.

"Stop it, right now." Louisa's coldly authoritative voice broke up the melee causing them to drop their respective ends of the sewing machine with a simultaneous plop.

"Tell her, Louisa. Tell her that's mine. Atie would've wanted me to have it," whined Mel.

"No, I was supposed to get it. I'm the oldest, so I should have first choice of what I want. That's how we did it when Mama died."

"Yeah, and you and Callie stole everything Mama wanted for the rest of us to have, you hear? You two are vultures as bad as the rest of them."

"Clio, it's certainly nice of you to come over and meet my daughter, Emily. I'm sure she's very impressed by your first meeting." Louisa directed her comment at her gray haired aunt, panting with exertion.

She sputtered, "I was trying to…you just have no idea what this woman is trying to…she's stealing…"

"Look here, both of you, there is to be nothing taken off this property, do you understand? The attorney and I have to go through Aunt Atie's papers before we know exactly how things are to be disposed. Atie has specified exactly what she wants to go to whom. If I find anything gone from this house, I will have someone arrested for burglary, got that? This kind of bad taste will stop right now, do you understand?"

Clio and Mel started to spit out explanations. Louisa held up her hand and said, "I don't want to hear it. If you can't be civil to each other, I want you both to leave. This is ridiculous to have two grown women arguing like undisciplined children.

"Besides, which, I don't know why either of you wants this sewing machine. Neither one of you knows how to sew."

Chapter 13

Dwayne Ed stood at the fax machine as it slowly burped out another paper. The fax machine was the only item in the office that didn't have a layer of dusty grease on it, but that was only because it was the newest addition to the room. In due time, it would be coated with the same greasy dust as the computer, telephones, copy machines and typewriters. When Dwayne Ed's mother had run the household, pristine order and hygienic cleanliness prevailed. Even Laurel, when she had moved into the home, had restored the house into tailored neatness. Her leaving induced the household to inattentiveness to its surroundings, so clutter and filth became the reigning decor.

"They're interested," he said to Jonas, standing beside him, as he read the message. "What we need to do is make this the best display we've ever done. We need a big show, something that will make those Yankees stand up and take notice. Then, they'll see how valuable Dwayne Ed Twerms can be to their operation. Something really big. We know how to do it. We've done it before. We'll show 'em we haven't died off." He slapped Jonas on the back gleefully. "This'll be great. Let's get the boys and start planning."

"Tell me what to do," replied Jonas in his deep voice.

Stacks of papers piled in front of the tattered, tapestry drapes prevented them from ever being opened, so it was difficult to see in the room. The desk lamps cast a dirty glow to the surfaces on which they sat, but there weren't enough of them to outshine the dimness.

"Contact everyone; tell 'em we'll meet at the regular spot. Don't forget to tell 'em about that road. That oil company used it for their drilling, and we need to cut around it. Remind 'em that road is too public anymore. You may need to get the tractor out and start a new one."

"No problem."

"This'll be great. Those bastards from the north are going to see the south rise again," Dwayne Ed gloated.

Chapter 14
▼

Two discoveries were made just before 1920 on the Easter Ranch. One was oil; one was deafness. Neither one was needed. Hugh Easter's great-granddaddy had built substantial affluence in the cattle market, so oil seemed to be just some pocket change to put into the equation of the family fortunes. Discovering oil was not unwelcome, however; discovering deafness in the family was. This was not only because of the effect deafness has on one's learning, but also because there was no provision for educating a deaf child short of packing him off to the east.

Irene Easter, great-grandmother of Hugh Easter, was not one to let her children become part of a world she didn't know or hadn't visited. Rather than ship one of her boys out to the land of the outsiders, she decided to take the oil money and open a school for the deaf in Easter County. She dragged into West Texas every progressive educator of the deaf she could find from across the country using the lure of high salaries and free housing. Then she set herself up as President of her hand picked board of directors and funded a foundation with enough oil profits to endow the Easter School for the Deaf for one hundred years.

Miz Easter's school made provision for the latest teaching discoveries of deaf education, so when other American schools for the deaf were tying children's hands behind their backs in an attempt to stop them using signs, Miz Easter and her teachers were out learning standard American

Sign Language. That way they could program their charges with as much English using as many sensory channels as they could pack into their little bodies. When Miz Easter's kids and young adults were reading college level texts and writing high school level compositions, many deaf adults who came out of the state deaf schools where they couldn't sign were only grunting simple speech.

For the most part, the world of deaf education laughed at Miz Easter and her school stuck out in the desert of Texas. They laughed until the first graduating class from Miz Easter's school moved on to Washington D.C. to Gallaudet College, the university devoted to allowing deaf students to reach their maximum learning potential, and graduated from there. Then they modified their derision. When some of Miz Easter's young men and women who graduated from Gallaudet and went into graduate studies in hearing universities, the laughter from the experts in deaf education ceased. Soon, Easter School for the Deaf became a model in progressive education for the deaf.

Miz Easter was quietly smug when it was apparent her gamble paid off, and she helped put West Texas on the map, but she was openly triumphant when her youngest boy, the one everyone said would be retarded, received his PhD in experimental psychology. She died a jubilant woman, and the Easter School for the Deaf lived on.

Chapter 15

"There are so many papers to go through; it's going to take longer than I thought it would. I was hoping we'd be out of here in a week at the most," Louisa explained to Emily as they drove to San Domingo the next day.

"It's not a problem. After today when I go meet Daphne, if you want, I'll help you. I called home, and David said he's really into his project, and Jojo and Lulie have two weeks more of camp, so no one is going to be there even if we went home after one week. Take your time," Emily placated her mother.

*   *   *   *

It wasn't long before Emily turned herself around and lost the direction she was supposed to be traveling. Although the Easter School had a small enrollment, over the years the campus had expanded from one building of classrooms and administrative offices and one building of dormitories to several buildings housing a gym, cafeteria, infirmary and maintenance. The campus resembled that of a well-kept small private college. As she pulled into a parking lot reserved for employees behind a maintenance yard, Emily decided she must have made her wrong turn at the entrance to the circular road which cut into the campus. Deciding it would be easier to walk to the administration building, Emily got out of the car and sought directions from a man getting ready to mount a riding mower.

Phoebe was waiting for her with Daphne in the lobby of the stone faced building that stood at the head of the circular road. Eddie looked like Laurel, but Daphne was Laurel's young twin.

With a shy smile the young woman with the honey blond hair said, "Hello, Emily. I am happy to meet you. My grandmother has told me about you."

Her voice had a flattened nasal quality to it, and her words were very carefully said as if she were afraid of losing them. The sibilants of her speech, because they were not crisp, gave her conversation a mushy quality. When Emily returned the greeting, the girl's blue eyes intently watched Emily's mouth, not her eyes.

Emily asked Phoebe, "I thought we would have to sign. I didn't know Daphne could talk." Phoebe glanced at Daphne to proceed with an explanation.

Again she carefully placed the position of her mouth as she explained, "I was not born deaf. I was born hearing, and I learned how to talk. I can talk, and I can read lips. Everybody can read lips, but deaf people rely on it more than hearing people. I like to sign better because it makes me very tired when I talk a long time.

"Since I knew how to talk before I got sick and became deaf, my teachers here have continued to practice me talking. They also make sure I say the sounds of the words right, so I don't have mushy speech. They say since I cannot hear myself talk, I will always have trouble making clear speech. By making me practice all those sounds, I can live in the deaf and hearing worlds. It is easier for you to hear me talk than have to have someone interpret what I say to you. But, it is hard, too. Sometimes my throat muscles hurt so much when I talk a lot. Some of my friends do not know how to talk because they have never heard talking."

And then, she made the same request her brother had a few days before, "Please tell me about my mother."

"I just did this with your brother. He asked me to do the same thing, tell you about your mother. I will be happy to do that."

"Did you meet Eddie? I miss him. He is the only thing I would go home for. Don't you think he is nice?"

"Yes, I do. I met him at my great-aunt's funeral, and then I met him at your grandmother's. He was very different. Nicer and better looking at your grandmother's."

"Yes. He is so good looking that the girls chase after him. Even here, when he visits, my friends always ask me for to meet him. I tell them it is no use, because Dwayne Ed and Jonas want him to marry Ruthie."

"Ruthie, who's Ruthie?"

"Jonas's daughter," said Phoebe. "She's a young, plain little girl. Jonas and Dwayne Ed are so close, they want to keep their alliance in the family. That's why I hope Eddie will get out of here and meet someone else. He needs to get away from his father."

"I like to tease him about it. He likes Ruthie, but he likes other girls at school, too."

Emily and Phoebe ate lunch with Daphne in the school's cafeteria. They visited Daphne's suite of rooms; they saw the campus classrooms and facilities, and they met many of Daphne's friends. There was an active quiet around the campus, people talking but not making noise. Faces were expressive as fingers whipped about in the air.

"Daphne, do you miss going home?" asked Emily.

Daphne's face lost expression as she stated matter of factly, "I do not miss it any. I do not like my father. The house is dirty. I miss my mother and my brother. Sometimes I see my brother. My father is mean."

Chapter 16

Louisa laid her cheek in the palm of her hand and looked at the stack of files she had gone through and the other stack of files still to be studied. That stack was still three times the size of the pile she had already examined.

Oil leases, land contracts, deeds on buildings, stock certificates, notes for mortgages held, schedules of stud fees for bulls, passbooks, certificates of deposits and various miscellany of monetary management comprised the cornucopia of Erato Ewell's wealth. Atie had so efficiently organized her holdings with notes to Louisa and John Utley for specific distribution of them to her heirs that Louisa wondered if it was productive to go through the items individually. However, the will stated she must, and a legality is a legality.

Emitting a sigh of frustration, she idly picked up one of the top folders out of the unanalyzed pile. Unlike the others that had been carefully labeled and dated, this one had nothing on the tabs, but it was well worn and smudged from being handled repeatedly. In it she found a standard, legal sized oil and gas lease on which had been typed information granting the mineral rights to several hundred acres of land in Dune County. Reference was also included in the deed to the exact volume of deed records that described the land. On the inside cover was written a note:

Louisa,

Make sure Mel gets this as it is the only inheritance I will leave her.

Erato Ewell

Attached to the mineral deed was a plat map of sections about one inch square with minute lettering in the squares, lettering so tiny that some of it could not be read with the naked eye. Louisa recognized none of the names on the deed except her Aunt Atie's, and she could only surmise the plat map must be that of the land described in the deed. She wasn't sure where the original map might be, so she went to find Atie's attorney.

To his secretary in the anteroom, she said, "Is John around?"

"Just go on in, Mrs. Daniel. He said to tell you whenever you have a question, go on in and ask him."

"John," Louisa asked as she stepped into an office lined with books and paintings of West Texas, "do you have any idea where the original of this map might be?"

He took the map and said, "These are used mainly by oil companies to determine the current ownership of the land. See, these upright letters show the landowners, and the slanted letters show the mineral rights owners. Most of the time on these maps, out here, you'll see small circles which show the results of drilling efforts. An empty circle is a dry well. A circle with half of it black indicates a show of oil but not economically feasible to produce, and a black circle indicates an oil well. I only see a few of those circles up here in the left hand corner which indicates there has been virtually no drilling on this big parcel of land down here."

Taking out a magnifying glass, John Utley paused in his explanation as he studied the map carefully. He looked at the map and then up at Louisa. "Wonder why there's no drilling on this parcel down here. I thought every foot of land out here that could be drilled had been. Where did this come from, did you say?"

"It's part of that stack of paperwork I'm supposed to look over. This came out of an unmarked file, but it had been handled a lot. There was a note from Aunt Atie instructing me to make sure Mel got this as it would be her only inheritance. It's part of a deed to mineral rights that Atie had purchased. Guess she wanted Mel to have the mineral rights."

"Is that right? I'll tell you, Louisa, if this parcel has never been drilled, then Mel stands to gain very much from the minerals on that land. Those completed holes up here in the corner may indicate there might be oil the further south you go. Some oil company is going to have a heyday if it has the opportunity to drill on untouched land with strong shows of oil surrounding it.

"To have mineral rights on land is, sometimes, more valuable than having the land itself. It means the minerals coming out of the land belong to the holder of the deed, and minerals such as gold, silver, oil, gas, water, and coal can be rewarding items to own. Many times, when land is sold, the original owner of the land will not sell mineral rights but sells only the surface ownership. To be able to buy mineral rights in an oil producing area like West Texas is a rare opportunity not to be missed. Atie was lucky to get these."

"Maybe Atie already contacted an oil company about drilling. Would she have done that?"

"She might. She might know some geologist or drilling contractor who could assemble a drilling partnership and promote a drilling venture. You have to have a geologist explore it and look for the most likely spot to drill."

"How do they know how to locate the drill site?"

"Good scientific research and persistent work. Now, you stop me when you've heard enough. This is the language of oil. Around here, we happen to love that language, but, if you don't get jazzed by the smell of crude oil, you probably won't be jazzed by the talk of it.

"Geologists use maps like these to show them where oil has been found in the past. Often they take seismic surveys, which are sound waves bounced off various underground structures, and look at cores of the subsurface rock formations. Through the use of well logs of existing drill holes, both oil wells and dry wells, they review geologic history of the area to see if there are any traps that would hold oil. Traps were formed by porous and permeable rock formations that were terminated in an uptilted formation by nonpermeable rocks. The oil generated by sea life, it's thought, migrated into the porous rock and rose through the ever present sea water. That oil then accumulated on top of the saltwater pool and remains there until someone can tap it. Drilling equipment can go so deep now, much deeper than it could even thirty years ago, so many of these areas that were drilled with few shows of oil in the past are being reexplored to see if oil is in deeper rock formations."

"And, if they think there's oil?"

"Then the oil company will try to lease the land from the mineral rights owner. Most oil companies have landmen who go to county courthouses and run records to determine mineral ownership on land tracts which their geologists have designated for exploration. Running records means the landmen are examining the chains of title from present ownership back to some point that determines complete mineral ownership. If the landmen can trace the ownership, then they can clear title and proceed to lease the land for drilling. The company takes that information and the geologist's information and develops a drilling partnership. The partnership allows costs to be spread, and, if the amount of oil is worth producing, the partnership reaps the profit.

"In laymen's terms—a few million years ago, oil was nothing but simple little sea creatures and bugs swimming around, and now those little bodies are worth millions. Just goes to show you how properties appreciate if you hang on to them long enough."

Louisa smiled at his joke as John paused, thought and then said, "Wonder why Atie would leave that to Mel only and not her other sisters. I didn't think Atie liked Mel."

"I assume the county clerk would have this volume of records, so I could look up the land?"

"You mean title chain? Are you talking about going to Dune County?"

Louisa nodded yes to both questions.

"Should have. Don't expect too much from over there though. I subscribe to a map library; I'll see if I can order the map for this area of land you're looking at. It'll be easier to read and might give us more information."

"In the meantime, it looks like a trip to Dune County might be in order," Louisa said.

She carried the map back to her stack of papers and read over the file again. The signature block contained a date within a month of Atie's death and several months after the codicil to the will forbidding Mel's inheriting any of Atie's estate was written. Louisa's first thought was to wonder about the stability of her aunt given the fact that her note had been written so close to the date of her death. If the codicil disinheriting Atie had already been written, why would Atie wish Mel to receive this land? Perhaps Atie felt guilty in leaving Mel out of the will and was going to appease Mel with a windfall of oil.

At least, she thought, it would be something on which to focus. It gave an aura of mystery, however farfetched, and would liven up Louisa's reading of documents. Perhaps the job wouldn't be so tedious if there were a puzzle requiring an answer. The thrill of the chase and all that.

Chapter 17

Emily had said her farewell to Daphne and Phoebe, who had decided to spend the remainder of the afternoon with her granddaughter, in the main quad of the campus. The school had been built in the residential section of San Domingo that lay in Easter County, so Emily decided to take a walking tour of the well-maintained Texas Victorian homes. She walked in relative coolness fostered by the shade of many pecan trees. Here there were no pump jacks to be found, only huge trees and green lawns that sported imposing three and four storied homes, some surrounded by shade porches, some with rounded towers, some with widow's walks around their cupolas, all secure in their moneyed stature.

Emily began her walk back to the parking lot behind the school where she had parked, took a wrong turn and became disoriented in the residential area she had been touring. A few more wrong turns brought her to a copse of dense, high bushes. Although she could see a cyclone fence protruding a couple feet over the ten-foot high copse, she could only assume the wall was one protecting the main quad of the school because the wall ran several blocks. Relieved she had come within the vicinity of the school, she hurried along the wall profuse with greenery.

As she rushed along the wall, she saw ahead of her about half a block a person emerge from the dense mass of bushes. Not wanting to be late to pick up her mother, Emily was delighted to realize there must be an entrance in the wall which meant she wouldn't have to skirt the three block long fortress to find the parking lot. Emily's rushing and the person's limping bridged the gap between them quickly, so Emily could see the person was a woman. But, she hadn't found the entrance, and Emily knew she had passed the area from which the woman came. Emily went back a few feet nearer the post of a street lamp and ducked into the forest of tall bushes.

Although there was no door, she had a very clear view of the quad near the area she had left Phoebe and Daphne. In fact, Daphne and Phoebe, expressions flitting across their faces as their fingers and hands made poetry in the air, were still there sitting on a bench under a shade tree where she had left them. Because the branches of the bushes on the outside of the fence were high enough, Emily could go forward a few feet before she had to exit the undergrowth. Still, she found no door.

Coming out of the green stillness, she was almost upon the limping woman.

"Excuse me," she hailed the woman, but there was no response from her.

Thinking the woman might be deaf, Emily rushed behind her and started to reach out to tap her on the shoulder. The woman, however, tried to walk faster, but the limp slowed her down. Emily was able to come in front of the woman and said, "Excu..." when she stopped abruptly. Shaking her head, she squinted her eyes shut momentarily. Slowly she opened her eyes and looked at the woman.

Thoughts jarred Emily's logic. *This is wrong. No logical explanation for this. I must be more disoriented than I realized. I've got to get to my mother. All this talk of lost people and relatives and the past has me rattled.*

Again, Emily closed her eyes and shivered as she continued to walk backward. The woman limping along and hunched over in concentration of the sidewalk held her arms to her body as if by squeezing all that she is back into herself, she could keep herself a secret from the world. She never looked up.

Emily reached out as if to stop her, and the woman skirted her outstretched arm, but Emily, continuing to walk backwards, stayed in front of her and scrutinized the woman. Keeping her head down, the woman muttered, "Go away."

Surprised, thinking she must be too aware of Laurel's children and too anxious about losing her car, Emily said tentatively, "Laurel?"

The woman kept walking and repeated, "Go away."

"Are you Laurel?"

They were coming to the end of the wall, and Emily could see the lot in which she parked, but she didn't want to lose the woman. However, also at the end of the wall was the corner of the street. It was bound to happen to Emily who had been walking backwards for a block and a half, and it did. When Emily stepped off the corner of the street, she fell. As she lay in a heap, the woman she had thought she recognized took off in a bounding series of hops.

Emily picked herself up, turned her ankle tentatively, and, although it was strained, decided she hadn't twisted it severely and turned to follow the woman. Emily looked across the street she had just tripped over at a business section of town, but she couldn't see the woman. She saw two gas stations on corners opposite each other. She saw a small strip mall with stores offering burritos, or tattoos or cellular phones or video rentals. She saw a plumbing shop beyond the strip mall, and she saw a grocery market next to the other gas station. She saw no woman.

She paused, leaned against a street sign to let her ankle relax. She was almost convinced she had made a consummate fool of herself by mistaking a stranger in a town strange to her for a dead woman. Almost. She wasn't sure, and, as the woman's face dimmed in her memory, Emily wasn't even sure why she had thought the woman was Laurel. Laurel certainly never limped. The fact that she could disappear so quickly was peculiar and made Emily wonder if, perhaps, she had seen an apparition superimposed on a stranger.

Laurel. How could that be Laurel? Older, for sure. Her hair wasn't that same honey blond; she was heavier. But, the college Laurel is gone, just like the college Emily. Spooky? You bet! Laurel hasn't been in this area for at least a decade. She must be on my mind because this is the last area I can place her, the last thread of her existence is here. That's all it is. That woman wasn't really Laurel. If she had been, she would have said something to me.

I think. I think she would have done that. She was my friend. She wouldn't not acknowledge me.

However, Emily wasn't really sure. She wasn't really sure that Laurel would have acknowledged her, nor was she sure that the woman was Laurel. As the throb in her ankle subsided, she continued to question what she had really seen. Wishful thinking? Was her curiosity chafing her perception, so she was manufacturing people out of trees? How stupid to think someone, especially a grown woman, would emerge from a copse of bushes like a genie from a lamp. And, to make that woman Laurel of all people. Laurel was gone. Wiped off the face of the earth. Her mother couldn't even find her, and if her mother used professional help to locate her daughter, what made Emily think she could find Laurel, or that Laurel would appear in Emily's sight?

This is crazy! I've got to find out for myself. If that is Laurel, and I miss this opportunity to help her, I'd kick myself from now until the day I die. What if she needs help? The woman looked like her last lifeline had been cut. What if...what if she's whacked out? No, scratch that. Laurel wouldn't be like that. She was too stable.

Emily lobbed the last thought into the deepest fissure of her brain. Ambivalence about possibly meeting Laurel settled over her. Her ankle mellowed to a dull ache. Louisa would be at Utley's office waiting patiently.

Even so, the identity of the woman continued to goad her mind.

Crossing the street, Emily, her decision made, walked determinedly past the gas station and the strip mall and the plumbing store. There was a side road between the gas station and the strip mall, right next to the tattoo parlor. There was an alley between the strip mall and the plumbing store. She proceeded up the road to find five, long, rectangular houses, different only in the color of paint that covered them, and a warehouse. The houses were a possibility. She then walked past the strip mall and down the alley. There she saw a car repair shop with a large twostory stucco house behind it. On the bottom floor of the house was an office, presumably for the car repair shop. Deciding to try the house first as being the easier to eliminate from her choices of the businesses and the five long houses, she stepped in.

A squirrel cage water cooler and no lights provided a pleasant coolness to the interior of the office. The living room of the house had been converted to an office by eliminating the wall separating the foyer and putting a counter across the back wall to the left of the room. At the counter sat a non-smiling, dark haired woman whom Emily approached.

"*Sí, señora*," said the woman.

"I'm looking for a friend of mine. She has honey blond hair, a little shorter than I am and walks with a limp."

<*No hablo inglés.*>

"Ooh," said Emily disappointedly. She hadn't used her college Spanish in so long, she was having difficulty recalling it.

"*Yo busco una amiga*, um, *blanca*, no *rubia, roto en su cadera*, um, oh," she said as she tried to imitate the limp she had seen the woman use.

The Hispanic woman looked at her in a blank of confusion.

Emily, frustrated, looked to her right, saw the stairs and dashed up them. She heard the woman yell, "*No, señora, no entre. Por favor, no entre.*"

Emily hopped two stairs at a time in her run up to a hallway where pine cleaner tried to quell the odor of the very old building. At the landing, she looked down a smoky yellow hallway that had several rooms all closed off by doorways. Out of the door closest to the stairwell came a burly, dark haired man clad in jeans and an atlas undershirt.

"Whadda ya want?" he growled. "You're not s'pose to be up here. Residents only."

"Please, I'm looking for someone, a friend of mine. I think she came in here. The lady downstairs doesn't speak English. My friend? Is she here?"

The man grabbed her arm, spun her around and hauled her down the stairs. Her feet bumped against the risers of the stairs as she was dragged down against the man's sweating body. "You ain't allowed in here," his voice rumbled. "Get out, now."

"But, my friend. I think she's here. I don't want to hurt her. I just want to talk. Please. Her name is Laurel. Is she here?" Emily's pleas, pervaded with desperation, were of no use as the man continued to wrench her along the foyer until he got to the front door. There he twisted her from him, placed his massive mitt on the square of her back and pushed her out the door. As she stumbled out the doorway, she looked back, before he slammed the door in her face, and she thought she saw sympathy in the eyes of the woman at the desk.

Her other alternative of checking out the row houses yielded little information or hope of finding the supposed Laurel. Two of the houses were homes for two ancient couples, one of which spoke only Spanish. One was empty; one was overpopulated by several small children being cared for by an extremely hassled mother, and one had a 'Daysleeper' sign on the door. Emily could see when the doors she knocked on were answered that the floor plan would make it difficult to hide anyone in the houses. The kitchen was at the back of the house, and the long narrow portion of the home was the living and sleeping area off of which was a small bathroom.

Discouragement and doubt played off each other in Emily's mind as she drove back to the center of town to pick up Louisa. Scanning the rearview mirror to turn into another lane of the road she was traveling, she saw Sheriff McIntire following her. She took a right turn earlier than intended, and it resulted in her anticipation of Sheriff McIntire's move because he followed her into the turn. Finding herself in a residential section of town, she wandered the streets. So did the Sheriff.

*   *   *   *

While Emily was playing follow the leader with the sheriff of Gold County, Louisa was thumbing through oil company leases in Atie's files. Not finding an active lease on the land for which she was holding out the deed to mineral rights, she decided to go across to the court-house and see if, perchance, they had an ownership map of Dune County. Since the counties were so amenable about sharing law enforcement duties, Louisa figured maybe they shared records also. If anything, it would give her a chance to stretch her sitting muscles by walking a bit.

*   *   *   *

"Can I help you?" drawled out a spiky haired, tiny, young lady as Louisa, looking confused, came down into the vault housing the deeds in the Office of Records.

"Yes, I think so. I have this deed, and it has the quadrants of a tract of land, but it's in Dune County. Would you, by any chance, be able to help me find this in Dune County? I mean, I know this is Gold County, but I thought, perhaps, you'd have the surrounding counties."

"Well, now, I'm not sure we can find the exact volume of deeds you're looking for in Dune County, but I can maybe help you if you show me what you've got," she said with smiling efficiency.

"We have so many old families in this area, that their lands are just everywhere. They marry and inherit all over this part of the state. All our Gold County records are there in those big old books over there." She pointed a one inch nail polished with two different shades of blue in the direction of a series of shelves with books about three feet by two feet.

Louisa nodded, and the young woman said, "Now you can just take yourself over there and look to see if what you want is there. I kind of doubt it, though, seeing as how you said it was in Dune County."

"Do you maybe have a map of Dune County? Maybe I could get an idea of where the land is from that."

"Yes, ma'am, we do, but show me what you've got. I've lived in these parts all my life. I should know just about every piece of land here."

Louisa gave her the copy of the deed. The young woman expertly scanned all the whereases and covenants of the lease and finally said, "I know right where this is. Do you know why I know where this is?"

"No, should I?"

"No, ma'am, but you're the second person asking about that acreage. There was another fella in here about two days ago. Isn't it interesting how things just go in cycles? Now let me show you where this is. Come over here to the map, and I'll show you."

Following the woman to the wall where the map of the area was, Louisa asked, "Do you know who it was?"

"Who? You mean the other person asking about this land. No, ma'am, I have seen him with my daddy before, but I'm not sure what his name is. Kind of a tall guy, a little younger than my daddy. Real good looking."

"That could be just about anybody in this area. They all seem tall and good looking."

"Yes, ma'am," she heartily agreed, "ain't it wonderful!"

Chapter 18

"You certainly look like you've seen the proverbial ghost. Does Daphne look that much like her mother?" said Louisa as she entered the car.

"Mom, would you mind driving?"

"Sure, honey," Louisa said. "What happened?"

Emily then began to chronicle the events of her afternoon.

She concluded with, "It doesn't even make sense that woman was Laurel. If she didn't die, why doesn't she let someone know?"

"Maybe it's safer to stay dead," countered Louisa.

"But, Mom, Phoebe said she loved those kids more than life itself. She's missed out on almost their whole growing up years. She wouldn't want to miss that."

"Em, honey, the kids are probably the safest they could ever be. If she came back, Dwayne Ed would use them as a weapon against her. From what you said, Dwayne Ed will never acknowledge Daphne, so she's safe and, obviously, loved by her grandmother. And, Eddie, he has his grandmother, too. She may able to foil Dwayne Ed's viciousness, so it won't infect the son.

"Besides, he's safe, too. As long as his father thinks he has his son under his belt, the kid is okay. It sounds like the kid and Gramma figured that out a long time ago."

"But, it's such a gamble. Laurel could be ruining that kid by allowing him to stay with his father."

"Sure, it's a gamble. But, Emily, it could be the safest gamble she's had to make."

"Okay, but there are some other things. If she's been in San Domingo all this time, someone's bound to know. Her mother and Maria Elena must know, and either they're very good at covering up for Laurel, or they don't really know she's alive. I think they don't really know."

"Not necessarily."

"How do you mean?"

"I mean, I agree with you about not knowing Laurel is alive, if she is alive. Laurel may not live here."

"But, I saw her. At least, I think I did."

"Emily, think. You wouldn't stay in a small city like San Domingo if you want to stay dead. Someone's bound to see you. You did; you saw Laurel. In all those years, someone's bound to see her and recognize her."

"She'd have to move away, but she could move to a large city close by, like San Antonio or even Austin. She could disguise herself, so she could still check on her children. Maybe the limp was a disguise. You said there was a clear view of Daphne and Phoebe when you looked through the fence where you thought there was a door. Maybe that's how she sees her children."

"Well, then, someone has to know she's here."

"Perhaps."

"Those people at that boarding home must know. I still think that's where she went."

"Perhaps."

"I could swear that lady knew what I was trying to tell her. My Spanish is really rusty. It looked like she felt sorry for me when that sumo wrestler threw me out of the house. It was kind of dark, though, but I think she knew."

"We could find out," suggested Louisa.

"Right, how? Go in and ask them?" said Emily caustically.

"Your frustration is showing. What do you think about having a low tire?"

"I think it's too hot outside to sit by the side of a Texas two-lane waiting for Sheriff McIntire to come by and tell us how he knows everything going on in three counties.

"By the way, he followed me up and down and all around the town, I forgot to tell you."

"I wonder if he knows the legal definition of harassment," muttered Louisa.

"Only if it fits in his way of running Gold County."

"Okay, let's go make a low tire. You said that boarding house had a car repair shop with it. Maybe we could have them check out the tire."

"How do you mean?"

"All right, think about this. You stay back. They don't know our car, and they don't know me. If the lady is at the front desk, I can tell her what I need, and then we'll know she's lying about not knowing English."

"We've got nothing to lose. Let's do it. After we let air out of the tire, you can drop me off in that neighborhood near the deaf school, and then we'll see what happens."

* * * *

Unless she had a twin, the non-smiling, dark-haired woman Emily had met was the same woman who greeted Louisa. "Can I help you?"

Louisa explained her predicament of a tire with a slow leak.

"I will have Pedro look at it for you."

Pedro was called from downstairs; he removed the tire from the car and looked for a leak to no avail. He went back into the office to give Louisa the diagnosis.

"Maybe it is so small a hole, I can't see it," he said apologetically. If it happens after we put some air into it, I will look again."

Louisa was effusive. "Oh, thank you so much. You just don't know what peace of mind that brings to me. You've been so helpful. Now, what do I owe you?"

The woman said, "There is no charge. Pedro didn't fix anything."

"But, there must be a charge, at least, charge for his labor."

"Okay, pay us five dollars. It only took him a few minutes."

Louisa continued her unctuous gratitude as she backed out the door.

After retrieving Emily, Louisa explained, almost verbatim, what had occurred.

"But, you know, Mom, it doesn't really tell us anything, about Laurel, I mean."

"That's true. It only tells us the woman was hiding something. Her English was flawless. It's not like she just crossed over the Rio Grande yesterday; she's grown up in this area, I bet."

When the subject of the alleged Laurel was exhausted, Emily remarked, "In all this, you haven't told me about your afternoon. Was it productive? Are you done with the papers?"

"Not productive, not done with the papers, but interesting." Louisa described the investigation of the deed to mineral rights she had found in Atie's papers.

"So what do you think?"

"I think the file was smudged and handled enough to appear to concern Atie. I'd like to go see that land, and I'd be curious to know who that man was who was asking about the land. I guess I hope if we go out there, he will miraculously appear, and we can find out what's significant about that deed, if anything."

* * * *

Screaming from Mel as the two women approached the Single Arrow ranch house caused Louisa to say grimly, "I wonder what relative she's trying to prevent from stealing today."

Louisa and Emily marched into the kitchen of the ranch house only to find Mel, her back turned and her straight black hair jerking with the punctuation of her taunts, screaming into the black telephone.

"Just what are you saying? I said I don't like the idea, it's too risky."

After a pause, she began a barrage of emotion, "It's bringing too many of 'em in here, you hear? I've done everything I could all my life to keep it going. We're just getting going again, and I don't want to see it flop, you hear? You got to have patience."

Another pause and the woman started in a high-pitched squeal, "Now, you listen here, you critter lower 'n a snake's belly. Don't you start in on that. It was your idea; I only carried it out. Don't you talk to…"

The caller must have hung up on her because she didn't finish her last statement. Louisa and Emily stepped out of Mel's sight into the kitchen and acted like they had just come in from outside.

Mel saw them as she moved into the kitchen from the phone nook, looked at them nearsightedly and said defensively, "I guess you'll be wanting dinner. Well, I don't have any made, so you'll just have to fend for yourself. I got somewhere I gotta be real soon, you hear?"

Trying to hide her delight in hearing the good news, Louisa said, "We can manage, Aunt Mel. We may even go into town."

"No need of doing that. Atie's got plenty here. Might as well use it up. Doesn't look like she's going to need it."

Louisa's face softened because she thought she heard a twinge of sorrow in Mel's voice. "No, I guess not."

"If you do go into town, you got to get us some more kerosene. You just about used up all we got." She glared at Emily, and Louisa decided sorrow wasn't really what she had heard earlier.

"By the way, that Maggie Barnes called looking for you girls. Guess she wants to have you over. If you work it right, you might get an invitation for dinner tonight. Then you don't have to take any of Atie's food.

"That Maggie Barnes is trouble. Lucky you don't have your man around here on account of she'd take him from you," she said to Emily.

"What're you talking about, Mel?" Louisa asked.

"Just what I said. That Maggie steals men. That's how she got her husband."

"What do you mean?"

"I gotta go. Don't get carried away with that larder, you hear?"

"We hear," said Louisa.

Chapter 19
▼

The government sent his disability check today, so Henry Wade took himself over to the San Domingo bar to lose himself in alcohol-induced apathy. Because he had the funds, he decided to take the bus. It would let him get started drinking earlier than he did when he walked to the bar.

The bus let him off two blocks from Toast's Bar. He walked those two blocks and worked up a sweat, whether from the exercise or the anticipation of a stiff drink, it would be hard to say. Toast, bulging forearms across his chest, stood watching the big screened television mounted in an upper corner of the wooden room. Turning as he heard the door squeak open, he gave a silent nod to Henry and moved over to the bar to pour a glass of cheap whiskey as Henry seated himself on a barstool padded in brown vinyl.

"Nah," said Henry in a voice burned rough by the gallons of alcohol riding roughshod over it. "I got my check today. Give me the good stuff."

"You got it," said Toast as he turned to the baseball game on the television.

Conversation between the two was as sparse as the decor of the bar. No pictures on the walls meant no broken glass on the floor in the brawls that occurred frequently; cheap pine furniture broke easily so fewer patrons were seriously hurt in those same brawls; bare wooden booths were securely anchored into the wall so they couldn't be ripped out easily. The neon and mirrored beer signs were at the eight-foot level of the ten-foot walls, so they couldn't be used as weapons. To play pool on the heavy slate table, customers brought their own cue sticks and took chances there would be enough balls to rack. It was a building designed for violence, and it had more than its share.

Toast had tried to talk to Henry when he first returned to town. He had been at most of the games Henry had quarterbacked and had watched the kid win the state championship for San Domingo High. Toast wanted to relive those days; Henry didn't. The only time Toast had ever seen Henry bark at anything was when he was pressed to tell about his glory days; it was as though Henry couldn't even remember them, he had blocked his San Domingo past so completely.

Dwayne Ed Twerms and Jonas Reed were the second customers of the day, but they didn't arrive until early evening. By that time, Henry was well on his way to semi-awareness. Dwayne Ed came up to Toast and handed him his flask.

"Fill it," he demanded.

Dwayne Ed watched intently as Toast carefully filled the flask with amber liquid. "Didn't spill a drop," said Dwayne Ed as he slapped a fifty dollar bill on the bar which Toast scooped up.

"The regular?" asked Toast as he proceeded to draw a beer.

Jonas nodded.

Dwayne Ed swaggered over to Henry at the other end of the long bar.

"Hey, boy," he said as he jabbed Henry's shoulder with his palm. Henry's response was to lift half his face off his arms laid out on the bar and look at Dwayne Ed with one baleful eye. He then went back to the cocoon of his folded arms.

Louder, Dwayne Ed said, "I said hey, you, boy."

Jonas smirked as Dwayne Ed commanded Henry's attention, but this second time Henry didn't look at Dwayne Ed.

Dwayne Ed slapped Henry's shoulder harder this time. "Hey, you piece of shit, look at me when I talk to you. You ain't showing respect!"

Henry's head stayed down while Dwayne Ed tried a new tack. "How come every time I come in here, you're here? You got any friends, scum? You got a girl, boy? I bet you don't have a girl. Why, I bet you are some kind of pouf. You are a sleezebag pouf."

Dwayne Ed started laughing while Jonas smiled, "Jonas, I believe we have our own drunken homeless person." He took gulps from the flask in between belly laughs and said, "Yeah, I can't believe in our neck of the woods, we got us a real live black pouf. Toast, did you know that—a real life piece of garbage? Now these maggots can go anywhere, not just the big cities. You better watch this here establishment; you don't want these trash people hanging around here. Scares away the paying customers."

Dwayne Ed lunged at Toast, grabbed his collar and screwed his sweaty, red face nose to nose with Toast. "If you keep encouraging this drunken warts of society to come to your place of business, I'll have to stop it. I don't want black boys in my town. You got that, Toast? This is my town—has been for generations, and ain't nothing gonna mess with my heritage."

Looking at Jonas, Dwayne Ed said, "Outta here, Jonas. This place stinks."

Chapter 20

"We just can't let you leave without some Texas hospitality. It just wouldn't be polite. Ty and I want you to come for dinner. What night could y'all make it?" Maggie Barnes said into the phone.

"What about Wednesday?" asked Emily.

"Oh, that would be just wonderful. Anytime after 6:00, and we can sit on the patio because it'll be cool enough. We are so looking forward to it.

"Now, we are the last ranch before Dune county ends. You just follow the main road that goes past your Uncle Luke's place. Your mama will remember his ranch."

* * * *

At dinner Louisa informed Emily that tomorrow she would be visiting the plot of land marked on the deed to Mel. "Maybe it's good farmland or something."

"We've been in West Texas over a week, and I haven't seen any good farmland. I've seen good oil land, and good cattle grazing land, and good desert land, but I have yet to see good farmland."

Louisa gave her an irritated look. "You know what I mean. Do you want to come?"

"You bet. It's for sure I don't want to stay around here with Mel. Guess we can pick up some kerosene, too. It'll maybe keep her off our backs. After that, what will you do?"

"Guess I'll go back to Utley's and read some more legalese. What do you want to do?"

"I think I'll park myself somewhere near that boarding house and see if the Laurel look-alike shows up."

"Bet she won't."

"Why not?"

"It's the week. My thought is she has to work somewhere, and she can only come in on the weekend. She's not going to want a high profile job, so she probably works below her capabilities. That way, no one will notice her."

Emily looked at her mother and thought about her assessment of the alleged Laurel.

"What a life. She was so intelligent. Such a waste."

* * * *

Knowing the heat of the day would beat them to their destination, they started out just after dawn Tuesday morning while the cool of the night still lingered. Instead of waking Mel who came in late the previous evening, they stopped in San Domingo at Lou's diner that was across the street from Toast's Bar. As they drank their coffee and sponged their biscuits in puddles of gravy, they watched Sheriff McIntire get out of his car, walk over to a huddled man, lean down to say something to him as he put the arm of the man around his neck to help him shuffle to the car. The man flopped his head on the back seat of the car, and the Sheriff drove off.

"That must be that fellow Phoebe Raines' neighbor told me about," said Emily.

"What do you mean?"

"A neighbor of Phoebe's told me Sheriff McIntire would escort some person, who drank the night away, home. You know, the sheriff with the x-ray eyes who knows everything going on in the county. Guess he provides a taxi service if someone's had too much to drink."

"Pretty nice service," Louisa shrugged.

*   *   *   *

The spiky haired woman in the County Records office had given Louisa fairly exact measurements to determine the location of the land specified by Atie's deed. The hillock Louisa had seen on the map was fairly close to the road, so she felt she had identified the land stipulated in the deed. They pulled off the road and parked behind the hill which was a little taller than the four wheel they were driving. There was nothing outstanding about the area to which the mineral rights had been granted. Louisa and Emily stood on lonely land with an abundance of hunched and warped mesquite trees, bumbling tumbleweeds and flighty lizards, snakes and horned toads. The sun grilled the sand so that ground heat rose up through the soles of the women's boots. They scrutinized the land in a three hundred sixty degree turn and didn't see anything any different than they had on any other scope of West Texas land.

"So, what do you think, Mom?"

"I don't know what to think. Atie never struck me as one to be remorseful about anything she decided once it was done. Why would she, at the last minute, give her sister deeds to mineral rights after she had cut her out of the will?"

After a pause, she said, "There's something missing, you know."

"Yes."

"Why do you think they aren't here?"

"Maybe no one has found any oil on this land."

"Doesn't make sense, Emily. Every few hundred yards in these three counties we've been in, it seems there are pumping units or active rigs drilling for oil. Doesn't it seem odd to you that no oil company has tried to drill this land in the last seventy-five years?

"Ever since they discovered oil in Beaumont in the early twentieth century, Texans everywhere are convinced they're sitting on the ultimate oil reserve. They're practically begging oil companies to come and poke a hole in their land. This Permian Basin has made so many rich oilmen since the early twenties, it just doesn't make sense no one has drilled this land. Pump jacks and oil derricks everywhere except here. Don't you think that's strange?"

"Yes, strange. Besides, we don't know that it's been seventy-five years without drilling. Maybe this is a dry pocket, and it was discovered to be dry long ago."

"That's right. Let's go find Dune County's records and see what the history of this land is."

"How are you going to know where to look? You don't have the deeds with you."

Louisa gave a triumphant smile as she pulled an envelope from her jeans pocket, "That's right, but I have something just as good–copies. San Domingo Courthouse has all the modern amenities, including a copier. Let's go."

Chapter 21

▼

San Domingo's Courthouse may have had all the modern amenities, but Dunton, the seat of Dune County did not. It was easily located as the town consisted of a few low lying, cinderblock buildings located on the main road. Not sharing the cinderblock architecture, the county seat was easily identifiable as it was a sandy colored brick square which served the multi-purpose of county records office, jail, courthouse and sheriff's office. Wind lashings had taken their toll on the old building because all the wooden frames had been replaced by anodized aluminum glass doors and double paned windows.

When Louisa and Emily entered the building, their eyes were drawn to a carved wooden staircase going up to the third floor. The craftsmanship of the stairs was demeaned by the cracked and chipped yellow and black asphalt squares covering the wooden floor. Mismatched aluminum office chairs were mixed with wooden Windsor chairs in the entryway of the building.

Emily pointed to the sign designating the sheriff's office and said, "Do you suppose they really have one, or has Bonham McIntire been appointed sheriff by proxy?"

"Somebody's in there, let's go ask."

Spread out on a wooden desk before an oily man were two *Soldier for Adventure* magazines and several gun catalogs riddled with grease circles from the cold French fries he was still chomping. A half full bottle of beer kept company with several empties on the desk. He didn't look up when the women walked in but said, "Yeah, whadda ya want?" Louisa said,

"We'd like to check some land ownership. Is the clerk of records here?"

The sound of women's voices brought his head up. "You're looking at him," he snorted.

"I thought you were the sheriff."

Mocking her, he said, "I thought you were the sheriff. I am, so what do you want to make of it. I do it all here."

"Could we just see the land records?"

His black eyes narrowed, "What for?"

"Land records are public records; we want to look at public records. Therefore, would you please give us access to the records?"

He put his hands on the desk to leverage himself out of his chair. As he did, a tray of French fries fell to the floor, but he didn't bother to pick them up. He scratched his stomach when he finally stood and checked the side of his belt to make sure his overstocked key ring was hanging there. His body listed left and then right as he walked slowly down the hallway and opened the records office.

Surveying the office, Emily asked, "How long've you been sheriff here?"

"'Bout ten years."

"Did your predecessor put any papers away, or do we have to go through more than ten years of unfiled information."

Annoyance flushing his face, he stepped towards Emily and started, "Now you look here, missy."

He then stepped back as though he decided Emily wasn't worth the expended energy and nodded toward the room after the women stepped in and said, "There's the records." Then he slammed the door and heaved on back to shop for guns.

"Think he'll let us out?" Emily asked her mother.

"He doesn't know who we are; why should he keep us here?"

"I bet he knows who we are. Everyone here seems to know better who we are than we do."

"Could be. Since the older records are cataloged, let's start from the beginning. What we'll do is look up this land on the deed and find all the names we can that are associated with it. This may only be a piece of someone else's land, but we'll try to find the history. Then I'll locate the last known addresses, and we'll see what we can find."

In a county like Dune where people have kept their land in their families since the discovery of oil, there's not much to search out. Sometimes titles will change when there's a marriage, and a name is added to the title, but, most often, the basic landholding remains the same. Emily and Louisa spent the morning and the early afternoon to discover the land that they had seen that morning was originally part of the Twerms ranch and had been deeded to James Bliss in 1934.

Further search indicated no other ownership change in the land, and the last known address for James Bliss was in Okmulgee, Oklahoma. Tackling the last ten years of records that lay in piles and boxes was the toughest part of the morning. They couldn't find any record of a newer address for James Bliss, and they couldn't find any record of a mineral rights deed filed in the name of Erato Ewell. There seemed to be no connection between James Bliss and Louisa's aunt.

"It could be in any of these boxes, Mom. We just have to look harder."

"No, let's go. I can start trying to find James Bliss, and he could tell me if he ever sold the land. If we need more information, we can come back."

"Right, like I want to find out what kind of weapons Sheriff Cholesterol bought while we were gone."

"This county is probably easy to manage; there's not a whole lot of people in it. He's just a little bored, so he has to entertain himself."

"Seems he could do it by organizing his records a little better than this."

"And," her mother added, "start eating fresh vegetables."

They let themselves out of the room and walked past the sheriff's office. He didn't look up as he grouched, "Y'all leaving?"

"Yes, thank you for your help," Emily said with exaggerated sweetness.

He grunted, and Louisa said as an afterthought, "Sheriff, are you related to the Twerms?"

"Who wants to know?"

"Just curious. I thought I saw a family resemblance."

"My name is Sheriff Twerms; my cousin is Dwayne Ed. Is that what you want to know?"

"Thought so," said Louisa as she and Emily walked out the door.

* * * *

Sirens and lights greeted them as they crossed the Gold County line.

"It appears our ever vigilant Sheriff McIntire is loose again," said Louisa as she pulled over.

His greeting was not pleasant. "I've told you two you just can't harass any of the citizens around here. If you can't quit bothering people, you'll have to leave. I've told you you can't do that. If you don't stop it, I'll lock you two gals up."

Louisa exploded, "You can't do that! It's illegal, and we aren't bothering anyone."

"Wrong. This is my county. I can do anything I want. Leave people alone."

"We need information; I can get anything I want off public records." As an afterthought, she added, "We weren't even in *your* county, Sheriff, so we have no idea what you're harping on now."

"You were in Dune County, and you were asking about Dwayne Ed. Sure sounds like you're up to no good. What kind of information you want about him?"

"None of your business," Louisa snapped.

"Don't take that tone with the law," warned Sheriff McIntire.

"Maybe you need to review the law." Louisa knew she was pushing her luck as she started the engine of the car and drove off in a crunch of gravelly sand.

"Would you like me to drive? I can keep it under the speed limit, so Sheriff McIntire won't have a real reason to arrest us," suggested Emily.

Louisa slowed the car down after Emily called her attention to the speedometer's needle lying almost horizontally on its right side. As the car slowed, her anger cooled. "No, I can handle it. You know, one would think Sheriff McIntire would cozy up to people more desirable than Dwayne Ed."

"Maybe he moonlights for Dwayne Ed."

* * * *

To avoid Mel's snooping and tirades about using the telephone, Louisa and Emily made their calls at attorney Utley's office. A call to information in Okmulgee, Oklahoma provided a phone number for a James Bliss, but a call to that number provided only Mrs. James Bliss. The softness of the voice didn't afford much clue to the age of Mrs. Bliss, so Louisa had no idea, at first, if she had the Mrs. Bliss of the 1930's.

Louisa began the inquiry. "Mrs. Bliss? Are you Mrs. James Bliss from Texas?"

"From Texas?" the woman chuckled. "Oh, my, no. Jimmy and I left Texas in the '40's. Said he wanted to go where cows have green grass to graze, not that old scrub in Texas. We've been here almost sixty years. Well, not Jimmy. He died about five years back, but I still consider him right here by me.

"I got my kids here. Well, not exactly here, but one's in Tulsa and one's in Oklahoma City, and one's in Norman. They come and see me."

Now she knew her age, and Louisa smiled at the openness of the woman. "I'm calling about the land in Dune County, Texas."

Understanding in her voice, Mrs. Bliss said, "You must be one of those oil people. You're always calling me trying to get onto that land, but I keep telling you that's for my kids."

"Are you still saying you have the land?"

"Why, yes. Jimmy saved that land, so our kids could inherit it. He said if oil was there today, it'll be there tomorrow. Our farm up here took good care of us; we didn't need any more money. Besides who wants to fight with those Twermses? Jimmy had his fill of Twermses. That daddy was just as bad as the granddaddy, and I bet that son is just as rotten."

Instead of agreeing with Mrs. Bliss on the condition of Dwayne Ed, she explained, "I'm not from an oil company, but I am the executor for my aunt's estate. In her papers was a deed she's holding for mineral rights to your land. I was over there today, and nothing is happening on the land, so I thought there might be a problem with the title. Did you sell her those rights? Her name in Erato Ewell."

"Oh, no, dear. That's my land, and I know better than to sell the mineral rights. Mr. Twerms lost that piece of land to Jimmy in a poker game in 1934. We'd never sell any of it." She chuckled when she said, "That's probably the only thing Twerms couldn't control completely. After oil was discovered, he offered to pay Jimmy three times its value.

"We'd never sell though. That Twerms was mean about it. After he set our house on fire, Jimmy brought us here. But, he'd never sell."

"What do you mean 'set your house on fire'? Are you sure it was he?"

"Oh, my yes. He bragged about it all over San Domingo. He'd always been above the law, and he knew it. Bet it's still that way, way out there in the middle of nowhere. Bet that grandson of his is above the law, too."

This time Louisa couldn't help but agree, "I think he owns it. Thanks, Mrs. Bliss. You've helped very much."

"No trouble, dear. I'm real sorry the land and rights aren't yours. Your poor aunt probably thought she was doing right by you with those mineral rights. I'm just real sorry."

"I wouldn't worry about it, Mrs. Bliss. My aunt knew just what she was doing, and she did right by all of us. It was nice talking to you, though, and very helpful."

After Louisa repeated the information to Emily, she said, "Mrs. Bliss was very concerned because Aunt Atie wanted to do right by us with those minerals. I told her she's done right by all of us. She obviously wanted to do wrong by Mel, but we don't know why. If she cut her out of the will, she must have known Mel was up to no good. I wonder what it is."

Chapter 22

▼

Henry Wade drank away most of his disability check and wouldn't get another one for about three weeks, so he had to walk to Toast's. Since he had to walk, he wasn't the first one to arrive at the bar. Some others got there before him. Some others, who weren't people he recognized as frequent patrons of the bar, had settled themselves into the hard wooden booths.

There were five men, two on each side of the table and one sitting in a chair drawn up to the end of the table. Three of them wore black leather jackets, but two had succumbed to the heat of the evening and shed their jackets. Primitive tattoos, made with the blue ink of a ball-point, decorated the scrawny muscles of their arms. Shaved heads, pallid skin tones and paranoid shifting of their eyes halted anyone extending southern hospitality to the group. Their curiosity of a newcomer coming into their midst made them look up to see who the new arrival was. However, their curiosity didn't appear to be appeased because they continued to stare at Henry as he nodded to Toast and took his regular seat at the bar.

Henry could see them looking at him in the cracked mirror that hung behind the bottles of liquor at the bar. He even caught the eye of one of the men dressed in a leather jacket and sprouting stubbles of hair on his shaved head. The man looked away before Henry dropped his gaze. He talked softly to his companions who moved in closer to huddle around the pitchers of beer. Although Henry and Toast couldn't decipher their muffled conversation, they could hear the lack of a Texas drawl. These boys were from the north, but after Henry had imbibed his first bottle of cheap liquor, he didn't much care from where the strangers came.

Chapter 23
▼

"You have the directions?" asked Louisa.

"Right here, but it can't be that difficult to find. Maggie said it was on one of those farm-to-market roads off the main highway. Said we couldn't miss it. She said the ranch has one of those big security lights that even if we get lost, we'll be able to see it in the dark. All we have to do it follow it."

"You can't miss it. That's almost a curse, sure to doom someone into getting lost."

"We'll try not to, okay? Let's get that kerosene first."

Twilight was just beginning to pull its purple shade down on the torrid day as they turned onto the Barnes road from the farm-to-market road. Emily and Louisa had found the kerosene in town and stowed it safely in the back of the SUV. Following the landmarks to the house without getting themselves lost made the trip out to the Barnes ranch carefree.

"Hey, we're getting good at navigating the Texas desert," exclaimed Emily. "We don't even need a compass."

"If we can get out of here in the nighttime, then we'll really have passed muster."

* * * *

The youngest of the Barnes boys greeted them at the door with a wide-eyed stare.

"Is your mother home?" asked Louisa.

The boy answered with a silent nod.

"Would you tell her Louisa and Emily are here?"

Again he nodded at them.

"We came for dinner," said Emily.

He nodded at them.

"Maybe we should come in?"

As he nodded again, Maggie whooshed up behind him, wiping her hands on an apron. "Now, Worth, honey, you go play with your brothers. Thank you for coming to the door." She reached down and turned his shoulders to point him in the direction going to the back of the house.

Maggie looked at her guests and said apologetically, "He doesn't talk much. He doesn't have much of a chance with his older brothers helping him out. They anticipate his every need. He likes to help me out though, so I let him answer the door."

They stepped into a log cabin unlike any with which Abe Lincoln would be familiar. Shaker style furniture and oak antiques filled the ballroom-sized living room. A Shaker table large enough to seat sixteen ran the length of the dining room.

"Ty is out on the land; he'll be here in time for dinner, so why don't you come with me to the kitchen? You can sit and have a drink there if you don't mind."

They followed Maggie through the dining room to a kitchen which included a strapping oak harvest table, a stainless steel twelve burner gas stove and oven, two dishwashers, three workstations complete with sinks and dried flowers and herbs hanging from the rafters.

The informality of being in the kitchen broke the ice of conversation much more quickly than being in the formal living room would have. With iced tea in hand, Emily remarked, "You must like to cook, Maggie. You've got a kitchen big enough to cook for a restaurant."

"With my children, I better like to cook. You just wouldn't believe how much those boys can eat. I told Ty when we built our dream home,

I wanted a huge kitchen because I spend just about my whole life in it. So, he built it just like I wanted. He's so nice."

"How did you meet?" asked Louisa.

"Well, we never met exactly. We just all grew up together. We probably met in the church nursery. I mean that's how we all knew each other. We just grew together."

"Who's 'we all'?"

"Well, let's see. There were a whole bunch of us who were always together, especially in high school. We knew each other from church, but we all went to San Domingo High, so we all ran around together. There was Hugh, Ty, Jonas, Maria Elena, Bonham, Ruth, me, Dwayne Ed, Cindy, Henry. Some of those people I don't think you know. There were a few others, but they've left the area. We just stayed together. Kind of took care of each other."

She quit chopping the apples for the salad and looked up at Louisa and Emily, but she didn't see them. It was as if she had turned her eyes inward to scrutinize a scene played inside her head. She said, "Our parents were relieved we were together all the time. They felt there was safety in numbers. Even when Ruth and Maria Elena and I were up for Homecoming Queen, and I got it, we stayed together. We just took care of each other." She paused for a few minutes, and Emily and Louisa looked questioningly at each other as the silent interval continued. Maggie, confusion pervading her statement said, "Then high school was over, and we all went away, and we never got it back when we came home. We never took care of each other again."

The arrival of Ty bumped her out of her musing. As he washed up at the sink at one of the workstations, he asked, "What were you talking about?"

"Not much," said Maggie brightly. "How you and I met. I told them we never actually met; we just always knew each other."

"And, loved each other."

"Oh, Ty, you say the sweetest things," tittered Maggie.

After they stared dreamily at each other for a few minutes, Ty went to round up his brood for dinner.

Chapter 24

Toast had locked the door of the bar a half hour ago.

"Henry, you gotta go home."

Henry raised his head which had been cradled in his arms on the bar and looked at Toast and said, "Yeah, yeah, gotta go home. Home, home, gotta go home. Wish I could go home."

Lifting the passthrough of the bar, Toast came around to Henry, put his arm under Henry's arms and heaved him off the stool.

"Come on, I'll walk you out. Maybe the Sheriff will come by tonight and pick you up. You gotta get out of here, though, because if he finds you in here, he'll have me for breaking the law. Can't stay open past closing hours."

"Yeah, yeah," mumbled Henry as he shuffled along with Toast out the door and onto the sidewalk. "Can't stay open for the drunks. Gotta close."

"Yeah, gotta close," said Toast as he supported Henry while locking the door behind him.

Henry slid down the wall of the building housing the bar. His head lolled around his neck until his chin dropped onto his chest. He slumped against the building for a bit, started coming around slightly and thought as he rolled his eyes up at the dimesized moon, *I hate this life. So useless, such a waste. I hate this life. No, not life. This isn't life, just dirty, sleazy waste. I hate this drinking. I hate this bar.*

He looked at the glittering stars merrily mocking him sitting like discarded rags against the building.

I hate this life. I hate this bar.

He laughed to himself and then out loud. *But, where else can I go? Everything I need is in this bar. No place to go.*

Head sagged to the side, eyes closed, Henry heard the motor slow, then halt to a stop near him. Just like Toast said.

Here comes the Sheriff. Sheriff's coming to pick me up and take me to my house. My house, what a laugh. I hate my house. Here comes the Sheriff.

He heard the footsteps coming closer.

Sheriff must be in a hurry tonight. He's stomping fast, so fast, sounds like there's two of them. Sheriff's coming, better get up. Get up, get up out of the gutter.

As Henry tried to lift himself to a standing position, a hand reached under his armpit while another grabbed his collar. The hands roughly hoisted him out of his standing position. Henry could only look down. In the frail moonlight he could see the boots of the two men surrounding him. The first gut punch leveled him, so that he barely felt the kicks of the booted men that followed.

It was not the Sheriff who had come to get him this time.

Chapter 25

"Maggie must be a whiz at organization if she can get seven kids to be as mannerly as those kids are," remarked Emily to Louisa on the way home.

"If she's so good at organizing, why couldn't she organize her instructions on how to get out of here better?" grumbled Louisa.

"Tell me you don't mean what I think you mean."

"If you want. It wouldn't be the truth, though. We are lost, unequivocally lost."

"Let me see the directions; I'm sure we just need to make a little adjustment." Emily switched on the map light and studied the handwritten paper of lines and arrows Maggie had drawn.

"I think we're past the adjusting stage, Emily. I wouldn't even know where to begin to make a little adjustment," Louisa said as she scanned the very dark expanse around the car. Neither would Emily, but she didn't think voicing that opinion would decrease the tension in the car.

"Perhaps we can just turn the car around and start back at the Barnes' house. They can tell us where to start. Ty might even guide us out," returned Emily hopefully.

"Okay, we're going to run out of gas pretty soon. Now, just point me in the direction of the Barnes' house. It seems we came from that direction, and if I turn down that road, we should be able to find their place."

However, Louisa's left turn onto a dirt road did not materialize into the Barnes road. When they had followed it longer than they wanted to admit, Louisa turned down another dirt road. This one was narrower and more cratered than the previous one. Emily looked at the inky murk outside the car. She helplessly gazed ahead at the sandy stream the headlights illuminated. What landmarks there were could not be distinguished in the meager starlight. It was too late in the evening for a low moon, so its paltry light was of no help in determining where they might be.

Emily glanced obliquely at her mother and saw shadowed determination on her face. At least, she hoped it was determination; it could have been anxiety; it could have been fear, but Emily chose to believe it was determination. Quiet reigned in the automobile as if a sound would cause the car to falter from its tenuous track of delivering Louisa and Emily to Atie's ranch.

Louisa saw the light first, but they said simultaneously, "There it is."

Louisa added, "We must've really got off track to have found Ty and Maggie's place this far from where we thought we were. All we've got to do is follow that light. That must be the security light they told us to look for if we got lost."

Emily's relieved chuckle came out breathlessly as she said, "If you'll get us there, I'll hop out and go ask one of them to guide us out of here. If we get lost again, we may not make it home until tomorrow night."

They continued to follow the orange glow until they came to an even poorer road than the one they had been using. Taking it slowly because there were potholes that would usurp the underpinnings of any vehicle that decided to drag race over them, the women progressed to the Barnes ranch. Two large barns stopped their progress and marked the end of the road. There were two pick up trucks parked off to the right side of the first building, and they parked their four wheel to the left side of those trucks.

"We really did go out of our way. I bet we're at the back of the ranch. Those barns must be storage buildings, and they must have grain or equipment in them," Louisa stated as she turned off the motor and shut off the lights.

Emily had hopped out of the car before Louisa could tell her she would go with her. "Stay there, Mom. I'll be right back," Emily called behind her as she rushed off toward the glow.

Louisa leaned her head against the headrest and waited with her eyes closed. She jerked herself out of a doze after about fifteen minutes. Alarmed because there was no Emily, she glanced at the clock to reaffirm she had really fallen asleep. She pulled on a lightweight, navy sweater she had been carrying in the car and proceeded to step out of the car to look for Emily. As quickly as she exited the driver's side door, a hand reached out and slammed it shut.

"Get down!" hissed a voice.

Louisa asked loudly, "Who are you?"

The same hand clamped over her face, "Quiet, Mom, be quiet. Get down and come with me. You won't believe this. Come on, but you've got to be quiet."

"What's going on?"

"Just let me tell you, if this is the Barnes ranch, they sure are different than we pegged them. That light we saw is not a security lamp. Come and look."

Emily led her mother around the second of the outbuildings past two mesquite trees that had intertwined themselves into a knotty clump. Standing behind the mesquite lattice the two women looked out onto an area of about one hundred yards encircled by cars and trucks. There were some mesquite trees randomly distributed in the clearing of sand.

"Look at that."

Louisa gasped an intake of air. The glow that had guided them to this spot was a fire. It was a fire that had been deliberately set. Flames the color of a Texas sunset ripped into the air as they incinerated two twenty-foot wooden crosses. To the left side of those burning crosses was an incomplete shorter cross with only one side of its cross beam in place. Surrounding the flaming crosses were several people in white, dunce-capped masks and robes with crosses on their left breasts. Some of those were on horses also dressed in white-sheeted armor and masks. Interspersed among the white costumes were four or five men outfitted in leather jackets. Cropped hair and shaved heads gave these men a feral appearance, so the dichotomy of flowing white and black leather against a crimson background presented a picture of confused surrealism.

Louisa began, "Those are…"

"…Ku Klux Klan," finished Emily.

"And skinheads."

Emily and Louisa hid behind the mesquite screen as they watched the men on horses strut around the short-haired men. The Klansmen would tease their horses too closely to the hairless men causing the men to fidget as they tried not to display fear of the animals towering over them. As the unseated men squirmed, the horsemen would veer the animals away from the men and come at them again.

A tall, white shrouded figure came up to one of the horses, grabbed the reins at the side of its face, and shouted, "You boys quit pestering our guests, you hear? You brought these boys down here to show them something, and it wasn't how to be playful. Go on, get out now. Go do your business, you hear?"

The horsemen rode away from the men they were heckling, and the Klansperson walked toward the crosses as Louisa and Emily watched in wide-eyed revelation.

Emily whispered to her mother, "I didn't think this still went on. I thought the Klan was pretty much wiped out a few years ago."

"It was, but those hate groups are still around. Same ideas, different packaging. Shhh, here comes someone."

Two men, one in Klan drapery and one sweating in a leather jacket approached. Emily and Louisa clustered closer to the wall of the building and further away from their shield of mesquite.

"So what do you think? Pretty effective, isn't it?" said the drape to leather in a voice expecting praise.

"My men came all the way from Idaho, and this is all you can do? You told me you'd be able to show us how to promote the cause. I can open almost any history book and see this kind of crap. Fucking burning crosses will not do a goddamned thing," the man with the shaved head said.

Defensive sputtering was the Klansman's reaction. "What the…? What in the hell are you talking about? My men've spent ten fucking days organizing this. You came here to see this, and you're going to goddamned well see it. My people are the best. If you think you fucking know it all, you've got another thing coming. This is the finest. We've done this shit for decades. It's always worked."

"It ain't working now, bud. This shit stinks. Bombs, weapons, that's what it takes. You promised something big. We haven't seen it yet. I'm taking my boys back north." The man in the leather coat turned heel and walked away.

Chapter 26

▼

The man in the white fool's cap chased after him, "Wait. Wait! There's more. Don't leave. There's more. What the fuck do you want? I can get it. You want bombs, guns, heavy artillery? I can get it. Stay for the fucking show, and then we'll talk."

To a group of other white-swathed men, he yelled, "Okay, boys. Now's the time. Go get 'em."

Emily and Louisa approached the mesquite blind more closely as a group of five white sheets went to the back of a deuce-and-a-half sized truck parked at the outskirts of the area. The others in the clearing had gathered in a semi-circle around the burning crosses, but they were focusing on the half formed cross. The men in leather pushed their way to the front of the crescent of people. A hush of expectation engulfed the group, so all that was heard were the flames on the crosses slurping the air around them.

The five white drapes came from around the back of the truck in a formation of two abreast with the fifth Klansperson at the head of the foursome. He was holding a thick rope coiled in the center of his hands. As the foursome approached the group, Louisa and Emily could detect a fifth person surrounded by the quartet being coerced into walking within their group.

"No!" exclaimed Louisa as she looked at the third structure. "That's not a cross; it's a…"

"Gallows," interrupted Emily.

"We've got to do something."

The women looked wildly around them. Emily ran toward the car. Louisa asked, "What're you going to do?"

"What would you say is in those barns?"

"Could be anything—grain, equipment, hay, stables. I don't know."

"Let's hope it's hay. You have any matches on you?"

"No, but there's a cigarette lighter in the car. What do you want them for?"

"I want to start a fire."

Louisa looked at the barns and said, "If you want to get a fire going, we have kerosene in the car."

"That's right. Good idea, Mom. You go get the cigarette lighter turned on."

"How are you going to get it to the hay? Kerosene is slow burning, so you've got to get it soaked through. Once it goes though, watch out."

"Come on. They're stringing up the noose. That guy doesn't have much time."

Louisa stopped to look at the man standing before the crowd. Hands were bound behind his back and manacles kept his stance closed in. His head was so far down on his chest, it looked almost as if his neck had already snapped. The crowd was listening to a Klansman orate before them, but the words were lost to Louisa in the black void of darkness.

"Let's do it," she said to Emily as she followed her to the car.

Emily switched on the ignition and pushed in the cigarette lighter. She then went to the back of the car and retrieved the can of kerosene. With the back hatch opened, she started rummaging in her purse. Louisa came around and reached to close the door.

"No, hon, what are you doing? They might see the light."

"I'm looking to see if I picked up some matches at one of the restaurants we've been. Maybe I threw them in the bottom of my purse."

"Oh, okay, but, hurry. Maybe all those people are too busy watching the entertainment to be over here. I'm going inside the barn. If you find matches, wait until I come out and then we'll start the fire."

"Check to make sure there are no animals in there."

"Yeah, okay." Louisa took the kerosene can, looked into the barn, empty except for hay stacked in the byres and stalls, entered and started splashing the oily kerosene onto the hay.

"Did you find anything?" asked Emily standing by the door waiting for Louisa to come out of the barn.

"Lots of stacks of hay. Should burn well."

"Here we go." Emily took the cigarette lighter and the matches as Louisa followed her to the doorway. "The cigarette lighter's out; use these matches."

Louisa took the matches. "Go make sure we're not too late."

Louisa didn't see her daughter's facial twinge at what she might see if they were too late, but she felt it. When Emily returned, Louisa held a rusted horseshoe close to Emily's face before she ripped a few matches out of the book, lit them and held them to the hay.

"Almost tripped over it as I walked back there. We may need it. Could be all we have for defense if we run into any of those guys."

"Maybe it's a good luck charm," said Emily.

"Right, for that guy in the noose."

Anticipating Louisa's question, Emily said, "No, we're not too late, yet. I think we've seen that guy. Do you remember when Sheriff McIntire picked up that drunk at the bar when we had breakfast?"

"Yes, you think it's he?"

"I'm not sure, but the man is black and has the same build as the one at the bar."

Louisa stood at the doorway of the barn, lit another match and then lit the book of matches. She gently tossed those onto a patch of hay soaked with the kerosene. Hot flames hissed as the hay became a mini-conflagration that would make an arsonist proud. Waiting just a few seconds to make sure the fire was battling the hay, she exited quickly. Mother and daughter walked away from the burning, furiously, they hoped, building and crept around the second building to their mesquite haven to watch the proceedings.

Another Klansperson, shorter and stockier, had taken the place of the first speaker and appeared to speak forcefully as he wrestled the air with his fists and arms. As they waited for the fire to consume the building, Emily and Louisa saw a leather-coated man come up to join him. His hands flailing in the air, he seemed to be answering the invective of the second speaker.

The man in chains lifted his head but quickly dropped it back to his chest. Someone stepped forward from the half circle of people and followed the speakers' leads by hitting the air with his fist. The speakers at the front of the group stepped forward to answer the person who was speaking from the crowd. Cinders and chunks of charred wood were falling from the crosses, but nothing had hit the crowd yet as it stayed an adequate distance away from the burn area. A lanky male in black leather and chaps advanced from the crowd and stepped toward the four Klansmen enclosing their quarry. The men forced their prisoner upon a five foot ladder below the gallows, and the leather outfitted man picked up the noose that had been formed at the end of the heavy coiled rope. After much prodding with a rifle produced from the folds of the sheets of one of the men, the man to be hanged lifted his head. At that instant, the man holding the noose slipped it around his neck. The man with the rifle then attempted to force him up the ladder. He refused several times until the rifleman turned the weapon, so the butt of it faced the back of the man.

He then raised the rifle butt into the air and brought it down into the man's kidneys. The victim's knees buckled but he didn't collapse to the ground. Seeing the rifleman raise his weapon in the air to hit the man again forced him to climb the ladder with the noose lying loosely around his neck. Four of the men retreated from the ladder, but the person in leather stayed close. The crowd remained silent as the man was forced to his degrading, meaningless death. No one stepped forward to plead his cause, and his body stance was limp with faithlessness and lost hope.

"We can't have been too late," Emily wailed quietly. "They're going to kill him. We've got to get help."

"We don't know how to get out of here. Maybe we should just run out there," Louisa shot back.

As the four men approached the ladder again to kick it out from the doomed man, the sharp pop of gunfire was heard. The Klansmen hesitated and looked around. More popping shattered the night as heads in the crowd turned in unison in the direction of the popping, but nothing was seen. As they settled back to the action at hand, another series of shots was heard. At the same time, one of the Klansmen shouted, "Fire!" and pointed in the direction of the shack Louisa and Emily had set ablaze.

Emily and Louisa looked to their right and saw the fire roiling across the roof of the barn gaining momentum as flame chased flame and synthesized into a hot, glowing star. Each looked at the other and smiled triumphantly. In perfect timing with their moment of victory came an explosion that set the crowd into random disbursement. The pyrotechnics were worthy of an Independence Day celebration. The orange glow that had lit the proceedings shifted from the crosses that were now ebbing into blackened spines to the barn that was now threatening to burn its neighboring building.

"We've got to get out of here," said Louisa.

"Yes, but look over there."

The women glanced at the gallows to see the same man who had put the noose on the chained man take the rope off his neck and lean down to undo the manacles with a key he produced from his pocket. As soon as the now free captive climbed down the ladder, the captor kicked it away. Another burst of gunfire from the barn and a roaring explosion were the final incentives to send the crowd fleeing the area. Masks were whipped off heads as the Klanspeople looked around wildly to pinpoint their vehicles while running towards them. Just as the crowd scattered toward its transportation, so did Emily and Louisa.

"How are we going to get out of here? We don't know the way," asked Emily.

"See that line of cars? We're going to follow them."

"Mom, they'll kill us when they realize who we are."

"Emily, how are they going to know? They're so panicked now, they wouldn't know if they had Santa Claus and his reindeer in their midst."

Under a barrage of artillery fire and flames, Louisa guided the four-wheel into the column of cars. Just as Louisa had predicted, people were scrambling for a quick exit, and no one cared who they might be, if they even took notice.

Chapter 27

Eddie couldn't get the leather jacket off fast enough. Hurried fingers fumbled at the ties of the leather chaps, so he couldn't budge them off his legs until he slowed his nervous hands to a speed at which they could manipulate him out of the leather uniform his father thought was so appropriate for him to wear. After tonight when he had passed the hazing of initiation into white supremacist bullyism, his father was going to tattoo him with the markings of Aryanism—whatever that was. He had heard his father and Jonas talking about it. He could ditch the leather easily, but it would be hard to ditch the tattoos. It would be a constant reminder of the hatred his father had nurtured so fully in his house. He had only to wake up every morning and be reminded of that hatred; he didn't need any outward signs on his body of it.

Get me out of here. I gotta get out. Away from him. I hate the man. Tonight was too much. This is the last I'll ever have to take from him.

Eddie continued to yank at the ties, fingers uncoordinated in his rush to shed the leather, the sign of all he hated. Bullets popped in the background. The fire lighting the darkness surrounding the clearing overpowered the fire dying on the crosses. People screaming as the fire fed on the dry wood of the barn rushed chaotically in thoughtless patterns looking for an exit from the bedlam created by the whizzing bullets. Sheets were ripped off bodies and thrown to the black ground where they lay in white puddles.

Eddie hurled his leather garments down in a fit of loathing for what they represented in his life. The key to Henry Wade's shackles with which he had been entrusted fell out of the pocket when he tossed his jacket onto the sand. Using the confusion for cover, he ran to the pickup and used the keys in the ignition to start the truck. He then headed for the line of spectators who had been fortunate enough to find their vehicles and beat it out of the inferno now threatening to spread to the mesquites near the burning barn.

He knew where his father kept a few thousand dollars in cash, money Dwayne Ed used for some of his dealings requiring non-traceable payments. If he could get to the house quickly enough, before his father and his cronies got there, he could escape the hell his father had created for him—forever. Eddie had seen his father talking with those white supremacists from the north. They were arguing, but then who didn't argue with Dwayne Ed? Dwayne Ed never met people; he confronted them.

Mr. Easter said you didn't have to end up like your parents. Just because they were one way doesn't mean you will end up like them. Never, never do I want to be like my father. Mr. Easter said I was like my mother, and she was decent. Please, please let me be like my mother. If I leave now, maybe I won't be like Dwayne Ed. If I can keep him away from me, I'll have a better chance.

Daphne will be okay; she hasn't had to live with him. She won't be like a Twerms; she'll be safe. But, if I stay here, I'm afraid I'll end up like Dwayne Ed. That's what the books say—get rid of the bad influence. Get away at whatever the cost.

As the gaps in the line of fleeing cars widened, he shot out from his position and took a back road he knew. He rumbled down that road until he quickly veered onto another road furrowed with miniature valleys over which the truck ricocheted. Only a half-hour more, and he could make his escape from the life Dwayne Ed had demanded his son live. Only a half-hour more.

Chapter 28

The ladies reached the main road, the road for which they had earlier searched so long in vain that night, by staying with the queue of cars on the back roads. When Louisa steered the car left to start heading north, she jammed her foot on the accelerator and sped down the highway.

"We're coming into Gold County; maybe you better slow down before Sheriff McIntire finds us," cautioned Emily.

"Good. Let him come. If he doesn't find us, we'll find him. That rally we saw tonight was despicable."

"It wasn't in his county."

"It sure seems conveniently his county if he needs it to be."

Her mother was right. Emily was silent until she noticed Louisa taking the turn opposite to the one that allowed them to skirt San Domingo and get to Atie's ranch.

"Are we going to get breakfast?"

Louisa answered tersely, "Later, maybe."

In central San Domingo, the only early morning activity was the humming of the halogen streetlights. Louisa squealed into a parking space at the courthouse square, got out of the car, slammed the door and marched down a flight of lit stairs to an office whose sign designated it 'Sheriff'. Emily had no choice but to follow her mother.

Louisa opened a steel door with a glass pane in it to a very large square room. Although lath and plaster walls designated the building as old, the tax money from oil production that appeared to be plentiful in Gold County had given the room a new facade. Instead of gray steel institutional office furniture, the room was carpeted with a beige short napped carpet on which were placed oak desks and chairs. Computer stations were at every other desk, and a multilined phone system was interspersed throughout the office. Tastefully patterned soundproofing covered the chalk colored walls. There were three conference areas with half walls of glass to the right of the room. The only indication that this was not a big city business office was an iron cage located in the far left corner of the room and, next to that, an iron door that looked as though it could be the security door for a bank vault. A deputy, in his khaki uniform, was dozing, feet up in one of the office chairs that sat in front of a microphone and sound unit. Louisa, with Emily shadowing her, stomped into the office and demanded of him to see Sheriff McIntire.

"He ain't here, ma'am," said the deputy with a start and a resounding plop of feet on the floor.

"Do you mean to tell me the ever watchful Sheriff Bonham McIntire is not at his post? Or, is he out harassing some poor resident of any of the three nearby counties? Or," Louisa paused dramatically, "is he at some rally? Maybe a Klan rally?"

The deputy gave her a puzzled look as he said, "Klan? Ma'am, we ain't had a Klan rally in twenty five years. My granddaddy used to talk about 'em, but I ain't heard of one out here for a long time. You okay, ma'am? You're mighty stirred up about something."

Turning to Emily, he asked, "This your ma? She okay?"

"No, she's not. If you had been where we were tonight, you probably wouldn't be okay either."

"What're you ladies jabbering about?"

Emily didn't have to answer the deputy because just then Sheriff McIntire walked in, and Louisa began to lambaste him.

"So, you know everything that goes on in three counties, do you? You, who claims to be so organized that nothing escapes you. You with your finger on every pulse beat of Gold, Easter and Dune counties. You are such a wonderful sheriff that you can spend your spare time harassing two visitors because you have everything else under control."

Louisa's voice went up an octave as she continued, "Well, just let me tell you, Mr. Sheriff. Do you have any idea what was going on tonight in one of these three well managed counties? Or were you there? Is hanging someone your idea of law enforcement, or is that just another one of your highly developed harassment techniques? You ought to be…"

"Just a minute, Miss Louisa. What're you talking about hanging? You have to tell me what you're trying to say."

He turned to Emily. "Can you tell me what she's talking about?"

Emily said quietly while her mother clamped her lips together in a stubborn scowl, "There was a hanging tonight. Actually, it wasn't completed, thank God. We got it stopped just before they were going to kick the ladder out."

The Sheriff's face blanched as he asked her, "What do you mean tonight? And, what do you mean, you 'got it stopped'? And, what were two ladies like you even doing there? And, where were you? Where did this hanging take place?"

Emily began, "We were at the Barnes ranch for dinner and got lost coming home. We thought we had retraced our steps correctly and found the right road, but it led to some land that wasn't the Barnes ranch. There were a bunch of people dressed like idiots in Ku Klux Klan sheets and some skinheads, at least, I think they were skinheads."

Obviously struck by a new idea, she turned to her mother, "Mom, did you see any pumping units in that area?"

Her mother thought and nodded.

"I wonder if it was that area we went to the other day. You know, the Bliss land. You think it could've been?"

"Perhaps."

Louisa proceeded to continue with the story to the Sheriff and his deputy, "They had some black person whose neck they had put a noose on. Emily thought of a way to start a fire in a barn. It turned out it must have been a shed to store live ammunition because the fire caused it to shoot off just as they were going to hang this guy." She started to laugh as she launched into a description of the people in scattered confusion running from the wayward bullets the shed was shooting.

Sheriff McIntire interrupted her. "A black guy? Can you describe him?"

"Not too well," said Emily. "His face was lying on his chest because the situation was so hopeless. For all I know, he could've been that guy you pick up at the bar."

"How'd you know about that? Henry Wade? You think it was Henry Wade? You sure it was tonight? That's wrong; it can't have been tonight. Henry Wade, are you sure?"

Louisa popped in exasperation, "Sheriff, how do we know? We've never met the guy. All we know is we've seen you scrape up some drunk out of a gutter. It could be him; it could not be him. That's your problem. You and your misinterpretation of executing the law. You can brag all you want, but you're nothing more than a penny ante sheriff from Podunk, USA."

Sheriff McIntire was backing from Louisa as he put his hat on his head. "Put them in the holding cell," he said to his deputy. "I'll be back."

Appalled and horrified, both women said, "Jail?"

"You can't lock us up," shouted Louisa.

The Sheriff turned in his rush out the door and smirked. "Oh, yeah. Watch me." To the deputy, he repeated, "Lock 'em up."

The Sheriff left, and the deputy took the keys and put one into the lock of the holding cell door. It swung open with a grating creak.

"Come on, ladies, in you go. You heard Sheriff McIntire."

"He can't do this," stated Emily without much conviction.

"Yes. Yes, he can. This is his county. He can do anything he wants, and if he wants to lock you two up, I got no choice but to do what he says. He's the boss."

"What about our phone call? We're allowed a phone call," said Louisa.

"No'm, only if you're arrested. You ain't been arrested yet. If you get arrested, you get to go to the tomb where the jail cells are." He twitched his head in the direction of the vault door. "It's cold, dark and wet. Sheriff's bein' nice to y'all. Now, get in."

Chapter 29

Enough of the lower level of the courthouse peeked above ground level so the occupants of the county jail office could see the first iridescence of dawn.

Emily lay her head down on the ticking pillow on one of the two cots, "If they had let us have our one phone call, I wonder if we could have called California and talked to David. Wonder what he would say.

"I'm so tired, I could sleep anywhere."

"I think I'd have called Detective Bob Washburn. He'd never do something like this in Pleasant Creek. I think I'd call him just to have him talk about proper law enforcement to teach old Sheriff Pompous how it should be done. He would never let his police department get away with some of this garbage that that sheriff has pulled.

"We never got any breakfast, I'm sorry. I bet you're hungry."

But Emily didn't respond; she had already fallen asleep. Louisa followed suit on the other cot. Neither woman woke when another deputy came in, nor did they wake when they heard the call come over the dispatch system. They did, however, rouse when a deputy let out a loud war hoop. "What? Come again." He listened for a few moments and said, "Right. I'll get someone out right away. You want Utley out there, too?"

After hearing a response overlaid with static, the deputy replied, "You got it."

"Did you hear that, Manuel?" asked the deputy to his peer as he dialed a phone number after calling for a back up unit.

"What happened?"

The deputy held up his hand to silence the other officer as he said into the phone, "Dr. Utley? This is the sheriff's office. We need you out at the Twerms ranch."

He paused as he listened to the response.

"Guess so. You need to bring your kit. This is an official call."

Another pause.

"Well, sir, the Sheriff says it's Dwayne Ed."

After listening again, the deputy said, "No, sir, doesn't appear to be an accident. Whoever did it used an ax."

Another pause to listen.

"Yes, that's what I said. Sheriff said there's blood all over and Dwayne Ed's hardly recognizable."

He finished the conversation with, "Yes, sir, as soon as you can. He's waiting for you."

As he hung up the receiver, the deputy looked at his peer, "Sheriff called in and said Dwayne Ed Twerms has been killed."

He paused and said in bewilderment, "Said he was hacked to death with an ax."

The announcement was cold water to Louisa's half-aware state. She sat up and said to Emily whose eyes were rolling open and then closed because she couldn't come to consciousness easily.

"Did you hear that, Em?"

"Hmmmm?"

"Em, they said Dwayne Ed was killed."

"Dwayne Ed?" she questioned sleepily, eyes still closed.

Louisa went over and aroused her with a slow shake of her shoulders. "Emily, Dwayne Ed Twerms has been killed. We saw him last night, and now he's been killed."

Emily gave her mother a confused, sleepy look, finally comprehended what she was saying and asked, "Are you sure it was he we saw? In those draperies, it might have been anybody. You're talking about the guy who came away from the group, right? That heavy man with the skinhead arguing about what they were doing?"

"That's the one. I'm almost sure it was Dwayne Ed. Who else would organize something that gruesome?" She repeated, "He's been hacked to death."

"Hacked to death?"

"Yes, wake up. That's what I'm trying to tell you. We saw him less than eight hours ago, and, now, he's dead."

"Who killed him?"

"How would I know? I'm in this cage with you."

Emily shook the last of the sleep out of her eyes.

*   *   *   *

During the morning the deputies paid little attention to the women hanging on the bars of the holding cage except to bring them a brunch of biscuits, gravy, hash browns, sausage and fried eggs for breakfast.

Wiping up the last of the egg with a bit of her biscuit, Louisa said, "I don't know if I just carboloaded or poured a quart of 10W-40 down my system."

Looking at Emily's plate, Louisa said, "You didn't seem to have any problem doing either."

"Yes, but now it's past lunch time, and I'm still hungry enough to eat again. I wonder if they'll bring lunch in time for dinner."

Chapter 30

The women never did get lunch because the Sheriff arrived in the early afternoon.

This time Emily stepped up to bat Sheriff McIntire around. "Sheriff, I have a hard time understanding how you can put two people in jail without any reason. Everything I know about American government says that isn't right. You are setting yourself wide open for lawsuits if this is how you carry out the law in this county."

Sheriff McIntire held up his hand and said tiredly, "Ladies, I don't want to hear it. Dwayne Ed Twerms is dead, so you won't have me following you around anymore."

"What do you mean following us around? Are you admitting you were harassing us?" asked Emily.

He turned away from his detainees to instruct his deputies in how to set up some paperwork. While he answered questions, Louisa picked up the questioning. "Well, were you, Sheriff? Were you harassing us? And, what does Dwayne Ed have to do with following us around? You make it sound like he was the reason you've been so annoying."

As the deputy sat down at a desk with a computer, Sheriff McIntire retrieved a ring of keys from his deputy, returned his attention to Louisa and Emily, and unlocked the grate to let them out of the holding cell.

"Come with me, please," he requested as he led them to a large room. Pulling in a third chair, he offered the other two to the ladies.

When each person was seated around the table, Sheriff McIntire washed his hand over his face as if to erase the tired lines off it and said, "Ladies, Dwayne Ed Twerms was the meanest man I have ever known in my life. Those Twerms have been around since before statehood, and they've all been mean, but Dwayne Ed has probably been the meanest.

"When I heard you were looking for Laurel, I didn't know any other way to protect you from him except to follow you and hope you'd get out of this area before he decided you were too close, and he didn't want you around. There's no telling what would've happened then, and I couldn't have that, for your sakes or my county's sake. When Jonas called about your visit and complained about your being on the ranch, I knew you were messing around where you shouldn't have been. You two were headed right up trouble's path, with a capital T. I had to do something.

"Right now, I've got a problem. You have information I need about last night, so, if you wouldn't mind, I'd like to ask you some questions."

He took the ladies' surprised silence at his explanation as an agreement to answer his questions and began. "Can you identify any of the people there?"

Emily said no, but Louisa said yes.

"What I mean is, I think we could identify the people, but they had those godawful outfits on, so it would be hard to say for sure."

"What about the black man you saw being hanged? Do you know who he is?"

"We already told you who we thought he might be," said Louisa.

"Are you sure you can't tell me more exactly who that person was?"

"No. Why do you keep asking?"

The Sheriff paused while debating how much information to give the women. "I can't find Henry Wade. I've got people looking for him, but he's disappeared."

"Why do you think it was he?" Louisa asked.

"He's the easiest target for something like this. Anyone in town would know where to find him; he's always drunk at Toast's. Bullies start with the easiest target to torment, and he's one of the easiest."

After a silence the Sheriff asked again, "Any other ideas who you saw?"

"We saw Mel, my aunt."

"You sure?"

Both Emily and Louisa nodded.

"She was out there bossing people around like she always does."

Emily said, "I didn't know women could be in the Ku Klux Klan. I would think those half-thinking men would find Klanswomen an affront to their questionable manhood."

"Women can hate as mean as men. Years ago, some of the most active members of the Klan were women. A gal named Elizabeth Tyler paired up with a public relations fellow named Edward Young Clarke and got the Klan going in the twenties. They made mucho bucks out of it—just goes to show what marketing can do for a bad idea."

The Sheriff chuckled as he continued, "The Klansmen wanted the Klanswomen to be their hostesses, while the Klanswomen wanted equal say in Klan activities. Sometimes the internal politics were as dangerous as the external politics."

"I hope my other aunts aren't involved," Louisa remarked.

Sheriff McIntire hesitated slightly and then said, "A couple of them are. When all your aunts were younger, they were involved somewhat, like most of the women in this area. There were units of Klanswomen all over the country, Indiana, Oregon, California, New York, all over. Your younger aunts were half-hearted about staying in the Klan when they realized it wasn't just a social organization and got out of as soon as they could. Clio and Callie and Mel were the ones who held up your family's end of it."

"That's par. How do you know so much about all this?"

"When you've got trouble, it pays to find out as much about the enemy as you can. I've read a lot about those hate groups because Dwayne Ed has, had, been so keen on trying to get the Klan started up again here. He wanted the Klan to come alive because that was part of his world; he doesn't like the different style hate groups because he doesn't understand them enough to control them. He knew there's not a whole lot of people here who think with hate like him, so he'd been looking for outside help to come in and make his group strong. He came up with some money somewhere. I've known about his wanting to reactivate a klavern for a while.

"Anyone else you recognized?"

"Dwayne Ed came near us when he was arguing with some skinhead. Must have been the leader of the skinheads, but I don't know if we'd recognize him."

"But, you knew Dwayne Ed was there?"

"No doubt. He was really mad the skinhead didn't think his extravaganza was worth the trip they had made to watch it. He acted like he expected something much more outstanding, but I don't know what that could be."

"I'll tell you what it was. Those new white supremacist groups want bombs, counterfeiting and murder of representatives of the federal government. A hanging is old hat to them. They aren't trying to scare the little people; they're trying to topple the U.S. government and set up one run by white Aryans.

"Dwayne Ed probably got him down here with a lot of blow and go about what a wonderful organizer he was and how he could promote their joint cause. Only trouble is Dwayne Ed is—was—too selfish and selfcentered to realize he's old hat.

"Anyone else you thought you knew."

"Just those people. Those sheets cover a lot."

"That's right," agreed Emily. "We didn't know any of the skin-heads, though. I don't think we've ever seen them."

"That's because they came down from the North. There may've been some Texas skinheads from the bigger cities. They've only been here a short while, probably came in just for the big show, so I couldn't get much i.d. on them."

"You talk like you knew this was going to happen."

"I figured something was going on." He smiled his cocksure smile as he reminded them, "I know just about everything going on in..."

"...these three counties," Emily finished, but she smiled back at him.

There was a pause, and Louisa said, "Maybe we did know one of the skinheads. The man who put the noose around the fellow's neck wore chaps." She glanced at Emily who nodded in understanding. "At Atie's funeral, Dwayne Ed, Jr. wore chaps, you know."

Emily thought about her mother's observation and said, "I wondered when I saw that but didn't want to say anything. You think it was he? I hope not. For Laurel's sake, I hope not. I guess he could've shaved his head, though."

*   *   *   *

"Okay, Sheriff, now it's *your* turn," said Louisa after a pause in the questioning.

"What do you mean?"

"We told you what we know. Now, you tell us what you know. Where did you find Dwayne Ed? And, how did you know to go out there?"

"You two are real nosy, you know that? What makes you think you have any claim on that information?"

"We stopped someone from being hanged. I would think that gives us a really strong claim," said Louisa.

"Yeah, yeah, maybe so. When you told me what had happened, I went out to where I thought Dwayne Ed might set up a rally. There's a section of land that doesn't have much activity on it, and that's where those rallies are usually held. The owners of the land left here years and years ago, so they wouldn't know what their land was being used for."

"Bliss land," confirmed Louisa.

"How'd you know that, Miss Louisa?"

"Mel sold the mineral rights to Atie. Atie found out she had been scammed, and she willed the deed back to Mel. But, Sheriff, you can't say anything about that until the will is read. Okay?"

"Sold mineral rights to Atie? Atie should've known better. She didn't get senile or anything. I'm surprised the old gal fell for that. So, how did you ladies find out it was Bliss land?"

"We went to the county records office in Dunton."

"So, that's what you were doing there."

"And, saw the sheriff, polite and helpful as he was," ridiculed Emily.

"Yeah, that's Sheriff Twerms. He and the desk have been spliced together for years. He's the reason I try to keep up on what's happening in Dune County."

"So tell us about Dwayne Ed's death," reminded Louisa.

"No one was at that land when I got there; they had all left. The barn you set on fire and the one next to it were demolished, but shell casings were all over the place. Since no one was there, I went to Dwayne Ed's house, and found him there."

"How could you recognize him?" asked Emily.

"What do you mean?"

"Being killed with an ax, wouldn't he be unrecognizable?"

"How'd you know about the ax?"

"Your deputy said something when he took the call."

"Yes, ladies, there was enough of him to determine it was Dwayne Ed."

"Who do you think killed him?" asked Louisa.

"How should I know? The coroner just took him away."

"Aren't there tire tracks or fingerprints or the weapon? Where's the weapon?" Louisa asked.

"Nosy, nosy. The weapon is nowhere to be found. It could be tossed anywhere. There are a thousand and one tire tracks, and the fingerprints that are all over are ones you'd expect."

"And, the skinheads? Where are they? Maybe they were so angry they killed Dwayne Ed," suggested Emily.

"Maybe."

"So where are they?" persisted Emily.

"I don't know."

"But, you know everything. That's what you keep telling us."

"We're looking for them."

"Who's 'we'?" asked Louisa.

"The department."

"Don't you think you'd better get on it?" asked Emily.

"Don't you think you better go on to the Single Arrow?" responded Sheriff McIntire. "I've got a murder to investigate."

Louisa and Emily got out of their chairs to walk out of the office. Emily put her arm to stay her mother as she walked out the door. "Wait, Mom, I want to ask the Sheriff something."

"Sheriff, we went to Ty and Maggie Barnes' house for dinner before we found that rally."

"Nice people. They would have you for dinner; Maggie's real hospitable that way."

"Yes, it was nice, but that's not the point."

"Ae you going to make a point?"

"No, I'm going to ask a question."

"I've told you all I'm going to tell you about Dwayne Ed. I'm tired, and I've got too much to think about. Murder messes up my county, and I don't like messes."

Emily ignored his warning to back off. "Maggie said a bunch of you here in town grew up together, from the time you were little kids. She made it sound like even your parents grew up together."

"That's right; this is a sparsely populated area. Most of our families go back several generations, before statehood, even. It's not so bad now with telephones and the internet for keeping in contact, but when there weren't many of us close together, we relied on each other even more than we do nowadays. We still rely on each other, but not like before when we couldn't get in touch with each other easily."

"Okay, but then she said all of you who had been so close just stopped seeing each other. She made it sound like one day you were all buddy-buddy, and the next day an earthquake or something had split you guys apart."

Sheriff McIntire flinched.

The weariness drained from his face to be replaced by palpable sadness. He leaned his head back on his chair and closed his eyes. After a silent interval, he said in a low voice, "When you're young, you think nothing will hurt you. You're convinced you are invulnerable, so invulnerable that not even evil can touch you. Your strength is in your quickwittedness at being able to dodge the worst life can offer.

"Louisa and Emily, it is one of the worst lessons of adulthood to learn, without any warning, how corrupt life can be—it was so pitiful."

"What was so pitiful?"

Bonham McIntire, eyes still closed, melancholy dousing his face, quit talking. After a few minutes, when they realized he wasn't going to say anything else, Louisa and Emily did walk out of the room.

Sheriff McIntire got out of his chair, shouted to the deputy to order him a sandwich, walked into his office and shut the door.

Emily and Louisa left.

Chapter 31

"If I drive us, would you mind a detour over to Easter School," asked Emily as they headed toward their car after lunch.

"If you want. I can fall asleep in the car if I need to. Do you want to tell Daphne about her dad?"

"No, I want to go to that boarding house and tell them to warn Laurel to stay away."

"Obviously, you must not believe you didn't see her."

"Obviously."

* * * *

The garage doors of the repair shop were down, so Emily parked the car on the street and left her mother sleeping while she went to try the front door of the boarding home. It opened, and the same woman who claimed to speak no English sat at the counter. Her bouncer was also there.

The husky man approached her in a decidedly unfriendly manner as he said, "I told you we got nobody here you know."

Emily addressed the woman. "Please, I won't ask you about Laurel, but she needs to know Dwayne Ed is dead. Tell her to get out if she's here, and if she's not, get word to her to stay away."

The woman, jolted out of her feigned monolingualism, asked, "What do you mean Dwayne Ed's dead?"

"Someone murdered Dwayne Ed with an ax. If she's around, Sheriff McIntire will know. You've got to warn her."

Emily started to go, but turned and said, "Please."

She received a slight nod from both of them.

* * * *

She had started her angle off the side of the street when she looked in her rearview mirror and saw the Sheriff's car pull in behind her.

"Aw, nuts," she cried.

It startled Louisa out of her nap. "What's wrong?"

"I thought Sheriff McIntire said he wouldn't follow us around anymore."

"He said that, that's right."

"Then explain to me, why is he behind us now?"

Louisa looked in the side mirror to see the Sheriff looking at them. Emily abruptly pulled the car onto the street to get away from him.

"Maybe he's not following us," said Louisa. "Maybe he's looking for Laurel, too."

"Oh, great," said Emily.

* * * *

"Where y'all been? I been worried sick about where you been, you hear? Sat here all night long waiting up for you," harped Mel.

Louisa looked at her and said acidly, "All night long, Aunt Mel? Waiting for us?"

When Mel nodded her head, Louisa said, "You may have been up all night long, but I hardly think you were waiting for us."

"What're you saying? You calling me a liar? You're being disrespectful to your elders, you hear? I waited up for you."

"Before or after the rally?"

Mel looked warily at her niece. "How'd you know about that? You weren't there."

"Now tell me about the mineral rights you sold to Atie. That was to finance the Klan, wasn't it?"

Mel looked at Louisa defiantly and then hung her head.

"That was pretty rotten to dupe your own sister, Mel."

"She has all that money; why shouldn't she give some for a good cause? The Klan is keeping America pure; she should've stayed in it with Clio, Callie and me. She should've supported it."

"Obviously, she didn't feel its motives were as patriotic as you seem to feel."

"When I get my inheritance from her, I'm giving some of it to the Klan. Then I'll be Grand Wizard; Dwayne Ed is out."

"There is no inheritance, Mel. You're out of the will."

Mel heard, looked at Louisa and flew at her, fingers bent into arthritic claws. Just as one hand raked down Louisa's cheek, Emily threw herself at Mel's knees and landed her great-aunt in a heap at Louisa's feet. Emily ran to the kitchen and came back with a wet cloth.

"Mel, I want you out of here right now. You are to have no access to anymore of Atie's estate," hissed Louisa.

Mel screeched at her, "I've taken care of all of this for Atie. I have every right to be here. Atie owes me. I'm her sister."

"No, Mel. Apparently, Atie felt you canceled that relationship with your scam. Now get out of this house."

"No! I belong here. I'm entitled to these things; they're mine. I want them, you hear?"

"If you aren't out of here in one hour, I'm calling the attorney and filing a restraining order against you. Then I'll call Sheriff McIntire to forcibly throw you out because you're trespassing.

"Emily and I will help you pack."

Emily and Louisa, holding the wet cloth on her throbbing cheek, accompanied Mel up the stairs, watched her pack, escorted her to her pickup truck and made sure she drove off. In that period of time, Mel said not one word.

Louisa went to clean her facial lacerations. Emily went to call Uncle Luke to tell him what happened and ask for help in changing the locks on the doors.

Chapter 32

Brother Johnson was suffering anemia of faith. In all the funerals he had preached in his ministerial career, he had never had trouble rationalizing a deceased's entrance into heaven. He had been proud of his ability to come up with at least one just-right trait for each person's funeral he had conducted. Sometimes, he was fortunate and came up with more than one qualifying grace in which case the sermon was a masterpiece.

Dwayne Ed Twerms was different. Dwayne Ed had wallowed in more dirt than Adam and Eve's serpent, so even poor Brother Johnson's search for redeeming values couldn't lift the murdered man out of the abject filth he had called home for his soul. Brother Johnson's homily reflected that failure. It was too short because Brother Johnson was afraid he couldn't preach around the evil Dwayne Ed without the congregation present realizing how much he disliked the man. It was devoid of entertaining vignettes of hell because Brother Johnson was positive that's really where Dwayne Ed had been consigned. It was lacking in emotional upheaval because Brother Johnson considered it a waste of his energy for a man who had spent so much of his energy in brutal ruthlessness.

Looking back on it, Brother Johnson was sorry for the wasted opportunity to bring more of the flock into the fold by his inability to stage a fist shaking, *Bible* whacking, evil denouncing event. As many people attended Dwayne Ed Twerms' funeral as had attended Atie Ewell's funeral. Unlike Atie's funeral where some people genuinely mourned the woman, Dwayne Ed's funeral appeared to be one where people wanted to make sure the man was genuinely dead. They seemed to be so relieved to be rid of him, they didn't mind having their entertainment curtailed. It was standing room only in the back and sides of the aisles of church.

* * * *

A phone call from Emily's husband, David, had kept Louisa and Emily past their departure time, so, as was their usual custom for scheduled events, Louisa and Emily swooped into the church about fifteen minutes prior to start time, too late to get a choice seat in the congregation. Looking around the church painted to remind one of a child's concept of heaven, pale sky blue walls and cloud white pews, pillars and trims, they spotted one lone space in a pew. They did manage to squeeze two seats out of one at the end of the last pew, so they didn't have to stand, but the density of bodies and the heat of the day left them panting for cool air. A forest of women's hats and men's heads prevented them from seeing the Twerms' family pew, but they knew Daphne and Eddie had to be up front, and their grandmother had to be close at hand, if not actually with them.

It was a quarter hour past the scheduled start time before the pale blue and white church swelled with the first rendition of "Amazing Grace" and "In the Sweet Bye and Bye", and Brother Johnson began his tepid eulogy. A few sentences into his dialogue, Brother Johnson saw one side of the double door open just enough to let a woman limp into the back of the church. Sheriff McIntire followed quickly and let the door silently shut as he stood behind her against the wall of the church. The congregation was so intent in satiating its curiosity as to where in the afterlife Brother Johnson was going to relegate Dwayne Ed Twerms that the entrance of the woman whom Sheriff McIntire accompanied went unnoticed.

* * * *

Disappointment in the lack of vivacity of Brother Johnson's sermon was beginning to register in the crowd. Heads were beginning to turn to survey the population of the church and note who was attending. Discreet whispers were filling Brother Johnson's dramatic pauses. Children were beginning to fidget in the overcrowded pews. Emily attempted to scan the front of the church to watch Eddie and Daphne's reactions to what Brother Johnson was saying about their father, but the wall of heads stymied her viewing them. She slowly turned her head to look at the back of the church. She paused momentarily when she saw Sheriff McIntire. As her head completed her arc of observation, her eyes swung back to the Sheriff because her mind registered a familiar presence.

In the mass that peopled the back of the church, it was hard to make out who was there because, although half faces and seemingly disconnected body parts were identifiable, people were not. She returned her gaze to Brother Johnson, but every few minutes, she would attempt to peek at the person the Sheriff seemed to be shielding.

Louisa whispered, "You aren't paying attention. What's wrong?"

"Look over at the Sheriff."

Louisa looked. "So? He got here late, too. He just didn't get a seat. Do you want to give him ours?"

"Right. Look at the person next to him. Who is it?"

Louisa and Emily both looked, but the person had drawn back behind the Sheriff as though she knew she were being examined.

"I don't see anybody special."

"I thought I saw Laurel."

"You're getting obsessed with her. Just listen."

Emily looked again, but Louisa jabbed her in the ribs with her elbow. The nearest pewmates looked at them pointedly, so Emily refrained from trying to determine if the person were Laurel. Curiosity made her fidget like the restless children in the church.

Rather than lose all these potential listeners of the Word, Brother Johnson announced the singing of "Rock of Ages" to be followed by the final respects to Brother Twerms and a closing reading from the Good Book. "Rock of Ages" wasn't even finished before people had jumped into a line to pass by the closed coffin of a hated man.

The woman next to Emily said as her husband rose to join the group lining up before the coffin, "Jess, you cain't see him. His head's all bashed in, so they got the coffin closed."

"Don't matter, hon. Just knowing he's dead's enough for me. Let's go look."

She reluctantly joined her husband.

To Louisa, Emily said, "Do you want to go up?"

"Not particularly, do you?"

"Not to see a closed casket, but I'd like to go see if that's Laurel. Want to come?"

"Only to appease you. You're seeing Laurel everywhere. Maybe you can meet this person and realize she isn't Laurel."

Louisa followed Emily to the end of the line that was now wrapping itself around the inside perimeter of the church. The soft sibilants of whispers and quiet talking hovered about the line of people. A few people, most notably Eddie, Daphne and their grandmother, stayed in the pews, but most were anxious to get out of their crowded seats and move about. Some of the congregation moved to the front pew to offer quiet words of comfort to Dwayne Ed's family; most of the group couldn't think of any to give. Sheriff McIntire and his charge had jockeyed a position about halfway in the line, but the Sheriff stood so his woman companion could not be seen well. Louisa and Emily moved to the end of the line.

"Wish we had gotten closer," grumbled Emily. "If we were behind her, maybe we could talk to her."

"I do, too. Then maybe seeing her would close it off for you because you'd realize that woman isn't Laurel."

"I know. I know."

As the line moved forward, Emily tried to focus on the picture of Dwayne Ed sitting on the casket. It was a portrait that had been taken about twenty years ago when Emily first met him at Laurel's wedding. It made him look quite handsome, much as Laurel must have first seen him. Her concentration on the picture was broken by a guttural shriek. Emily looked to her left as did most everyone in the church to see Daphne jump out of a pew and rush behind her grandmother to the area where the coffin stood.

Phoebe, following her granddaughter, stopped slightly before Sheriff McIntire and said questioningly, "Laurel?"

"Is that you, Laurel?" she asked again.

The woman looked at Phoebe, then at Daphne and further back at Eddie. She looked again at Phoebe and nodded.

Daphne's hands signed rapidly to her grandmother, but her mother returned the answering signs just as rapidly. Daphne's eyes widened in delight at her mother's signs, and she catapulted herself into her mother's arms. Phoebe tried to join the hug. Her short arms didn't quite reach around the two of them, but Laurel disengaged one of her arms from Daphne and included her mother.

The hushed whispers heard in the church became loud questions as the congregation watched the interplay of Laurel, Daphne and Phoebe. Brother Johnson radiated beaming relief at the sight of a longlost mother joining her daughter and son. His funeral oration had just been given a reprieve because he could now talk about the goodness that comes out of bad. He could parallel the goodness of a mother being returned to her children after having been separated from them by an evil father. He was basking in the upcoming chance to inspire this gathering of people who were disappointed with his previously lackluster sermon. He decided the new theme would be out of bad comes good.

*   *   *   *

The crowd's eyes followed the movements of Daphne, Laurel and Phoebe as they signed rapidly. Facial expressions and laughter told of their happiness at being together again. Emily watched the women, but glanced over to the pew where Eddie was standing. As he watched his sister and grandmother greet his mother, his face darkened. His eyes narrowed as he observed the trio. Laurel looked up at him over Daphne's shoulders and saw the animosity on his face. She let go of her daughter and limped over to the pew.

Her honey blond hair was now streaked with gray, so it looked as tired as her eyes which were encircled by gray rings. Deep lines cut her forehead and mouth, and her limp added sluggishness to her cautious movements. Her brown skirt was old enough to wear an aged sheen. Although her blouse was white, it's longevity was marked with a yellow cast and nubby pills where her sleeves rubbed against the blouse front. Heavy brown oxfords looked as though they had provided years of quality service for her feet.

"Dwayne Ed?"

He didn't answer, so she asked tentatively, "Eddie?"

"Who *are* you?"

"I'm your mother."

A brooding frown greeted her. She slowly extended her hand. He quickly slapped it away.

"Dwayne Ed, Eddie, don't you remember me? I'm your mother; we haven't seen each other in so long. Don't you remember? I'm your mother."

"You are not a mother. You are not my mother. My mother would have been around. She would have made sure my sister and I were doing okay. She wouldn't have let us stay with him." He threw his index finger in the direction of the coffin.

"Eddie," said Phoebe. "She's come back."

"Come back from where? In ten years, you couldn't come back before now? You couldn't save us from Dwayne Ed? I hate you. I wanted you to come back; I didn't want you to be dead. I used to wait for you to come home. I wouldn't believe it when everyone said you were dead. I wanted you to come home and be my mother.

"I don't now, though. I don't care if you're dead or not. I hate you. If you had come back, Dwayne Ed wouldn't have hurt us. He wouldn't have made life ugly. I hate you, and I never want to see you again."

Watched by horrified eyes, he stalked out of the church.

Out of everything bad comes good?

Chapter 33

Brother Johnson spread his hands in dismay. Even if he could round up the distracted flock, he would never be able to round up their undivided attention. There was no way to compete with the show the assembly had just received. Knowing he knew that they couldn't be brought back to the fold, members of the crowd talking in excited bursts began to disperse out the several doors of the church like gerbils routing themselves out of a maze. The organist's attempt to aid Brother Johnson in corralling his audience by pumping out "Onward Christian Soldiers" wasn't much help. Instead of rallying them to the pastor's call, it only helped them to march out the church.

They all, with the exception of the Twerms family, paraded to the Easter Ranch. Knowing the Twerms homestead was barely habitable for its residents and certainly not hospitable for guests, Hugh and Maria Elena Easter were hosting the funeral reception which was hardly funereal. To be rid of Dwayne Ed Twerms was worth giving up a day's labor to celebrate, and most of the citizens of Gold, Dune and Easter counties were happy to partake of that celebration.

While Louisa had drifted off with her Aunts Polly, Cora and Lalie, Emily found herself talking with Maria Elena.

"Are you sure, Maria Elena, you had not one clue Laurel was in the county during parts of those years?"

"I'm absolutely positive, Emily. I even feel a little hurt because she and I were close friends, and I thought she would tell me, especially if she needed help. I think I am a little hurt she would not contact me. She's been gone a very long time."

"Did anyone know, do you think?"

"I would guess there's only one person who knew, and that would be the…"

"…Sheriff. Of course, it would," agreed Emily. "He knows everything else, it seems."

"Maybe her mother knew," suggested Maria Elena.

"If she did, she can keep a very tight secret, or she's a consummate actress which would be hard to believe because her emotions seem to be at surface level."

"The Sheriff is over there talking with Hugh. Shall we find out if anyone else knew she was alive?"

As Emily and Maria Elena, carrying plates so heaped with food the portions disfigured each other by running together, moved toward the Sheriff and Hugh, the Barnes and the Reeds joined their conversation. Emily and Maria Elena walked up just in time to hear Maggie exclaim, "Ruth, you look just wonderful. I haven't seen you look this good in so long. You must be feeling good."

Ruth smiled at Maggie. "I do feel good. Better than I've felt in a long time."

Ruth wore a red gingham fitted sheath with red pumps. Her brown hair formed a soft, curly cloud around her face. She still carried herself warily as though she were convinced her shoes would slide in mud and knock her off balance, but her eyes didn't shift uncontrollably as they had when Emily first met her.

"I am so happy for you."

Maggie surveyed the group. "Why this is just like high school. We're all together. This hasn't happened for years."

Sheriff McIntire smiled, "Except for Dwayne Ed and for you, Emily."

"So, should I leave, or is this easier for you to keep an eye on me here? Maybe you'd like me to go get my mother, so you can watch her, too."

The group laughed, and Hugh asked, "What have you been doing to this little lady, Bonham? You aren't going to get a lawsuit brought against the county, are you?"

Bonham looked at Emily and said, "Well, ma'am? You going to file a suit? After all, I was just looking out for you, just like I do all my county's inhabitants."

"Speaking of which, Sheriff, what were you doing at the boarding house Laurel Raines stayed at? I saw you there after Dwayne Ed was murdered. Did you know she was alive? Were you *protecting* her, too, with your constant guarding?"

"You mean Laurel Twerms, Emily," corrected Maria Elena. "Did you, Bonham? Did you know Laurel was in this county?"

Pondering his answer, Sheriff McIntire looked at his group of friends. He said slowly, "I'm not sure."

Hugh asked, "What's that mean, Bonham? You either know someone is someone, or you don't."

"Let's just say I was never sure. A few years ago while I was patrolling that area, I saw a lady limping along the wall of the school for the deaf. Actually, I had seen her before, but I hadn't paid it much attention. Then one day, I realized that wall was the only place in town that I saw that lady limping along. That's not unusual, and I didn't think much about it the first few times. Sometimes, though, things will stick in your mind, like a fly buzzing around you. You want to bat it away, but it keeps coming back. Months would go by, and I wouldn't see that lady and I'd forget about her. Then I'd see her—usually on a weekend, and I couldn't get rid of the thought of her.

"After a long while, I began to think she looked familiar, and I couldn't bat her out of my head. It was like that fly coming around again. Finally, I figured my mind was playing games with me because she kept getting more familiar. Only I couldn't place her, and I liked to go crazy trying to fix her in my mind.

"I think it must have been one time that I saw Dwayne Ed Junior that I began to be suspicious of who that lady might be. I hadn't seen him for a long while, and when I did, he had grown and started looking very much like Laurel. Then it kind of clicked, and I watched for the limping lady more intently.

"The only problem was I had no way to check for sure to see who the gal might be. It took me forever to figure out where she disappeared. You got it much quicker than I did, Emily.

"I questioned people in the area across from the school, but it took me a lot of watching to figure out where she disappeared. Even when I questioned those people at the repair shop, they wouldn't tell me anything. There was no way I could get any information from them; they weren't doing anything illegal, so I couldn't even bargain with them. All I could do was keep my eye on her and hope Dwayne Ed never found out she was around.

"So you see, Hugh, that's how I mean I wasn't sure."

"But, you brought her to church," said Jonas.

"I did. You had smoked her out a little, Miss Emily, when you went over there to tell the shop owners Dwayne Ed was dead. I just had to give her the final push. It was her decision to go to church to see for herself that Dwayne Ed was gone."

"So you had to accompany her?" asked Hugh. "Was that official business or personal interest?"

Darned if Sheriff Bonham McIntire's self assured pomposity didn't desert him like a sinking ship. Standing in the circle of his friends he looked down at his shuffling feet in an attempt to hide the blush of embarrassment that made his ruddy face scarlet.

*   *   *   *

Louisa and her aunts were lost to Emily. She couldn't spot her mother in the clusters of people stationed around the grounds of the Easter Ranch. The ubiquitous politeness of the group she was in pushed Emily to the perimeter of the conversation. She withdrew to the edge of the shade of the pecan tree ostensibly to reorganize her plate of food, so she would have a general idea of what she was eating. Social dynamics dictated Emily should be a part of this group of people so close to her own age. The history of this group forbade it.

In the patchwork quilt of the lives of this generation of San Domingans were patches still be added or, at best, reworked. Emily felt as keenly as the members of this clique the need to pick up those patches and add to the quilt's design. Soon the courteous attempts to coerce Emily's presence into the friends' pattern were dropped, so Emily withdrew further from them and listened as she scanned the throng of people again looking for her mother as an escape from herself as a nuisance factor.

Maggie repeated her earlier remark. "We haven't been together like this since high school."

The rest of them smiled, unsure what to say next to advance the conversation. Maggie put herself into the middle of their circle, a position of notice she commanded comfortably.

She tried again. "Don't y'all remember all those marvelous times we had?"

Hugh nudged closer to Maria Elena and cupped her elbow. He agreed with Maggie politely.

"Don't you remember, Ty?" she tried again.

Ty, unsure of what to say, smiled at her.

Scanning the crowd, Ruth and Jonas looked as though they would like to will themselves into another knot of people.

"Like that time we went camping, remember?" asked Maggie. "We set up the tents and decided to go swimming. It was so hot that weekend, remember? We had so much fun."

They all nodded slowly.

Hugh said, "Until the fire."

Heads popped to attention, and nods of understanding made the round of the circle.

"Yes, that's right, but that was an accident. That breeze just got it going too fast," explained Maggie.

"So Dwayne Ed said," Hugh responded.

"You still can't think he started that fire. You heard his explanation."

"I heard it."

"That was more than twenty years ago, Hugh. Dwayne Ed told us what happened. He was there; he should know what happened."

"My point exactly."

Maggie surveyed the other faces in the group. "You all don't think Dwayne Ed started that fire, do you?"

Most of the people looked doubtfully at Maggie, but Jonas said, "Probably not. It just got out of hand. Dwayne Ed wouldn't hurt any of us; we were his friends."

Relief that someone agreed with her was in Maggie's voice when she said, "That's right. Dwayne Ed wouldn't hurt his friends."

Emily watched as Hugh, mild disgust on his face, quietly led Maria Elena away from the group. Jonas and Ruth followed them, so the group noiselessly broke apart. Maggie, her face ready to crumple into tears, shot Ty a glance who returned a helpless stare with a shrug of his shoulder.

Chapter 34

Instead of sending the mourners to the cool indoors of the Easter ranch house, the hot afternoon only slowed people down and induced a lethargic reverie as Louisa sat ensconced in the midst of her aunts, uncles and cousins. She listened to their catching up with daily events in their lives, heard their comforting Texas twangs and enjoyed the camaraderie of her family. The low buzz of various discussions allowed her to hone in on chunks of conversation as they piqued her interest.

Through half closed eyes under the shady pecan tree, Louisa watched a leaf slowly glide along an air current and float on the water of the swimming pool leaving a lingering trail of ripples along the water.

Polly was saying to Cora, "…but she was at the church. I thought for sure she would show up here."

"Then she'd have to answer all those questions. She never did say much, if you remember."

"She may not have said much, but it was sure said about her. I wonder how much of it was true."

"With her, probably all the negatives and none of the positives."

"You mean you heard some positives? I never did."

Louisa opened her eyes and turned her head toward her aunt. She remarked, "I thought Laurel was supposed to be a nice person."

Polly's face drew into a question mark and then cleared with understanding. "No, honey, we weren't talking about Laurel. She was, is, a nice person. We were talking about Mel. She, on the other hand, is not a nice person. Maybe you hadn't noticed."

"Right, I'd noticed all right. No matter what Emily or I do, she finds fault with it. It's a good thing she never had children; they'd be a mess with her finding fault with everything they did."

"But, she did," exclaimed Lalie.

Just as quickly as it was out her mouth, the aunts gave their sister a synchronous, pained look.

"Well, she did. She had a family, of sorts. I mean, she basically raised him and all. The old man wouldn't do it."

"The only reason she raised him was to keep her hooks into the old man," said Polly.

"Fat lot of good it did her," said Lalie.

"If Junior hadn't married Laurel, she thinks she would have all that money to herself. Was she mad when he came home with his bride! You remember, Lalie? She was fit to be tied. Said she'd never speak to him again," interjected Terp with a laugh.

Uncle Luke looked at Louisa and saw the puzzlement on her face. "Ladies, you better explain. For not wanting to air dirty laundry to Louisa, you've sure opened up the hamper. Go ahead and tell her."

"Mel raised Dwayne Ed Junior," said Terp.

"No, I thought his dad was taking care of him. There wasn't anyone around the house when Emily and I went there except Jonas and Ruthie. Jonas didn't act like he was there to raise Junior. He's there to help Dwayne Ed," said Louisa.

"That's right," Uncle Sam said. "But, you're talking about the latest generation of Dwayne Eds; we're talking about the last generation. There have been five Dwayne Ed Twerms, but they all go by Dwayne Ed and Junior. The granddaddy has always died before the grandson is born, so we just call the daddy by his name, and the younger one Junior. It's the only thing those Twerms men have done to help anyone out. They die early enough, so we don't have to mess with Dwayne Ed Twerms the third or fourth. Makes it a lot easier."

Polly picked up the story. "When Dwayne Ed's mama, the Dwayne Ed who is dead today, died, Mel couldn't wait to pick up where she and the old man had left off. She moved into that house right after the mama's funeral. She raised the little boy from the time he was about three. She's like his mama. That's why we're surprised she only came to the church. Seems like she'd want to see him off. Raised him to be as mean as she is."

Uncle Luke said, "I don't know about that. He probably would have been as mean as she is even if she hadn't raised him. That old man was a mean son of a bitch. 'Scuse me, ladies."

"That's the God's truth. And, he was as mean as his daddy before him. Never knew a meaner bunch of people, not a nice one in the whole lot of Twerms men," Uncle Pete agreed.

"Wonder what that says for this Junior," said Lalie.

Murmurs of agreement went through the group that had abandoned its individual discussions and now focused on the discussion of the Twerms lineage.

Louisa addressed her question to the group as a whole. "How did the mother die?"

Discomfort made each member of the cluster squirm. Uncle Luke grabbed his chin and rubbed it as he thought of an answer. "We aren't rightly sure."

Polly said, "She died of rattlesnake bites."

"Must be pretty common around here, I would think," said Louisa.

"It is," agreed Pete, "but…"

"But, what?"

"That gal never hardly went out of the house. She hated it there on that ranch in the middle of nowhere; she was a city gal. She wouldn't leave the house for hardly anything. Just laid on the sofa or sat on the porch almost all day. Rattlers usually won't mix where there's a lot of goings on. They'll crawl up to a house, but you don't usually find a whole bunch of them near a house."

"One bite could kill someone, though. Maybe she couldn't get to a hospital in time."

"Maybe."

"That's what Pete is trying to say," said Cora.

"What do you mean?"

"There were too many bites to be just one snake."

"You mean someone planted them on her?"

"It looked that way. That's what the story was."

"Snakes crawling all over her. She must have panicked knowing they were rattlers." Louisa visibly shuddered. "Why didn't she run?"

"She was locked in a room."

Louisa shivered again. "Who would do such a thing? That'd be awful."

"We aren't sure who would do it. That's what we don't know," explained Polly. "It's just what some people said happened. You know, in an area like this, talk about our neighbors is one of the most interesting things we do."

"Gossip, you mean," said Sam.

Polly tapped him on the shoulder. "Sam, now you quit that. It's not gossip, not mean talk. It's just passing news along to another person about each other."

"The juicier, the better, and the faster it's passed," said Luke.

"So you think the husband did that to her?" asked Louisa.

The aunts and uncles hesitated before agreeing all at once. "Seems to be, could be."

Sensing there was more to the story, Louisa stated, "And, someone else. There was someone else, right? Who else killed the mother?"

She looked around the group, none of whom was volunteering information. "But, you know, right? Who was it? Was it Mel? Do you think it was Mel? Is that what you mean by picking up where they left off? Mel and the father had been having an affair?"

Lalie shrugged in agreement. More leaves floated onto the pool water and drifted toward the insurmountable pull of the skimmer as Louisa ruminated on the discussion.

"Why didn't she just marry Dwayne Ed's father before the wife came along?" she asked.

"Because Dwayne Ed's daddy didn't like her. He went to the city and found some business associate who was hard up for cash and bought his daughter for his son to marry. The son didn't have a choice," said Uncle Luke.

"Luke Moss," squealed Lalie, "he didn't buy her. That sounds like white slavery or something."

"You got a better way of putting it?"

"Well, yes. Yes, I do. He gave her a dowry. The daddy provided a dowry for Dwayne Ed's mama."

"A quarter of a million dollars back then was a hell of a dowry. Sounds like he bought her to me. Just like he bought, or tried to buy, everything else. Course, it was probably better that way. If he couldn't have bought her, he probably would have just stolen her."

Lalie cocked her head, looked at him and nodded.

* * * *

As funerals go, it wasn't quite up to expectations. Instead of a life story being laid to rest, more questions were raised about Dwayne Ed and his life. However, as a party, it was acceptable. The atmosphere was hardly one of saddened bereavement; it was more of gladdened relief. So, the funeral reception lasted late enough into the evening that all the dishes brought to feed the minions of Dwayne Ed harbored nothing but air hardened crumbs, swirls of unidentified gels and elastic vegetables swimming in leaden sauces.

Louisa and Emily finally connected and told to each other the glimpses of covert knowledge each had discovered of the lives of the inhabitants of Gold, Dune and Easter counties. When Louisa related the alleged details of the elder Mrs. Twerms' death, Emily said, "Come on, Mom. That would be impossible."

"What do you mean?"

"Who's just going to have a couple dozen rattlesnakes locked up to use as weapons?"

"Around here? Lots of people."

"Right," said Emily disbelievingly.

"Emily, haven't I ever told you of the annual rattlesnake hunts?"

"What do you mean—like the Gilroy Garlic Festival?"

"Exactly, or the Watsonville Artichoke Festival. Around here people gather every year and have a big festival where they hunt rattlers. Then they kill them, skin them and eat them."

"Give me a break. Eat them?"

"They jelly them, pickle them, roast them like chicken. They're supposed to taste like chicken. They use the skin for leather. You can buy just about anything you want made out of rattlesnake skin. It's quite a deal around here. They have weigh-in contests to see who can catch the most snakes. Guess who's won the contest most of the years?"

"I don't know, Mom, but I bet he's a real sneaky snake."

"Punny, Em. Aunt Mel usually weighs in the most; she's got a real talent for catching them."

"Figures. Poor things. That's another mark against Mel, killing nature for no good reason. She's such a snake in the grass."

"Guess I should have seen that one coming. Anyway, that's how someone could have rattlers as weapons—they could catch them."

"And, eat them. Do you suppose that's what Mel has been feeding us, peanut butter and rattlesnake sandwiches?"

"Not jelly, jellied. Like a sauce to preserve them."

"Whatever you say."

Emily thought about what her mother had told her. She thought about what she had learned watching Dwayne Ed's peers.

"It didn't answer much, Mom. The stories I heard about Dwayne Ed only made me more curious."

"About Dwayne Ed?"

"Him and the group of people he ran around with."

"And, his mother and his relationship with Mel."

"I suppose if you think about it, we could have suspected there was some tie in with her. After all, we did see her at that rally, and she chased him away when he was harassing those skinheads."

"But, Em, they all but said she was a murderer. She and Dwayne Ed's father. Seems like if there's that much gossip going around forty years later, they would have, at least, been questioned."

"Don't you remember what Mrs. Bliss told you? She said that family always ran that county. If that lazy Sheriff Twerms is any indication of how Dune County is run, it's not surprising that family could buy, steal or coerce themselves out of any trouble."

"Wouldn't you like to snoop around Dwayne Ed's house?" suggested Louisa.

"Looking for what, exactly?"

"You never know what might fall into our hands. There might be something kind of interesting."

"Sounds like most of the Twerms' skeletons are dancing out in the open. We just have to keep our ears open for the rattle of their bones," Emily said thoughtfully.

"It could be awfully interesting."

"Maybe we wouldn't have to snoop around."

"How do you mean?" asked Louisa.

"Maybe we could ask and get in the front door—such as it is."

"You mean without breaking our necks on that porch? Who're you going to ask to get in? Sheriff McIntire may not be on our butts anymore, but he's not our long lost best friend either."

"Forget Sheriff McIntire. You forget Laurel was, and is still, Dwayne Ed's wife. She owns the house."

Louisa snapped her fingers. "That's right. Have you talked to her at all? I heard she wasn't even here. The kids didn't come, either. I bet he never had her declared legally dead. You heard Hugh Easter talk about how he didn't want to think of her. He didn't have her declared dead because that would mean some kind of investigation. If he killed her or thought she was dead, he wouldn't want anyone asking about her."

"I heard that, too, and I haven't seen her. Tomorrow I think I'll track her down. You want me to try to get keys?"

"Silly girl, do you need to ask?"

Chapter 35

"Hey, Sheriff, long time no see," Toast hailed Bonham McIntire as he walked into the bar the morning after Dwayne Ed's funeral.

"How you doing?" Bonham tipped his hat as he removed it.

"Not bad. Not bad at all. You here on business or just visiting?"

"A little of both, I suppose. I've got some pictures here for you to look at. See if you know these guys."

He pulled a stack of six four inch by six inch black and white photos from his shirt pocket. Toast spread them out on the bar and studied them in the dim light provided by the open front door. He picked up a beer mug, pulled the lever to fill the stein with amber and suds and handed it to the Sheriff. He then went back to studying the pictures.

"I don't know them, Sheriff. I mean, I don't know their names or anything. I seen 'em, but I don't know 'em."

"Where have you seen them?"

"Here. Right here in the bar. A couple of these guys here in the picture have long hair, but they didn't have it when I saw them. I recognize them though even without the long hair. They all wore leather jackets, and when they took them off, they had funny tattoos on their arms, like they'd done it themselves. They were here maybe a week ago. You know, the night the Klan had that big rally. They kept coming in for about three days before that. They talked real quiet, so I could never hear what they were saying. Every time I'd go over to refill their drinks, they'd shut up like they thought I was being nosy.

"By the way, what happened with that rally? I heard they got Henry. You think these guys killed Henry?"

No answer from the Sheriff as he sipped his beer didn't deter Toast from talking about Henry.

"You know, he ain't been around. You think he's all right?"

"What do you mean?"

"I mean for a guy who's spent all his time drinking his life away and then not to show up, there must be something wrong."

"How long's it been since you've seen him?"

"I haven't seen him since the day before that rally."

"Shoot, man, why didn't you tell me?"

"Think he's in trouble? Maybe those skinheads got him. Did they? Is that why you're here? I hope not. Henry was a good guy; he sure was a good customer. You remember when he played football at the high school? I went to all those games just to watch him."

As Sheriff McIntire nodded his head, Toast said, "Oh, yeah. I forgot. You used to run around with him. Whatever happened? You think the Gulf messed him up like that? He was really messed up. You think that was all the Gulf? Every once in a while, you hear those stories about some people getting it bad over there. Not like Viet Nam, but still, who's to know what goes on?"

The Sheriff nodded looking into his beer stein before he took a long drink.

As he set the stein down, Bonham asked, "Were you there? At the rally?"

"Nah, had to work. Mostly what I heard was from people who came in the next day."

"You sure? Sure you weren't there?"

Toast started wiping the counter with a rag. "Well, you know, I thought about it. Had a couple people tell me they were going over there. I was kinda curious, heard about those things, ain't never seen one. But, it got to be late, and being at one of those things is just asking for trouble, so I bagged it and went on home. Heard some things, though, afterwards."

"Like what? What'd you hear, anything important?"

Toast continued wiping. "You know, the usual. Dwayne Ed and his buddies, stirring up trouble. Again. He's always in the middle of trouble. Guess I kinda figured he'd be in the middle of this horseshit. Heard about ol' Henry. That's bad. Bad for all of us. Never could figure out what night that rally was gonna be. First I heard one night and then another. Guess that was good because it was just gonna be trouble. If I didn't know the exact night, I couldn't very well go, could I?

"So did these guys kill him?"

"Don't know. FBI has a couple of these guys; they don't know what happened to Henry, or so they say. We're still locating the others. I just wanted to make sure they were the ones who were here in town. We're still trying to find Henry."

"After all he's been through, I'd turn tail and run as far away from here as I could. Sure is a shame. All that talent and all. Bet he could've played pro, maybe with the Dallas Cowboys or someone like that. Bet you were sorry to see him so messed up, huh? He would never talk about his football. Guess it made him realize how much he'd lost. Sure is a shame."

"That it is, Toast, that it is." The Sheriff made his final drink long enough to drain the stein. He put two dollars on the bar and said, "Thanks for the drink, Toast, and the information."

"Hey, make the drink on the house," Toast called after him.

"No, Toast, can't do that. Keeps it cleaner this way. See you around."

"Yeah, Sheriff, no problem," Toast said as he gathered up the money.

Chapter 36
▼

Emily hadn't tried to contact Laurel since the funeral to tell her she'd like to visit her. Deciding Laurel would probably be staying with Phoebe, Emily had dropped her mother at attorney Utley's office and driven to the Dune County section of San Domingo. As she crossed the tracks into Shanty Town, she saw Sheriff McIntire's car on the opposite side of the tracks going out. He waved at her, and she nodded her head at him. The few wrong turns she took on the unmarked streets of this not so desirable area of San Domingo allowed her to survey the newest graffiti on the misaligned fences. When she located Phoebe's house, she parked her car, took a deep breath to steady herself against…

What? What, she wondered, *could she possibly have to be uneasy about? All she was doing was visiting a friend she hadn't seen in twenty years. They hadn't parted on bad terms, so there should be no hard feelings to overcome. Laurel had been through some rough times, but, surely, she would welcome Emily's presence as someone she could talk to and rely upon. Surely, that would be the case. Hopefully, that would be the case. On the other hand, Laurel could look upon Emily's presence as an intrusion into a part of her life in which she did not wish her friend to participate.*

Emily started the car and retraced the path she thought she had taken earlier. Just as she was about to cross the railroad tracks that would take her out of Shanty Town and, most likely, away from her last opportunity to reconnect with Laurel, she stopped. She then u-turned the SUV and headed back toward Phoebe's house. Again she stopped. This time she stopped a few blocks from Phoebe's house. She didn't quite make it to the street on which Phoebe lived.

I should have called. This isn't right to not give her warning that I'm coming, that I want to see her. She's been through so much; this isn't fair to spring something else on her. What if she doesn't want to see me? What if she doesn't want to bring in the past? A life that was easier for her; a reminder of what could have been? What if she hates me? Not that she would mean to do so. But, she hasn't been with her children for almost ten years. She hasn't had a life with her family for so long. It's only been two weeks without Jojo and Lulie, and I'm missing them more than I'd miss my right arm.

And, I have Mom here. Laurel didn't even get to see her own mother, at least, not that I know of. She's been a woman without the most precious people in her life. All because of a cruel asshole of a husband. Thank God I have my David.

But, then, maybe that's why I don't want to see her. Maybe Dwayne Ed changed her so much that I won't even know her. Maybe she's not the Laurel I knew or want to know. Maybe he made her go off the deep end, and she belongs in a psych hospital, and I won't be able to handle her needs. And, then what kind of friend would I be?

After all, she left her family. Her family. Her kids. Her mother. What kind of woman could do that? Just charge off and leave without a word. Nothing should separate a mother and her children. The Laurel I knew wouldn't do that. She loved her family when we were in school. Her father and mother were the dearest people in her life. She talked about them all the time. Laurel wouldn't leave her own kids, not the way she loved her parents. When her father died, she was devastated. She could barely attend classes that semester because she felt so broken by his death.

Emily, sweating in the heat of the car, leaned her face against the steering wheel with a deep sigh. As if it would jostle her thoughts into some kind of logical order, she shook her head against the wheel. Nothing made sense when she thought about Laurel. Here was a woman who had shared so much with her those two years in college. Both of them had families in faraway states, and both of them had families they cared for deeply. They, unlike so many of their dorm mates and sorority sisters, didn't have the luxury of the family washing machine only a town or so away. They didn't even have hard to live with families that made a distant college a welcome refuge. But, they had each other, and because they had a shared respect and love for their families, they had a strong affiliation.

So, why would Laurel leave those two beautiful children? How could she leave them in the hands of that poorest excuse for a father knowing the harm he could inflict on them? Why wouldn't she stick around and protect them, even if it killed her in the end?

Emily, still unaware of the sweat dripping down her face, clenched her fists and jammed one against the steering wheel with a gut-wrenching groan. As she opened her eyes, she jumped with a screech. There was a woman pounding on the driver's side window.

As the lady pounded the window, she yelled, "Open up! Open the window!"

More than hearing the shouts, Emily saw the exaggerated movement of her mouth. It took a few moments for Emily to realize the lady at her window was Stacy, the friend for whom Phoebe had such hope. Stacy, her black hair bound by pink sponge rollers around her hairline, kept pounding. Turning the engine on, Emily pushed the button to turn down the window.

"What're you doing, ma'am?" asked Stacy. "Man, lady, I could cook bacon and eggs on the hood of your car, it's so hot. Why're you in this car? You need to get yourself somewhere where it's cool. You cain't do this to yourself. Making yourself sick."

"Oh, Stacy. If you only knew. If you only knew."

"You goin' to see Miz Raines, ain't you? That's where I seen you before. You remember me? I remember you; you was looking for Miz Raines' house."

Emily nodded, "I remember, Stacy. I'm Emily. I remember you."

"Miz Raines' house is over there, a couple streets over. She's got her daughter with her. You a friend of hers, right? Miz Raines said you two knew each other. That's how Miz Raines knows you, through her daughter. That gal's been drug through hell and back and drug through again. Ain't nobody should have a life like she's had. Not having her babies. Cain't see her own mama. Havin' to put up with that bastard of a husband. Oooo, and he was a mean sonofabitch. Ain't nobody nowhere in these parts likes him. Killin' him was too good for him. Whoever done it ought to get a medal.

"Ma'am, if you're truly a friend of Miz Raines' daughter, then she needs you. Don't matter when you seen her last, she needs you now. I don't know what you was doing driving back and forth like a headless chicken, but, ma'am, you gotta help that poor lady out. She needs all the kindness she can get. And, if you're a friend, then you got kindness to give. Don't matter when you last seen each other."

Emily smiled. "I expect you're right. I just haven't seen her in so long. Don't know how she's going to react. What if she doesn't want to see me? Maybe too much in her life has gone wrong."

Stacy stood at the driver's window and slowly shook her head, "Don't matter, Miss Emily. She just needs kindness. Just needs to know people's lookin' out for her. Don't matter if you never see her again. Right now she needs that kindness to give her strength. God puts people in other people's lives to teach 'em and help 'em. You got the strength, and that lady needs some right now. Maybe that's why you're here. You think you came for somethin' different, but maybe you're here to help that poor lady get her life back. You go now, go help her."

Emily shrugged in agreement, "I think you may be right. You answered my dilemma. Thanks, Miss Stacy."

As Stacy stepped away from Emily's car, she tapped the door and smiled. Emily backed away, and Stacy waved reassuringly.

But, Emily still, even when she parked her car in front of Phoebe's house, was unsure of the reception she would receive. Unsure of Laurel's stability, unsure of her own reasons for needing to see Laurel. It certainly wouldn't be to catch up on the last few years. Laurel would hardly want to remember those, as painful as they had been. Maybe Stacy was right. Maybe the timing for her visit to West Texas was fortuitous, maybe the reason she was here was to help Laurel. It seemed to be more than coincidence. After all these years. All these years without seeing a very dear friend. And, now, that friend literally pops into her life.

Chapter 37

When beset by indecision, make a move one way or the other. Emily got out of the car, marched up the path lined with the lighthearted zinnias and knocked at the screen door. As she stood on the wooden porch, she could hear voices talking in one of the rooms of the house. She knocked on the screen door again and listened to it rattle against the doorjamb as she rapped. Phoebe came from the back of the house, gave her a slight grimace and went back into the room. Emily heard Phoebe's voice talking earnestly, but she talked too softly to allow Emily to decipher what she was saying. Laurel, with her faltering walk, emerged a few minutes later.

Before Emily could greet her, Laurel said, "I've been waiting for you."

She looked at Emily through the screen door as though she were deciding whether to open up and let her friend in. In the house or into her life, Emily couldn't decide. Emily stood her ground and returned Laurel's gaze. Slowly Laurel slid her hand up the wooden frame of the door, even more slowly unhooked the jamb and finally invited Emily in. They stood for a few moments considering each other, and, finally, Laurel made a slight opening of her arms. Emily stepped into that opening and Laurel grasped Emily tightly and for a long time. Still holding onto Emily's arms, she stood back and said, "I've been waiting for you, but I didn't know if I'd want to see you. I'm glad you came. If we had waited for me to make the first move, I might not have ever seen you.

"I know you must have a terrific amount of questions to ask. I'll answer them all. I knew you didn't like my going off to marry Dwayne Ed, and I knew you didn't like him when you met him. I guess I thought you wouldn't like me anymore for doing that. And, if I really dig deep, I suppose I was angry with you for not supporting my decision, and I felt you weren't giving Dwayne Ed a chance. Same with my mother. I was mad at her for two years because I thought she was rotten to Dwayne Ed. You don't know how many times I've kicked myself for not listening to the two of you. Go ahead, ask me anything; I'll answer it."

Emily did have questions to be answered. There was half a lifetime's events to recover, but all Emily asked was, "How are you holding up?"

"Thanks. Thanks for asking how I'm doing now. I'm doing okay. We had Daphne here for the evening, and I got to talk with her. Couldn't keep my hands off her. There were times I thought I'd never get to be close to her and hug her. There were times I thought I couldn't not tell the family I wasn't dead. In the beginning, it all seemed like it would be so easy to protect them, to stay away from the kids. If I weren't around them, their father wouldn't hurt them. That's why they do it, you know."

"Do what?"

"Fathers will hurt children to get back at the mother. The fathers hate the mother so much, so they hurt the thing closest to her. Dwayne Ed liked to watch me suffer when he made the kids suffer. Most of the time I could keep them away from him; sometimes I couldn't. When Daphne got so sick and ended up deaf, he blamed me for making her retarded. You've seen her; she's anything but retarded. But, he said the child grunted all the time, so the meningitis damaged her brain instead of just her hearing. Every time she'd get frustrated, she'd throw a tantrum because she couldn't tell us what was wrong, and he'd haul off and hit her. He never listened to the doctors who told him she was deaf only, that she'd learn through sign language and be a productive and fine person. He never listened. Finally, Hugh talked him into putting her in the residential deaf school. That's where you saw me."

"I know. I was surprised you were there. Both my mother and I kept talking me out of the fact I had seen you. It seemed improbable after all these years you and I would find each other. Only trouble is I couldn't forget your face walking down that street. I didn't even know you were this near my mother's family. I never thought to look at the counties in this part of Texas, to see how close they actually are to each other. If I had, maybe I would have put it together and looked harder and earlier for you."

Laurel smiled sadly. "It didn't take very long to figure out Dwayne Ed wasn't the nicest person. By the time I faced up to it, I was pregnant. My mother would've taken me in, but he wouldn't let me have the kids. They were Twerms, and they had to stay in Dune County. Even Daphne, he wouldn't let me take her. He didn't want her, but his supposed manhood would have been threatened if he let his wife run away from him and take the kids. It was too risky. Also about that time, I realized your relatives were on the ranch next to us and in the next county. Only I was too embarrassed for you to find out about my husband and marriage. You would have every right to say, I told you so. You can still say that."

"No, that's done and over with. You've got a second chance; you should make the most of it. Your kids are almost grown, all of you need each other. If you dwell on what happened, you'll lose your chance to be a family now. Now you won't be by yourself. You must have been very lonely these last years."

"I had Pedro and Hermalinda; they were nice to me."

"Those are the people at the repair shop?"

Laurel nodded. "They found me in the road. Dwayne Ed pushed me out of the car one night, and I went down the side of a hill about halfway between the Easter's house and the county line. He had been drinking heavily, and he decided he wanted to make love. I told him I hated him. I hated him because he had made such a fool of us at the Easters' house where we had gone for dinner. I hated him for the drinking. I hated him for the abuse he put the kids and me through. I just hated him. So, he got rid of me—just threw me away. Opened the car door and tossed me out, like an old piece of gum.

"It was a few days that I lay down that hill; I was passed out most of three days. We figured I must have had a concussion. When I finally came to, I climbed up the hill at night. It was so slow because my hip was broken, and I was all banged up. Whenever I moved, something else in my body just ached. I cried every time I moved, and I was so thirsty.

"The thirst was as painful as the bruises and my hip—sometimes even more so. I never thought being thirsty and hungry could hurt so much, but it does. Sometimes when I felt like I couldn't hide anymore, when the loneliness got really hard, I'd remember how much it had hurt crawling up that hill. I'd like to think I stayed hidden because of protection for the kids, but you know what? A lot of the reason to stay away was because of Dwayne Ed and how much he hurt me. I can still feel the thirst and hunger.

"I tried to sleep in the day; that way no one would see me. It was such a relief to get to the road, but after I got there, I wondered why I was so glad because I didn't know where I would go next. I couldn't go back to the house because Dwayne Ed would find another way to kill me, and I didn't know what would happen to the kids if he killed me. I hid under a tree and then started crawling the road at night. These county roads are all deserted at nighttime, so it was pretty safe.

"One day toward dawn, I passed out on the road. I guess the dehydration was killing me. Pedro and Hermalinda found me and wanted to take me to the hospital, but I wouldn't let them. Dwayne Ed has people all around this part of Texas who let him know everything that's going on. It was too risky; I had to keep quiet to save the children. Hermalinda and Pedro became my only haven in this whole tricounty area. Dwayne Ed would never have anything to do with them because they weren't one of the old landed families, and they didn't have any money, so they were relatively safe from him.

"They still risked a lot for me, though. I was there that day you came in. I was behind that counter waiting for you to leave. I didn't know what you wanted. If Dwayne Ed found out I had been around all this time, he would have killed me—and the kids. I'm sorry."

"It's okay. Were you here all the time? Did you stay in San Domingo?"

"Heavens, no! I stayed and worked in Texas. I took jobs doing housekeeping and maintenance at night in big corporations, places like the hospitals and the universities and government buildings. When they wanted to promote me, or it looked like I was getting noticed, I'd go find another social security number and get another job. It used to be easy to get a social security number. I'd just go to a graveyard, find a tombstone with a birth date about the same as mine and use that name. As long as I kept moving around Dwayne Ed couldn't ever find me. If he ever looked. I think he figured I was dead, so it didn't matter. He didn't need to look for a dead person whose bones were lying at the bottom of a cliff picked clean by those buzzards.

"But, then it got harder because computers with their databases have closed up graveyards as a source for social security numbers. Now, it's too risky to use a graveyard."

"So, what'd you do?"

"Borrowed someone's. I'd go to the library and search the newspapers and find someone who was born about my same year. Then I'd write the state and ask for a new birth certificate and tell them I lost mine. Sometimes it worked; sometimes it didn't. After I got the birth certificate, I'd apply for a copy of my social security number. I'd have the employer take out extra pay, so the taxes wouldn't hit hard whoever's number I was using, and I wouldn't work very long using that number. Just long enough to get food to eat and a place to stay. Sometimes I could work for cash only. Then people didn't care who I was. And, sometimes, it was dumpster food and a park bench. I think I know all of the soup kitchens between here and Dallas and Houston."

"Bet your mother was happy to find you, wasn't she?"

"She hasn't quit talking to me. She's given me blow by blows of everything she knows about the kids. She's got scrapbooks and pictures of them, all organized. She said she did it, so I could live all the parts of their lives that I'd missed. She never gave up; mothers are like that. They never give up. Guess I should have listened to her when she told me not to marry him. Should have listened to you, too."

"Then you wouldn't have your kids. Out of all that bad, you've got some good—Daphne and Eddie."

Laurel nodded as if she didn't believe what Emily was telling her. As Emily watched and waited for her to continue, Laurel dropped her face into her hands, took a gasping breath and said, "I don't have Eddie."

"Laurel, I'm sure he'll come around. Seeing you at that funeral was highly emotional for him, too. He just reacted to all the crises that have been occurring to him. He still needs you, especially now."

"No, you don't understand. I don't have him because he's run away. He's gone. No one can find him. Bonham has people looking for him in the whole state of Texas. He even contacted police in the big cities. He's gone. He's left here because of me. He didn't even tell Daphne where he was going, and he and she would tell each other everything that happened in their lives."

"How long?"

"You mean how long has he been gone?"

Emily nodded.

"Since he ran out of the church. He's gone. Mother went to the house last night; she thought he might have gone back there. No one was there though. There was a note telling us he took one of the pickups, and he took a bunch of money Dwayne Ed had stashed somewhere.

"I don't care about him taking that, I just want him home," she wailed.

Emily reached out to her friend whose gut wrenching sobs would surely cleave her body from stem to stern. Carrying a box of tissues, Phoebe came into the room and took her daughter from Emily and held her while cooing comforting noises to calm her down.

"Laurel, Eddie's a very young man trying to make sense out of very adult situations. He's tried to fend off his father's weaknesses all his life. Seeing you synthesized all those fears and hopes, so he panicked. I bet he's at the house now."

Laurel nodded. "Maybe. Mom said we could check the house tonight again."

"Are you going to be moving in? Will you be living there?"

"Living there? In Dwayne Ed's house? Why would I live there?"

"Laurel, it's your house now. You and Dwayne Ed are still married, you know. You are the surviving spouse, and I would imagine you inherit all the property. That house is yours. Dwayne Ed's assets are yours."

She blotted her face with some of the tissues her mother held out to her, "I hadn't thought of that. Maybe you're right. I suppose I should find out if he divorced me."

"Why would he do that?"

"Maybe he wanted to marry someone else."

"Laurel, he thought you were dead. Besides, who would marry that dissipated old toad? Did you ever see him as he got older?"

"No, I don't think so."

"Probably just as well. You'd be appalled at what you had married."

"He was so romantic in Houston. He was such a disappointment after we got married."

"Where do you think Eddie might have gone?"

"How would I know?" Laurel wailed again. "I don't know the first thing about my teen age son. I haven't been around him to even know what his personality is like. All I know is what Mother has been able to fill in. Now, he's left, and I may never get to know him."

"Honey," said her mother, "I'll go back to the house and look for him. I got that set of keys from Jonas, but I didn't want to go back to the house this afternoon because I was worried about you."

She turned to Emily and explained, "Jonas has been keeping an eye on the ranch; his house is very close to the ranch. He had just come back from checking the place and hadn't seen Eddie, so I figured it would be okay to come and take care of Laurel. Daphne was here, too, and I wanted some more time to be with them."

"I'll be glad to go and look for him at the ranch, if you want," volunteered Emily.

Phoebe looked relieved. "Would you do that for us? That would be so wonderful and such a big help. Let me get the keys, and you can go over there now."

"You'll call, please?" asked a hopeful Laurel.

"I'll call as soon as I get over there and look. Phones are still on, do you think?"

"Unless Jonas turned them off already. He took care of much of the management of the ranch, so I wouldn't think he'd have them turned off because he still needs supplies and all that. Would you like Mom to call him and ask? If you don't want to go out there, I suppose we could call Jonas and ask him if Eddie's shown up. He might know by now. I'm sure he's made a daily check."

"No. No, that's no problem. I'm happy to do this for you. You'll feel better having someone not as close to Dwayne Ed doing a job for you. If the phones are off, I'll call you from my aunt's ranch. Anything else I can do for you?" Emily put her hand on Laurel's shoulder.

"No, going all the way out there is a big relief. Thank you."

"It's no problem; I've got nothing else to do."

Chapter 38

▼

"Do you think I got them under false pretenses? Should I feel guilty?" Emily asked her mother after she had picked her up from the attorney's office and explained why they were going to Dwayne Ed's ranch.

"Under the circumstances, it was probably easier for them to not have to think about why we were being nosy. Phoebe and Laurel have got so much on their minds. It probably is better having someone in their own camp look for Eddie. Jonas may be above board and all, but he was Dwayne Ed's right hand man, so Laurel has a right to distrust him. All in all, it's better to do it this way."

"Nice tactful answer, Mrs. Social Worker. Just what I'd expect from you. You've been in the business too long."

"Tactful answers give me much insight into my clients. Are we going to the ranch now?"

"Do you mind? I know it's hot, but I told Phoebe and Laurel I'd get over there and look for Eddie."

"If it's this hot, maybe no one will be around because they won't want to come out of their air conditioned buildings. Maybe Jonas has already made the rounds, and we can search to our hearts' content without being disturbed."

The air conditioner was forcing out its maximum amount of cool, and that cool air was only just taking the bite out of the hot interior of the car. Both Louisa and Emily wore a sheen of moisture on their faces as they tried to get comfortable in the acetylene atmosphere of the day.

Setting out on the highway, Louisa remarked, "A storm's coming up. See it way off in the distance."

Emily looked up from the road she was following south to the Twerms ranch. Only the faintest line of indigo bisected the sky.

"How did you see that? You sure those are clouds?"

"I felt it first. Can't you feel the quiet in the heat? Nothing's out this afternoon, only two crazy ladies from California. I bet even the horned toads are hiding under some rock. That's why it's so hot; all the moisture has been sucked up into those clouds. When it's this quiet, you know the storm will be heavy. I hope we make it to the house before it hits."

"Come on, Mom, that storm is miles and miles ahead of us. We've got plenty of time."

"No, we don't. These storms aren't like the ones at home where you wait days for it to come off the ocean. These roll in fast and usually roll out fast."

"At least it'll be cooler. That rain will cool things down."

"For a short while. Then it'll be muggy, and you'll wonder why you thought it might be better. But, for a while it will leave a little moisture in the air so you won't feel like you're wearing beef jerky for skin. We'll just watch it come in."

When they arrived at the house of the Twerms ranch and stepped out of their car, there were no skittering lizards and toads as there had been the last time they paid a visit to the ranch. The only sound on the ranch was the subdued hiss of the pump jack as it coaxed crude oil out of its underground hermitage. The quiet made the decrepit house all the more portentous in its looming presence in the middle of nowhere.

While Louisa steeled herself to walk up the wooden slats to the porch, Emily took the keys out of her purse and took a deep breath, "Let's go; I've got the keys.

"It's just an old house. I don't know why it should seem so strange to go into it. I mean, it's not like we're sneaking in or anything. Laurel asked us to go and check. We have every right to be here."

"More or less. It's all that negative history that's seeped into its walls. That's what makes it eerie. That storm isn't going to help either."

Emily looked at the sky to see the faint line of purple clouds expanding into turgid hordes of massive blisters as they bolted toward the ranch. Black cankers engorged the purple and lavender clouds until the afternoon was engulfed in a premature twilight.

"We either get in the car and try to outrun the storm, or we get in the house. Now!" commanded Louisa.

They ran up to the house, the rotting wood of the porch giving spring to their steps, and stood at the door while Emily started to insert the key in the lock. The door handle turned as she steadied it to put in the key, and they walked into the house through the unlocked door. They made it inside the house just as the first bullets of rain attacked them.

"Mom, do you think someone is in here? That door should've been locked."

"Yes, well, perhaps. Some people around here may still leave their doors unlocked. Maybe Jonas figures no one will come around here because Dwayne Ed, if he has a ghost, will be nastier than when he was alive."

"Yeah, right. Even Brother Johnson was chicken when he had to talk about Dwayne Ed's afterlife."

Louisa and Emily continued their pointless discussion more as an armor against shadows lurking in the dank hallway than suggesting anything meaningful. The dim hallway was all the more murky because of the lack of afternoon brightness that might have ebbed into the house. Musty decay overlaid with the smell of rancid cooking grease molested their olfactories. Seldom wiped dust powdered the furniture and woodwork with a granulated opaqueness. The gloomy living room allowed them to see only bulky outlines of furniture. Piles of newspapers had become permanently affixed to the dining room table.

Pulling back the liver colored drapes in the dining room, Emily read some of the dates to her mother as she riffled through the piles. "Here're papers from 1990, a whole stack of them. Here's some from 1984. Look here, they're all in chronological order, dusty, but in order. I bet we could even find some from when Laurel disappeared. Bet that's how he decided she had died; he tracked her through the newspapers and never found any indication her body had been discovered. Wonder why he kept these others, though."

"Because," said her mother as she went through individual papers, "he was looking for information. See how he circled some of these stories, and folded the papers back to where he had underlined them? These are on white supremacist groups and how they are settling in the northwest United States. Here's some about the Ku Klux Klan rallies in the south. Here are hate crimes in California. Look, he has names and places underlined."

"Well, well, look here. I found it. He wasn't just looking for information; he was tracking Laurel's disappearance. Here's the series about Laurel and her disappearance. It's circled with exclamation points, and he underlined his own name. What's that mean, Mom? Why would he underline his own name when the article is about his wife?"

"Looks like he has—had—a very inflated view of his importance. Let's go look at some more of the house."

Emily and Louisa walked down a hallway with a fractured chair rail. Some of the tongue and groove wainscoting had been ripped off the lower portion of the wall, and the wallpaper on the upper portion displayed lacerations across its dirtied pattern. The kitchen was worth only a glance to see towers of dishes mortared together by numerous days of dried food. There was a window over the sink, but the light it permitted to come into the room would only illuminate the layer of tacky grease and filth that had settled over the food preparation areas. Switching on a light sent a brigade of cockroaches clicking across the linoleum floor as they sought refuge under dusty, darkened appliances. They walked back to a closed door passed earlier in their walk down the hall. They opened it and peeked in to see a room stocked with a computer system on an imitation oak computer stand, a fax and copy machine sitting near a multi-lined telephone, and file cabinets stacked with telephone books.

"This is where we want to look, but let's go upstairs first. Let's look at the bedrooms," said Louisa.

"There might be someone up there."

"I know. That's why I want to check it out up there before we get involved down here. Don't you think if there were someone in the house, he would have come down and looked for us? It's not like we've been creeping around in our bedroom slippers, you know."

They plodded up the stairs noisily. "If anyone is up here, maybe he'll run and hide and won't bother us," said Emily.

"Or, get a gun and shoot us."

"Now, Mom, we're allowed to be here; that person isn't."

"Shall we tell him that before or after he shoots us?"

"Not funny, Mom."

They started at the back of the upstairs hallway, not in as bad a condition as the downstairs hallway but still nothing to designate the area a decorating triumph. Opening one of the bedroom doors, they entered a crisply neat young girl's room done in pink and white rosebuds and lace with porcelain dolls and stuffed animals readied for play.

"Daphne's room," both women agreed.

"Probably hasn't been touched since the day she left for school. Wonder if Dwayne Ed wiped this room out of his mind the way he wiped his daughter out of his mind," commented Emily.

"What do you want to bet the room next to it is Eddie's?"

"Maybe he's in it."

"Maybe," said Louisa as she opened the door.

Brown walls and a blue rug were coordinated with a brown and blue plaid bedspread and curtains in a neatly kept room filled with books in shelves along two walls. A computer sat at the desk with a rack of computer games and programs next to it.

Emily walked over to the computer and felt the back of it, "Feels kind of warm to me. Could be my imagination, I suppose. What kind of books does he read?"

"A little bit of trash, some thrillers, and some classics. Do you think it's interesting that there are a few psychology and sociology books here? Those aren't all high school subjects, are they? I thought those were mostly college classes. At least, they were when I went to school." Louisa scanned the books with patient interest. A personal library can be as telling as a personal interview.

"I think they still are. Who was he trying to figure out, his father or himself?"

"Or, his mother or all of them. He has quite a choice."

The rain was hitting the house with a heavy barrage of beats against the outside walls. Louisa pointed to the window in Eddie's room. "Look, Emily, that rain won't even let you see the outside, it's so dense. We could be driving in that."

"No, we would be stopped at the side of the road, lost probably, waiting for it to let up, so we could find our way home."

"Shall we? We're stalling, you know."

"Let's look at the other bedrooms first."

The first room they peered into was devoid of personality with its beige walls, white drapes and multiflowered bedspread.

"Obviously the guest room," said Louisa.

"Who would want to stay as a guest in Dwayne Ed's house? I'd be afraid I'd come out of here in a depressive state. Or dead." said Emily.

Louisa closed the door of the guest room. "We have two more doors. Which has the grand prize, door number one or door number two?"

"I choose door number two," Emily said as she reached to open it.

They opened the door into a graceful room of Victorian mahogany furniture dressed in satin pinks and blues. One mirrored panel of the heavy armoire was opened to exhibit lace dresses and flowered straw hats. As ordered as a Gibson girl and spotless, the room couldn't have belonged to anyone but Laurel.

"You wouldn't think this ramshackle, rotten old house would have much personality, yet each of these rooms is probably a better picture of the people who inhabit them than they are themselves," said Emily.

"True. The outside of the house is as decayed as the family structure."

"They'd make a good case study for you, Mom."

"Thanks, but no thanks. I've got enough case studies at the office back home."

"Those kids' rooms make me miss Jojo and Lulie even more. I wonder how they're doing."

"I'm almost finished with the paperwork for Atie's will. When I'm done, we'll go home."

"When I talked with David last night, he said he'd be done with his big installation in a week. Maybe we can get home by then."

"We'll try. You know we're stalling. You wouldn't, by any chance, be afraid of looking into the last room, would you?"

"Not afraid, just uneasy. Here goes," Emily took a deep breath as she opened the door.

Red heavy drapes masked the windows, so what little light the storm permitted was completely blocked in the dark room. Louisa switched on the overhead light.

Emily froze at the doorway. "Oh my heavens. You've got to be kidding."

"Why should this surprise you, Em?"

Red velour fleur de lys on a gold background papered the walls behind the full bodied female nude paintings on two of the walls. A wide screened television sat next to video cassette shelves stocked with adult movies. On the ceiling over the king sized waterbed was a mirror, and blood red shag carpeting flooded the floor. On the dresser behind a stack of weekly tabloids and male magazines was a small picture of Laurel exed out by heavy black lines and dotted with pencil stabs.

"Not much up here; let's go down and look at that office we passed in the hallway."

Chapter 39

▼

"Wonder if the sheriff and his crew pried open the locks," Emily nodded toward the desk with drawers sticking out like uneven tongues.

"Locked drawers are an invitation to curiosity; it could have been the murderer," said Louisa as she pulled drawers out of their slides.

"What're you doing?"

"Whoever sprung the locks would find what they were looking for if it were in the drawers, so it's not worth looking really hard at the drawers. It might, however, be worth looking behind them for secret spots."

"Okay, but I'll go through these papers in the drawers, just in case they missed something. Then, I'll start on the file cabinets. Not much, some old news clippings about happenings at San Domingo High, some old bills. Here's a yearbook. Looks like one from the time they all went to high school. Here, I'll show you Dwayne Ed and why Laurel thought he was so wonderful. See? Look at him, good looking, don't you think?"

Louisa looked at the picture Emily held to her, "Best looking snake in the grass that I've seen."

"Look, here's Hugh Easter and Ty Barnes. Do you know what Maggie's last name is? I bet she was a beauty."

"I don't think I've ever heard her maiden name, but look for the Homecoming Queen picture. That would have it. Yearbooks always have a big spread for Homecoming Queen, and she told us she was the Homecoming Queen."

"Wow! I wouldn't mind having looks like those stare back at me from the mirror. Her name was Sutter, Maggie Sutter. Look here, Mom," Emily pointed to the caption and read, "…missing from picture, Ruth Lewis. Why do you suppose someone would be missing from her yearbook Homecoming picture? This was obviously taken the night of the dance; they have their formals on, but Ruth Lewis is missing."

"Maybe she got sick. Look at Maria Elena; she would have made a beautiful queen. Do we know the other two girls?"

"Maggie's mentioned Cindy before, but I've not met her yet, and the other one I've never heard of."

"Hey, since you and David do computers for a living, try to get into these files on this one," said Louisa has she turned on the master switch of the computer sitting on the desk. "I can't get into the files." Louisa poked various buttons on the keyboard.

"Is it password protected?"

"Guess so. Can you get around the password?"

"If I have the software, I could reinstall and get into the program. Did you see any software around here?"

"No."

"That's probably because Dwayne Ed pirated it. He's too mean and cheap to spend the money on it," muttered Emily as she rummaged through the drawers of the desk, opened the file cabinets and ran her eyes over the shelves. "This place is as disorganized as that records office we saw. It's amazing they could run the ranch. You can't find anything.

"If we knew some birth dates of the family, you could maybe get in. Usually, people choose significant dates for passwords."

"Do you know Laurel's?"

"Not off hand." Emily looked at her mother and asked, "Besides if he hated Laurel so much, why would he use anything about her?"

"Because he hated her so much. Wouldn't be very obvious using her birth date as a password, don't you think?"

"I guess. Try her name then. If he thinks hate for her is a diversion in passwords, maybe he used her name. If he hates her enough to use a date, why not a name?"

Louisa typed in Laurel's name and the screen opened up to reveal a menu.

"Smart cookie. That did it. Now what do you suppose I'm looking for?"

"Try the files and see if there's anything cryptic looking, something he wouldn't want people to recognize. If there aren't many documents in the files, you could look at each one."

"There aren't. Some of these look like ranch records. Here's a financial statement. Want to see how much Laurel's worth?"

"Sure, as long as we're nosing around, let's do it right."

Both women gasped as the bottom figure of a six-page net worth statement popped onto the screen.

"She's going to have a slightly different lifestyle than what she's been used to. Flip back and see where the holdings are."

"Looks like Atie's profile, second deeds of trust, oil royalties, gold stocks, bank stocks with major holdings, land, cattle et cetera, et cetera. Looks like money will not be a worry for her."

Louisa exited the financial statement and went back to the menu.

Emily pointed to a file with the word, Hardware. "Pull this one up and see what it is. Maybe Laurel owns a hardware store. That would be handy for running a ranch. You could get all your hardware supplies at wholesale."

Louisa opened the file and revealed a purchase order on which was written '4crhow rec'd 12/30,air'. The second line was similar with '5crAK47rec'd 1/15,air'. Another line read, '3cr LAWrec'd2/1, truck'. Noted at the bottom of the purchase order was '2000amm'.

"What do you think that is, Mom? Looks like he's written in code or shorthand. Any ideas?"

"Not really, but it sure seems a funny way to track business purchases."

"Kind of a sneaky way, don't you think? Maybe it's not legal hardware. Maybe it's not even hardware."

Louisa stared at the screen. "You're right, Em; it's not hardware. Those middle letters, you know what those are? Think about what was in that shed we started on fire."

"Ammunition of some type—lots of it," said Emily.

"That's right—lots of it. Why would there be so much ammunition that it had to be stored in a shed? Hidden behind that hay. If that were legal ammunition, why would you bother to hide it in a barn in the middle of the West Texas desert? Those middle letters are weapons' designations. Looks like Dwayne Ed was running a little business on the side.

"And, these purchase orders tell when they arrived and how they came," said Louisa. "Sheriff McIntire said Dwayne Ed was hot to get a Klan chapter going in this area. Maybe dealing weapons was how he was going to finance it."

"Or storm West Texas."

While Louisa looked at files in the computer, Emily went through the files in the cabinet.

"Most of these look like ranch records, Mom. You got anything there?"

"A couple more of those purchase order lists. Here's something labeled 'Land'."

There was a pause as she read the file, "My, my, what do we have here? Emily, look in that cabinet for a file called 'Land' or 'Bliss', something to do with that land we went and visited, the one where there was no oil drilling."

"Here it is, under 'Land'. Why do you want it?"

"What's in it?"

"Looks like a deed." She brought it over for Louisa to examine. "Isn't that a deed?"

"Sure is, it appears to be the same one Atie's mineral rights were written on. Look at this list. It's got a slew of names of people who live around here. I think this is the list of people to whom Mel must have sold mineral rights on Bliss land. You know what this means, Emily?"

"Sure. If Mel sold mineral rights to Atie, and Dwayne Ed has a copy of the deed and a list of possible buyers, they were working together."

"Makes you wonder how much they were working together."

"Or how stable their working relationship was; maybe Mel got really mad at Dwayne Ed."

"Mad enough to kill him? A classic love/hate relationship? Maybe. Let me pull that whole file, so we can hang on to this.

"You going to print that list?" asked Emily.

"Yes, it might be kind of interesting to contact some of these people and see if they're aware they were scammed."

The ackack of the raindrops blended with the cadence of the inkjet printer to form a hypnotic percussion, so Emily and Louisa didn't hear the door being pulled shut.

When the hard copy was completed, Louisa grabbed the paper out of the printer, held it over her shoulder and said, "Here, Em. Put it in that file, please, and we'll take it with us."

Paper still held over her shoulder, Louisa repeated as she looked at the menu for more files of interest.

"Emily, put this in the file."

When Emily didn't answer, Louisa repeated, "Emily, do you want this? It might be interesting."

A hand reached out and grabbed Louisa by the shoulder.

Chapter 40

"What in the…" Louisa turned quickly as she dropped the paper in her hand and bounced up from her chair.

"Don't move. Mom, don't move."

As Louisa eased back into the chair, Emily whispered, "Be quiet, and listen. Do you hear it?"

The heavy beat of the rain had all but drowned out the low rattling sound they could just now detect. As they strained to listen, Louisa asked in a low voice, "What is it?"

"Maybe I'm just a little freaked, but I would say we are listening to a rattlesnake, and I don't think he's in here to keep us company for the afternoon."

Louisa's eyes frantically scoured the room. "Did you see a snake?" she asked.

"I'm not sure. It's so dim in here."

Both Louisa and Emily froze their bodies and pivoted their heads as far as their necks would allow while they tried to examine the room using only their eyes. The dark room provided much opportunity for imagination, but little for actually spotting the rattler. Prickles started at Louisa's waist and ran up her back as surely as if small snakes were crawling her body.

Emily, eyes looking intently at the floor, tiptoed slowly to the door and took an interminably long time to turn the doorknob. The knob turned, but when Emily tried to ease it open, the door didn't swing outward. Emily pushed a little harder, heard the rattle again, looked back at her mother and shuddered.

In a slow movement, Louisa, eyes starting at the floor and raking the furniture and walls, looked around the room. The rattler, forked tongue alternating in and out of its mouth, eased itself out from under a bookshelf mounded with miscellaneous papers and eked toward Louisa's chair.

"Emily, don't move. It's coming toward me."

The snake, moving as if on a track of oil, flowed across the room. Louisa stared at the scaly diamonds decreasing the distance toward its prey quickly. Too quickly, Louisa decided. It can't move that fast, there are no feet to carry it. How can it go so fast? It's too close.

The ropey monster stared at her with its expressionless eyes, holding her transfixed. As the snake approached Louisa, she vainly swiveled her head looking for an object with which to decapitate the approaching danger. A shovel, that's what she needed. It's always a shovel; that's what gardeners use to behead these twining dragons. She looked around as pulsating diamonds bridging the gap moved closer and closer to her. *No shovel. This isn't a garden. Can't get on the desk, the chair swivels. No shovel. No decapitation. No desk. No refuge. Diamonds. I had diamonds once. In my wedding band. Diamonds, how lovely. Diamonds, lovely then, lethal now. Diamonds killed my marriage. Diamonds will kill me now.*

Here it comes; its forked tongue will get me. Diamonds with a forked tongue. Like my marriage. Diamonds with a forked tongue. He gave me diamonds and spoke with a forked tongue. Here comes the forked tongue diamonds. They're going to get me again.

"Mom, you've got to do something," cried Emily.

Louisa jerked around to look at Emily. No forked tongue spoke just now. *Respond. Respond, body. Move!*

Louisa stood up from her chair, reached out blindly and put both hands on the printer next to the computer. She pulled the printer hard enough that it was wrenched from the umbilicus attaching it to the computer. Lifting it over her head, she brought it down next to the coiled snake just as it struck at her leg.

"Mom, are you okay? It bit you."

"No, I think it got my boot. We'll check it later. Let's get out of here."

"No, Mom. Now, we have to look, now. Those bites get into the blood, and if you move, it'll travel faster through your blood. Look at your leg."

"Yeah, yeah." Louisa scrutinized her leg as she pulled the boot off her calf. "No fang marks, but that snake is still moving. That printer landed just next to it. It's not dead. We're out of here."

Fortunately, the doorjamb was as rotten as the house, so when they heaved together at the door, the frame dislodged. The slight opening created was enough to allow them to ease their bodies out of the room.

"Let's get out of here," Louisa said as she charged down the hallway. Emily started to retrieve the paper Louisa had dropped. Louisa looked back, lunged at Emily, reached out her arm and grabbed Emily yanking her away from the splintered opening.

"I said we're leaving."

"But that paper. We need that information."

"Not that badly. Get out to the car immediately. There might be more rattlers. They said lots of snakes killed Mrs. Twerms. Move it! Get out!"

They tore down the hallway to the front door and jerked it open. Doused by the pelting rain, Emily and Louisa ran to their car. Emily snapped the door locks open as each woman rammed herself into the front seat of the car, and they drove off, muddy water spewing off their wheels. Emily headed the car away from the Twerms ranch.

"Do you know where we're going? I haven't seen Uncle Luke's ranch. Seems like it should be close," said Louisa.

"I don't care where we're going. At least, we're out of that house. Somebody had to be in the house to close that door, and I don't want to find out who it was. I can't imagine that rattler calling that office home either."

"Get on a main road, and let's go talk to Sheriff Vigilance. All main roads seem to lead to San Domingo," urged Louisa.

"Or a hanging."

"Too wet."

The blurring rain shielded the road signs, so they traveled blindly on the road at as fast a speed as the slipperiness of the tarmac would allow. They thought they had just passed a sign pointing to San Domingo when Emily noticed red taillights ahead of them.

"See, Mom, we aren't the only crazies on the road. Look, there's someone else out."

"Must not be a native then. Can you get any closer to see who might be on the same road as we are?"

"Coming from the same direction as we are. I'll try."

Emily accelerated a bit to try to catch up with the taillights. As she did, the lights quickly swerved to the right off the road, uturned and proceeded to head towards Emily and Louisa's car. The spotlight, prevalent on so many pickups in West Texas, was aimed straight at them.

Emily stared at the action. "That looks like a pickup. See how high its lights are? Wonder why it changed directions? Can you see anything? That light is blinding me. Why do they have spotlights on the trucks out here? That's awful, I can't see a thing."

"Guess it wants to figure out who would be on the road on a day like today. They have spotlights for lots of things. If part of their herd is lost on the ranch, they can go out at night and find them if they have to. They also use it for days like today or dust storms—gives them a little more range. I would think, coming at us like that, they would shut it off. They know it's going to be tough for us to see."

As the pickup barreled toward them, a bolt of lightning cracked the sky. In the release time of the electrical flash, Emily looked and realized the vehicle had picked up an excessive speed.

"Mom, look how fast that dumb cluck's going. He's going to kill himself."

Louisa opened her mouth to respond, but as she did, the pickup crossed the middle of the road and aimed itself toward them. The pickup rapidly approached the SUV on the rain soaked highway. As it careened toward the four-wheel drive, Emily gripped the steering wheel in a seemingly long few seconds of indecision.

"Emily, it's heading toward us!"

The pickup raced toward them and accelerated faster. The vehicle closed the intervening space between them—too quickly to make a rational decision.

Emily looked at the space narrowing by the second. The flash of headlights and the spotlight dazzled her eyes into a reeling brilliance. She squeezed the steering wheel until even she could feel her hands hurt, but she couldn't focus on anything. Louisa grabbed the armrest with her right hand and the edge of the seat with her left hand. She went rigid with expectation of a bone jarring impact.

With only a few feet between the oncoming pickup and the women's four-wheel, Emily spasmodically twisted the steering wheel to the left. The SUV jerked to the left side of the road just as the pickup encountered the four-wheel. The right edge of Emily and Louisa's car tapped the pickup in the confrontation. Emily concentrated on bringing their car to a stop on the narrowly shouldered road. Louisa, staring at the darkness of the pickup as it heaved upward into a projectile on the side of the road opposite Louisa and Emily, shuddered.

"Stop the car," Louisa shouted.

"I am. I am."

When the car finally rolled to a stop, Louisa demanded, "Back up. Back up the car."

"Make up your mind. First I've got to stop; now you want me to back up. I still can't see really well. Hold on, I'm doing it."

"Look behind you!"

Emily stared into the rear view mirror and turned around quickly to get a wider view of what her eyes had caught in the edge of the mirror.

The pickup had flipped in mid air and landed on the cab. Like a turtle on its back with its legs flailing in mid air, the wheels of the vehicle continued to spin as the truck rocked in the rain. Emily quickly turned the SUV around and drove to the area off the road where the pickup lay with its squashed cab.

Chapter 41

The women vaulted out of the car into the rain. Lightning branded the sky as they thrust their faces into the cab.

"Oh, no," groaned Louisa.

Emily put her arm around her mother and stared through an intricate maze of cracked glass at the sight in the cab.

The pickup was old enough that it didn't have shoulder harnesses; it only had lap belts. Those hadn't been used. Lying in a heap of misaligned angles, head at a right angle to the body was Mel. Shards of glass jutted out of body parts, shards of glass from an aquarium used to hold a rattlesnake. Blood still spurted out of arteries, but it was ebbing even as Louisa and Emily observed Mel's splintered body lying topsy-turvy in the cab of the pickup.

"Oh, no," Louisa groaned again. Distressed, she turned to Emily in mute request for help. Emily pulled her closer and said, "We've got to get someone out here. If you want me to stay, I will and you can go, or you can stay, and I'll go. I think we've passed the Gold County line, so we'll try to get Sheriff McIntire to come here. You want me to stay?"

Louisa shook her head.

"Well, then, do you want to stay?"

Again Louisa shook her head.

"Then what, Mom? How shall we handle this?"

Louisa drew in a convulsive gasp of air. "I want us both to go. It's raining, and Mel is dead, and nothing will happen to her out here. We should both go. We can even call from the first phone we see."

"Okay, Mom. You're probably right. Come on, let's go."

"Too bad the Sheriff doesn't follow us around anymore. This is one of the few times we could use his tailing us," said Louisa.

Before they took themselves back to their car, each peered into the cab of the truck to prove to themselves they had actually seen Mel lying in a mass of bent and turned bones. She was still there, her head askew of her body, her eyes staring at nothing, her face beginning to relax into non-expression. Convinced they hadn't imagined the incident, they walked, arms around each other, back to their car.

As Emily started the engine, Sheriff McIntire drove down the road, pulled in behind them, got out of his car and came around to Emily seated in the driver's side. Before shutting off the engine, she pressed the button to roll down the glass and allow Bonham McIntire to hang his head in the window.

Rain dripped off the protective plastic of his hat and back. "What's the matter, ladies?"

"First time we've actually been glad to see you, Sheriff," said Emily. "Mel's in there. Dead. Her truck hit ours, and it flipped. It's pretty bad."

"You want to tell me what happened or let me guess?"

"We'll tell you, but tell us why you're here. I thought we weren't part of the unwelcome anymore."

"Laurel told me you were going over to Dwayne Ed's house to look for Eddie. Thought I'd come by and see how you two ladies were doing. Find anything out there?"

"Not Eddie. We didn't see him."

"Look, Sheriff, before we get started, come in the car. No use you standing out there looking like a duck in water" invited Louisa. "You'll catch cold. If you're sick, you can't go hightailing after people."

"Thank you, ma'am," said Sheriff McIntire as he entered the back seat of the four-wheel. "Now, you didn't find Eddie, but how about when you were snooping around? Find anything then?"

"What do you mean snooping around? Why should we snoop around?"

"Well, ladies, just let me tell you. If I had an open invitation to go somewhere where fishy stuff was going on, and that's what a key is, an open invitation, I sure wouldn't waste it. And, you two ladies have done more snooping around since you've gotten here than people have in the last seventy years looking for Amelia Earhart. So what did you find?"

"Nothing you probably don't already know about. Did you know Dwayne Ed was running guns?" Emily began.

"I knew."

"Did you know he was a real sleezebag?"

"I knew; so did the whole town. Didn't need to go to his house to find that out."

"No, we mean a sexually perverted sleezebag," explained Louisa.

"We all knew; that's why we worried about Laurel. It's also one of the reasons Hugh tried to persuade him to put Daphne in the Easter school."

"There was a rattlesnake in his office. In that cab is an aquarium. I bet it was used for a cage for a rattler. That snake bit me."

"Ma'am, you need to be in the hospital. Those bites are mighty dangerous."

"No, he got her calf, but it was covered by her boot. I made her check before we left the room," said Emily.

"Just one snake?"

"We didn't stay around to ask them to come out for tea, Sheriff. How do we know if it was one or twenty? Does it even matter?" asked Louisa.

"Some. Chances are that gal," the Sheriff pointed to Mel's truck, "is the one who planted that snake. She could catch more of them than most of the people around here at the Rattlesnake Festival. She has quite an affinity for them."

"So we heard."

"So, ladies, tell me what happened."

Louisa started the story of their ride home, and Emily filled in and explained points as her mother related the occurrences of the last few hours while Sheriff McIntire wrote it all down.

"Okay, ladies, go home. I'll call this in and get it investigated. I'll call you if I have more questions. When are you leaving?"

"It can't be too soon," declared Louisa. "I'm so tired of people dying. Now we have another funeral to attend. Three funerals in as many weeks is just not normal."

Chapter 42

Three funerals in three weeks in this day and age is just not right. Brother Johnson's thoughts echoed Louisa's of a few days ago. *It's just not right. And, to have the people be so different; it's not like their deaths were all related. Although it seems they should have been related because their lives were intertwined with each other's lives. A natural death, a murder and an accident. Just seems like they should all be together somehow, but Sheriff McIntire says no. He says there's no way they can be related. At least if the deaths were somehow part of each other, I could make a rip roaring sermon out of that fact—a sermon that would make the mourners sit up and take notice, one that would make them joyful that they came to hear me preach.*

That's really where the problem lay. He wasn't going to be able to deliver a stand-on-your-toes sermon. The people who would attend Mel's funeral were the same ones who had attended Dwayne Ed and Atie's funerals. He had used the main theme of his eulogy for those two sermons in too short a time to be interesting to his listeners; he didn't have a new spin for his old idea.

Tough business, this giving people the final send off.

Chapter 43

▼

"Hello," Maria Elena greeted Emily in the aisle of the WalMart beauty aids. "It's nice to see you again. I didn't know you were still here."

"Mom's almost done with her work. As soon as she meets with the attorney and accountant, they can read the will, and we'll be leaving."

"You must be anxious to return home."

"I miss my family very much. I can't say this has been boring, however."

Maria Elena agreed, "You certainly have had an interesting time. Come to the middle of nowhere and find a long lost friend and attend three funerals. When will you be leaving?"

"Within the next couple days, I would imagine."

"Hugh and I are having a barbecue at our house tomorrow. We'd like to have you and your mother come. It could be a farewell dinner for you two. I'm going to ask Laurel, so I'll be sure to include Phoebe. That way your mother won't feel out-generationed."

We'd love to come. Thank you, what shall we bring?"

"Since you'll be guests, nothing. Come and enjoy. I'll call you with details. Are you still at the Single Arrow?"

"Yes, Atie willed it to my mother, so we have a home away from home."

"Maybe we'll see you around here then. I've enjoyed your company. Let me know when you're coming back to town."

"I'd like to bring David and my daughters out here. This has certainly been an unusual visit."

As Maria Elena began to push her shopping cart out of the aisle, Emily said, "Maria Elena, I saw a yearbook from when you were at San Domingo High."

"That was so long ago. Did you look at how young we all were then?" Maria Elena chuckled.

"Weren't we all? We looked at the pictures of all of you. The Homecoming Queen shots were lovely. All of you were quite pretty."

"That's very nice of you. Thank you. It was so long ago. None of us ever talks about it, it was so long ago."

"Why?"

"Oh, time has passed."

"That's not what I meant. Why doesn't anyone talk about it?"

Maria Elena looked passed Emily and started to push her cart away again. "I have to get back. I better hurry if I'm going to finish shopping."

Emily put her hand out to stop the cart and said, "Maria Elena, where was Ruth that night? Why wasn't she in the picture?"

"Wasn't she? She was there at the dance. I'm sure I saw her with Bonham or Jonas. Yes, she must have been there in the pictures, but it was so long ago, I forget really."

"Most everyone I know goes through the yearbook over and over until it's memorized. You know she wasn't there. Why did she miss getting her picture in the yearbook?"

"Emily, Dwayne Ed hurt so many people. It didn't start with Laurel; it started long before that. We thought we had it controlled, we thought no one would get tied up with him. After Maggie, we thought we had fixed everything."

"Maggie, what do you mean Maggie?"

"Oh, Emily. You're bringing up so much old history. We fixed it all; we truly did. You don't really want to talk about this, do you? It happened so long ago."

"Possibly though if someone would talk about it, Dwayne Ed wouldn't be around to haunt everyone. If he hurt all those people, all of you are going to live with that hurt for the rest of your lives. Maybe by getting it all out, it would help get all of you back to being friends."

"We're still friends. I just asked you to dinner with all of us."

"Were you friends like that while Dwayne Ed was alive? How many dinners did you have with him around?"

"Some. We had a few. It's just that he would come drunk and ruin it for everybody. We tried to have get-togethers without him, but that was hard too. We all liked Laurel so much, it was hard not to include her. Laurel's disappearance was like the kiss of death for any social gatherings. We just quit trying to see each other."

"So, don't you think it would help everybody to get out all the hurt Dwayne Ed caused? Why wasn't Ruth in the picture?"

Maria Elena sighed and said, "Ruth was supposed to be queen that night. All of us were sure of it. It wouldn't be Cindy or me. The county schools had just become integrated, so Cindy was dealing with all that, and I was from a family from the wrong side of town. Susan, she doesn't live here anymore, was beautiful; so was Maggie, but after what Maggie did in breaking up Ty and Ruth, we knew she wasn't going to get it. Maggie really wanted it, too. Neither Susan nor Maggie was as pretty or nice as Ruth. That's hard to believe, isn't it? Ruth was prettier than Maggie. You'd never know it now, would you? We just knew it was Ruth who was going to be queen.

"I've really got to go, Emily. I'm sorry." Maria Elena pushed her cart away.

Emily followed and asked, "So where did Ruth go?"

"She never came. She never showed up."

"Why?"

"She was hurt."

"How?"

"Please, Emily, don't ask me anymore. I'm not trying to be unkind to you. It's just that we all promised we would never say anything. Please understand. We have to protect her."

Maria Elena left her shopping cart at the end of the aisle and walked away. "I'll finish shopping another day. I didn't really need all this stuff."

As the glass doors swished open, she turned to Emily and asked, "Come to dinner?"

"I wouldn't miss it for the world."

*   *   *   *

Sitting at Atie's long kitchen table, Louisa and Emily dined on the tamale pie Aunt Cora had brought for them. On the counter was a homemade pecan pie waiting for their dessert. In the refrigerator thick whipped cream waited to swathe the pie.

"This is the best tamale pie you're ever going to have, and you're eating like a teenager before her first date. What's wrong?" asked Louisa.

Emily put a bite of the chunky pie on her fork, brought it to her mouth and stopped. "Mom, tell me about the land scam that Mel arranged. Tell me everything you can about it."

As Emily put the food into her mouth and chewed, Louisa gave her a chronologically detailed report of the scam. After her mother finished, Emily sat back in the kitchen chair and looked at Louisa for a few minutes. Finally, she said, "Have you thought much about generations and their effects on other generations?"

"All the time. What do you think I do for a living? When I counsel, many times to solve the present day problem, my client and I have to go back to the past." Louisa thought about what she had said and continued, "It's interesting because we usually talk about the preceding generations affecting the succeeding generations. We don't think of the present generation as doing the affecting as much as how it's been affected. That's because we don't think about the future generations as much as we think about ourselves. Why're you asking?"

"I saw Maria Elena and told her about seeing her high school pictures. Her manners couldn't gloss over her trying to forget about those years."

"So, why the question about generations?"

"I think I know who killed Dwayne Ed."

"It wasn't Mel."

"Why do you say that? Are you protecting her?"

Louisa's face wrinkled in surprise. "Protect her? Why?"

"Don't know. Maybe the generations, with her being older and all. Or the family thing. Or maybe even speaking ill of the dead."

"Emily, being dead doesn't erase what she did. She left some kind of legacy, good somewhere, I suppose, and bad. Those negative actions are still hers."

"True. So, why do you think she didn't kill Dwayne Ed?"

"Wasn't her style. Wasn't sneaky enough. Killing Dwayne Ed with an ax was too blatant and too spur of the moment. She was the kind who liked to do things on the sly."

"Yeah, probably."

"So that kind of leaves out Mel's generation, doesn't it? Who killed the old boy?"

"Let me think on it a little. We have an invitation to the Easters' for dinner, with people from your generation and mine. Maybe by then, I'll have it worked out."

Louisa reached across the table and patted her daughter on the hand. "Let me know if you want any more input."

Chapter 44

It was like the first meeting of a couple after their final divorce decree. The group were quite familiar with each other's habits, but there was a formal air hovering about each of them that would act as a shield from any intrusion of emotion. Therefore, when Louisa and Emily arrived at the Easter house, conversation was trite and malleable. Each time the conversation danced close to one of the group's sensitivities, it was quickly changed to a non-threatening topic. But, there's only so much discussion about the weather, government, fashion, or food one can endure. So, it wasn't too long after the endurance threshold for light topics had been reached that the conversation turned to children. And, of course, that turned to specific children, and, of course, that spotlighted Laurel and her children.

"Have you heard from Eddie, Laurel?" asked Maggie almost in a whisper because she was unsure of Laurel's reaction.

Jonas and Ty looked down at their feet; Ruth and Maria Elena did a quick intake of breath; the rest of the group looked at Laurel.

"He called."

"He did?" asked a surprised Maria Elena. "What did he say?"

Laurel, with a little shrug of her shoulders, said, "He said he missed us."

"So he's coming home?" asked Maggie.

Laurel shook her head, "No, he doesn't want to come home."

Hugh asked, "Why not?"

Laurel started to tell them, rubbed her forehead with her hand, looked at Bonham and said, "You tell them."

Bonham stepped forward. "He apologized to his mother for what he said in church. He said he'd come home..."

"Oh, good," interrupted Maggie.

Bonham's face grimaced in her direction. "He said he'd come home when we find out who killed his father."

"What?" exclaimed Hugh. "That could be forever. What's that boy thinking? Doesn't he know his mother needs him? Someone needs to talk sense to that boy. You talk to him, Bonham? Did you tell him how irresponsible he's being? You tell him that's just like his daddy?"

"I talked to him, but I didn't tell him he was irresponsible or being like his daddy. I don't want him to hear any of that nonsense. Understand this, all of you. That boy is not going to be like his daddy. He has more going for him than that. He doesn't deserve to be treated like that. We're going to stop it right now. You all got that?"

"Well, do you? Do you understand what I'm saying? We're going to break that Twerms meanness with Eddie's generation. He's got his mama back, and we'll all help her. Isn't that right?"

Bonham received a tacit nod from each of his friends and then proceeded, "He's not coming back until we find out who killed Dwayne Ed because he thinks the people in the town figure he did it. He knows some of us knew how he'd sneak away from the ranch and do things against his father's wishes. He's concerned people will take that as an indication he might have been the one who killed his father. He was at the ranch at about the time his father was murdered. Said he was ready to leave that night, run way with any money he could take from the house. He was at the rally that night and could just as easily have axed his father."

"No. That's not true. I know he didn't do it." Phoebe stepped forward.

"How do you know, Mrs. Raines?" asked Hugh.

"Because I was there. I was at the rally. I've been going to those things for a long time. I joined the Klan, so I could keep an eye on Eddie. I was there, and I was the one...the one...who...I did it."

"Did what, ma'am?" asked Bonham.

"I...I did it. I...killed Dwayne Ed. I did it."

"Mother. You did? No, say that isn't true. You couldn't do something like that."

"That's right, Laurel, I did it. I did it to... protect Eddie. I was going to take care of him. That's right, to protect Eddie. I wanted him safe, so I killed Dwayne Ed."

"Ma'am, do you know what you're saying by telling us you killed Dwayne Ed? Do you realize what that means? Are you sure you want to say that? I'll have to arrest you," explained Bonham.

"Yes. Yes, I know what I'm saying. You need to arrest me. I killed Dwayne Ed Twerms because I hated him, and Eddie needed to be protected."

Phoebe Raines, silently pleading with the group to believe her, stepped out defiantly and held out her hands, "Arrest me. Put the handcuffs on. I'm the one who killed him."

Bonham and Laurel exchanged confused looks after which Phoebe said again, "I did it."

"Mrs. Raines, you couldn't have done it. You weren't a member of the Klan, and I know it as well as you do," Bonham said gently.

"No, I was a member. I joined to keep an eye on Dwayne Ed, so I could protect Eddie."

"Let me tell you again. You couldn't have joined because Dwayne Ed wouldn't let you come near him or his son."

"But, I killed Dwayne Ed. I know how to split wood. It was really easy to split open his head." Phoebe looked at the group. "The whole town knows how much I hated him. Look what he did to Laurel. I killed him."

"No, you didn't," said Sheriff McIntire.

Phoebe started to cry. "I did. I know I did. Please believe me."

"No you didn't," Emily said. "The Sheriff is right; you didn't kill him."

"What are you saying, Emily?" asked Ty. "Why don't you think Mrs. Raines did it?"

"Because I know who killed Dwayne Ed, and I know why."

"You're saying you know who killed him? I don't believe you. Does she, Bonham? Does she really know who killed him?" asked Maggie.

"How should I know? These two women seem to have stumbled on more information being here three weeks, than I've been able to find out in years. Why do you think you know who killed him, Emily?"

"Because I know why he was killed. When I realized I had heard why he was killed, it followed as to who killed him."

"What do you mean, Emily?" asked her mother.

"Daphne told us why he was killed. Not that she knew she was telling us. She actually told us before her father was killed."

"Daphne?" asked Laurel. "How would Daphne know?"

"Mrs. Raines, do you remember when she talked about how Dwayne Ed and Jonas wanted Eddie and Ruthie to get married? That they had planned it from the time Ruthie was born?"

"No, Emily. Stop. You're supposed to be my friend. You can't blame Eddie. He may be confused, but he wouldn't kill anyone, especially his father." Laurel rushed at Emily.

Sheriff McIntire reached out and grabbed Laurel and put his arm around her shoulder. "Just listen to her."

"It started me rethinking some things. We all thought, more or less, that Dwayne Ed was killed for some cruel act he had done as an adult. His murder happened the night of the hanging and rally, so, for a while, some of us assumed it had something to do with the hate group. The skinheads didn't do it because Sheriff McIntire claims they were caught going back to Idaho and questioned pretty thoroughly. They probably cleared out before he was killed and were tracked by law enforcement almost from the moment they left the rally. They didn't like what they saw there because it didn't help their cause. To them, that rally was ancient history; they've got a new slant on old hate. They thought they were going to find some spectacular way to overthrow the federal government. Of course, it would have been nice if the skin-heads had done it because it would be an easy way out for San Domingo. That way, one of their own would not be the murderer. But, everyone knew, deep down, that the murderer was here in town, in this group, this group that had been so close until the end of high school.

"Only the break-up of the group didn't occur because high school ended. It was easy to think that was the reason for breaking up, but it wasn't. It was earlier than that because the relationship was falling apart before that. Remember, at Dwayne Ed's funeral, when you talked about the camping trip and the fire? Remember, Hugh?"

"I do."

"What happened?"

Hugh debated how much to say as he looked at his circle of friends. Ty avoided his eyes, but the rest of them looked at him as they silently voted. Bonham nodded slightly, and Hugh began, "Dwayne Ed started drinking way before we picked him up to go camping that weekend. He wanted to drive, but we told him he couldn't, and that got him mad. Dwayne Ed was always mad, and you could hardly be around him, but we had all grown up together, and he was always part of the group. Our parents didn't realize how bad he was, and some of the parents were beholden to the Twerms for jobs or loans or their houses, so they didn't want to rile them. They encouraged us to keep him around."

"But, your family didn't owe his family anything, did it?" asked Louisa.

"My family? No, never had. We always could get by on our own. My daddy always stayed clear of any business dealings with any Twerms, and I learned from him to do the same."

"And, that day, what happened?" prompted Emily.

"Dwayne Ed got really nasty with his mouth, started calling the girls horrible names. I told him if he didn't cool it, I was going to hogtie him and dump him on his daddy's porch. Then we left him and went swimming. He wouldn't go. I thought that would give him a chance to sober up, and I was hoping he'd forget what he had done. Chances were, though, he'd remember."

"Were all of you there?"

"Sure, all of us and Cindy and Henry, too."

"Who are they? Is Henry that drunk we used to see in town?"

Bonham nodded.

"That's why you always picked him up, Sheriff?" asked Louisa.

"Yeah, he was a good friend. It was shameful to see him so low. Hugh, Jonas and I knew he'd never get back on his feet again, so we kind of looked out for him."

"So, go on, Hugh," said Emily. "What did Dwayne Ed do?"

"He set fire to the tents we had set up. We all saw the smoke; it was a real dry summer day. That fire could have spread and done some damage, but we got it out fairly quickly. Then we knew."

"Knew what?"

"How far gone Dwayne Ed was. We knew he was going to be just like his daddy and granddaddy and all the granddaddies before that one. Cruel and hateful. It wasn't going to do the group any good to have him around. I told him for the good of the group, we didn't want to have anything to do with him ever again, but Maggie…"

The group watched Maggie staring at Hugh as she shook her head and futilely looked around for a friendly face.

There were none.

Chapter 45

"Let me finish your statement," said Emily. "But Maggie was dating Dwayne Ed, and Maggie was part of the group, so Dwayne Ed was still around. Is that right?"

Maggie said, "Emily Kristich, I told you you were so smart. Now that you've gone and figured all that out, why do you have to talk about it? It's history; it's got nothing to do with killing Dwayne Ed."

"Oh, yes, it does. It's got everything to do with killing him because, you see, that's why he was killed. One of you killed him, and it has very much to do with this group of friends."

"One of us killed…oh no, you've got that wrong. No one would ever *kill* Dwayne Ed. We were all used to him, so we stayed away from him, and no harm came to anyone. We always looked out for each other. None of us had to kill him," Maggie protested for the group.

"Someone did, Maggie," said Hugh.

Emily turned to Laurel. "Do you remember the day you had me check and see if Eddie had shown up at the house?"

At Laurel's nod, Emily continued, "There was another reason for Mom and me wanting to go. We wanted to snoop around Dwayne Ed's records. We found Dwayne Ed was running guns, but you already knew that, didn't you, Sheriff?"

Sheriff McIntire nodded warily and said, "I did."

Hugh said, "Well, why, Bonham, didn't you do anything about it? That's illegal. You were elected to protect the county."

As the Sheriff started to produce an explanation, Emily said, "He did, Hugh, but, listen to what else we found. Go ahead, Mom."

"What? Oh, you mean the land?"

Emily said, "Yes, tell them about the mineral rights."

"Mineral rights?" Ty blurted out. "What do you know about mineral rights?" Maggie moved in closer to her husband.

"You know the reason we came out here is because I was designated executor of my aunt's estate. Part of the stipulation of the will was that I go through all the papers. That's why we've been here so long. I came across a file with little information in it except a deed for mineral rights. When Emily and I went to look at the land, we noticed there was no oil drilling activity on it which, as you are all very aware, is unusual in this area. It didn't make sense, so we did some checking. We called the seller listed on the mineral rights deed and found she had never sold the land; she was keeping it for her children. My aunt had been scammed."

"By her own sister, no less," said Emily.

"It looked like Mel and Dwayne Ed had been scamming together probably to raise money for starting up the Klan activities here in this area. Emily and I found a list of people they had tried to sell the land to. All of your names are on the list, but only one of you fell for it.

"When I went to the Gold County Office of Records, I found out someone else was asking for information about that same piece of land. You were that person, Ty. You'd been scammed, too."

The group turned to Ty and Maggie.

"But, I didn't kill him. I was mad enough to, but I didn't kill him. I went over there early that morning, but I couldn't find him. I realized what had happened when I contacted an oil company landman to see if he could get a well drilled on that property. Dwayne Ed had told me the rights had just come out of probate and had been tied up a long time. The landman looked up the land after I bought it through Dwayne Ed and told me the title to the mineral rights was clouded, not clear. That's why there wasn't any drilling. As soon as I got my deed, I contacted the oil company. That's when I found out. I went back to the records office to check on the coordinates of the land to make sure we were all looking at the same piece of land.

"I was mad, but I wouldn't have killed him—especially with an ax."

"Maybe Mel did it. Maybe Mel killed Dwayne Ed," said Jonas.

"Could be. She tried to do us in with a rattlesnake, but Emily seems to think someone else killed him."

"What do you mean with a rattlesnake?" asked Maria Elena.

Louisa told the group about the rattlesnake she and Emily encountered in Dwayne Ed's office just before Mel's accident.

"Well, see, there's your answer. It had to be Mel," rationalized Maggie. "I mean, she tried to kill you two times in one day. If she could murder her own kin, she could surely murder Dwayne Ed. None of us would kill him. We all knew about him; we could protect ourselves from him."

"Like Ty protected himself?" asked Hugh sarcastically.

Ty blushed, and Maggie became very quiet.

"There is another generation coming up. Who will be around to protect them?" asked Louisa.

"If you mean Junior, he's going to be okay. We've kept an eye out for him, and his grandma has balanced his daddy's insensitivity. She's a good woman," assured Jonas. "He'll be okay after he works out his feelings about his daddy. And, Laurel, she's okay. Got a kind heart. This next generation should be safe from bad Twerms."

"You sure about that, Jonas?" Emily asked.

"What do you mean?"

"I'll tell you what I mean, but we have to go back to the Homecoming Dance your senior year. Remember, everybody? All of you were there, remember? Cindy and Henry, the Homecoming Princess and the hot shot all-state football player; Bonham went by himself; Dwayne Ed and—it was suppose to be you, Maggie, right? You had always been with Dwayne Ed, but you thought Ty was more up your alley."

"Ruth, when Maggie got Ty to ask her to the dance, who did that leave you with? Bonham, why didn't you take her?" asked Louisa.

"If my daddy and mama could have paid for that dance with the love they gave their family, I could have taken fifteen girls to it, bought corsages and dinner for all of them. But, I couldn't even afford to rent a tux; I used my daddy's only suit, the one he was buried in."

Bonham looked at Ruth, standing so close to Jonas, no piece of paper could fit between them. "I would've taken you, Ruth, but I couldn't. You were the nicest girl in the whole school, and it would have been an honor, but I couldn't do it right, and I thought you deserved better. We all knew you would be queen. I didn't think it was fair to take you in Daddy's pickup. Dwayne Ed knew how I felt, so he asked you instead. I've always been sorry."

Maggie gasped a loud sob and huddled into Ty's shoulder. He looked over Maggie's blonde head and cautioned, "Ma'am, maybe it's time to stop. You're upsetting too many of us."

Ruth placated the group by holding out her hand to them and said, "No, we've never talked about this. If Emily won't continue, I will."

"Are you sure you want to do this, Ruth?" asked Maria Elena. "You don't have to, you know."

"Yes, we all have to. It's been a gangrene in this town too long."

"No, Ruth, we all swore we would never say anything about it. We're the only ones who know."

"We are, Maria Elena, and the rest of the town knows. They've known since it happened. Dwayne Ed told so many people, didn't he, Jonas? Jonas knew everything Dwayne Ed did." Ruth scanned the whole group. "You all knew that. Jonas was always with Dwayne Ed. Since the day of the fire, he was with him. He was always there with Dwayne Ed. Always, always, always. Jonas and Dwayne Ed. Jonas, Dwayne Ed's right hand man. Jonas, Dwayne Ed's lackey. Jonas, Dwayne Ed's servant. Jonas, Dwayne Ed's slave. Jonas was always with Dwayne Ed."

Jonas stared at his wife as she talked and said sadly, "Except when he raped you. I wasn't there then."

Ruth took his hand, held it against her cheek and closed her eyes as she said, "But you've been there ever since for me. I love you."

Maggie cried louder, and Ty derided Emily. "Are you happy now? You've pulled back the carpet we had swept this ugly, little scene under. You come out of that high falootin' state and think you can run our lives and ruin them at the same time."

Louisa defended Emily by saying, "You people don't see it, do you? Almost every one of you has said it, and you still don't see it. Let me recap a few phrases for you. Bonham, you talked about how you, Hugh and Jonas pick up Henry when he's down. Maria Elena, you talked about how you and all your friends here made up a story about Ruth's being sick. Hugh, you tried to tell Dwayne Ed to get lost after the fire. Bonham, you arrested Emily and me to protect us from Dwayne Ed. Ruth, you've been living with a lie all these years to protect this whole group from Dwayne Ed."

Maria Elena expressed the confusion of the group when she said, "But, we all knew what had happened to Ruth. Just because we didn't talk about it, we still knew. Ruth wasn't living a lie."

"Yes, she was," said Louisa. "The lie she lived with was acting like Jonas was Dwayne Ed's, as she put it, lackey. Jonas wasn't around Dwayne Ed because he was trying to help Dwayne Ed, was he, Ruth?"

Ruth's mouth fell as the tears rained down her face. She put both arms around Jonas' waist as she cried, "Jonas pretended all those years that he was Dwayne Ed's friend." She took her arms away from Jonas, turned to the group and said angrily, "Do you know why? Do any of you have any idea of what he did for all of us? He was protecting us from Dwayne Ed. Every time Dwayne Ed would try one of his nasty scams or tricks or cruelty, Jonas would try to block it in some way. For over twenty years, he's been protecting all of us, and no one ever knew.

"No one knew how much of his life he sacrificed for us to be safe from that bastard, Dwayne Ed. That mean, mean, nasty… and now, Dwayne Ed is dead, and Jonas can be free from having to protect us." She looked up at Jonas and smiled at him. As he tried to return her smile, he shook his head and started to talk, but only guttural anguish was heard.

"It's okay, now, Jonas. You don't have anyone you have to shield. It's good, now." His wife wrapped him in her arms again and held on for dear life.

Chapter 46

▼

"But, it's not so good now, is it, Jonas? You were so adept at protecting your friends, but there was one person you wanted to protect even more than your friends, right?" asked Emily.

Jonas nodded. His mouth shaped itself several times before he could say, "Ruthie."

"Dwayne Ed was the one who wanted Eddie and Ruthie to marry; Jonas didn't. He went along with Dwayne Ed until he could figure a way out. He thought there would be lots of time, but what, Jonas? What was the pressure? Why did you kill him the night of the rally?"

"Now, hold on just a minute," said Hugh. "He may have been around Dwayne Ed enough to hate him, but I don't think he's a killer."

"Hugh," said Jonas, "she's right."

Ruth led Jonas to a seat on the sofa and held his hand while he talked, "After that rally, Dwayne Ed was riding high. He really thought he had impressed those people from the North, and they'd come back and work with him to bring back the Klan. He was talking about creating an Aryan dynasty that would join forces with those bigots from the North and take over the United States. He claimed the first couple for the new order would be Eddie and Ruthie, and he wanted to draw up a legal document forcing them to marry in the next two years.

"She's only fourteen, and Eddie…Well, he's a, I'm sorry, Laurel, he's a Twerms. I think he's okay now. He and I have talked a lot about the world, and he seems to be thinking things through, but we've had five generations of Twerms, and they've all been mean. Who's to say Eddie wouldn't slip back to that viciousness? Dwayne Ed had already taken so much from Ruth, the one time I wasn't there to stop it. I couldn't have him take it from Ruthie, too."

Bonham interjected, "Why an ax? Why not a shotgun or something cleaner? Son of a bitch, he was a mess, Jonas."

"I keep an ax in the truck. I was the one who made the noose for Henry on Dwayne Ed's orders. I think I would have asked to do it anyway because I wanted to fray the rope and keep track of it until they tried to hang him. I was hoping it would break before it would snap his neck. I tried my pocketknife, but the rope was too thick. The blade of the ax worked well."

Jonas stared angrily at Bonham and said, "Have you ever seen anyone hanged, Bonham? Shit, it's a mess if it's done right, and it never is. Done right, that is. To do a hanging right you have to have had practice, and who around here is going to practice something like that? My granddaddy used to talk about a couple hangings he saw way back when. He said on one the rope was too long, and the guy's head rolled into the crowd because it decapitated him. In the other, the rope was too short."

He looked defiantly at his friends. "Ya'll know what happens when it's too short?" They shook their heads in mute despair. "The guy chokes to death. And, if they don't put a hood on him like Dwayne Ed didn't want to do, you see it. His face swells up, and looks like it's going to blow apart, and he's kicking trying to find something to hang on to. Who wants to see that let alone be a part of it? And then, then, when the hanging's done, the body just lets loose—shit and pee and sperm all over." He looked at the women in the group, "I'm sorry, ladies. I'm not trying to be crude, but that's what hanging is—crude. It's like the death is so degrading, the body protests it and craps itself up to match the degradation."

He asked again, "Who wants to see that? And, who would want to do that to Henry? He was our friend, and he got a bum rap. It wasn't fair what war did to him, and it sure wasn't fair to kill him—especially like that. It was sick, just another sick thing that Dwayne Ed was going to do.

"So, yeah, I tried to stop it. I tried to make the noose, so it would break. Poor Henry. I don't even know what happened to him. For all I know, those asshole bigots from the North might've gotten him. I hope not." Jonas gasped in a breath almost like a sob as he hung his head down.

After a few seconds, he lifted his head and faced the group. "Then, when we got back to the ranch, and Dwayne Ed started talking about making Ruthie a part of all that hatred and cruelty, I just snapped. That ax was right there in the back of my truck, and it was so easy to grab it and put it into Dwayne Ed's skull. The mess, Bonham? If it wasn't going to be Dwayne Ed killed in a mess, it was going to be Henry. For my money, I'd rather Henry live, and Dwayne Ed go, if I had to choose."

He looked at Ruth's hand holding his tightly and then at her and said, "I'm sorry. Dwayne Ed has hurt you so much. I'm sorry." She placed his face between her two hands and kissed him gently.

"Were you the one who put the noose on Henry's neck? The one in chaps?" asked Louisa.

"Chaps? How'd you know about that? Were you there?"

Louisa nodded, and Jonas looked for confirmation from Bonham. "How'd they get there, Sheriff?"

"They stumbled on it. I knew for days that rally had been planned. I thought I knew when it would be, but Dwayne Ed moved it up a night. When these ladies came into the office to tell me how badly I was running the county, it punched me bad in my gut. They watched almost the whole shootin' match.

"In fact," he chuckled, "they started the shooting that broke up the party."

Jonas smiled slightly but was solemn when he said, "That was good, though. That rope might have stayed strong. I couldn't make it too noticeably frayed. Someone might spot it. That person in the chaps was Eddie. His father thought it would make him real involved in the Klan if he took part in a murder. Eddie was sick almost the whole day knowing what his father was going to make him do. I still think Eddie will be okay, but I didn't want Dwayne Ed running Ruthie's life."

Jonas stood up, scanned the circle of friends, faced Ruth and said, "I'm sorry. I let you down again."

Ruth wrapped him in her arms.

As Ruth held on to him, each of the members of the group, starting with Hugh, came up to Jonas and shook his hand.

Chapter 47

Emily and Louisa had just finished packing their bags when they heard a knock at the screen door of Atie's ranch house.

"Hello," called out Laurel as she opened the door to walk in. "Emily, Louisa, are you all in there? You home? We came by to see you."

Mother and daughter each grabbed a suitcase and came down the steps to see Phoebe, Laurel, Daphne and Eddie standing in the foyer of the house. Phoebe had a basket in her hands, and Eddie was carrying a cooler in his. Daphne had her hand on a giant mutt of a dog whose ear-to-ear smile matched those of his family.

"Well, well, if this isn't a wonderful sight!" laughed Louisa as she greeted the family. "Emily, it's Laurel's family, all of them."

"So, I see. And, who is this?" asked Emily pointing to the dog.

"This," said Eddie proudly, "is Derrick. I raised him from a pup. That day you first came over to the house to see Dwayne Ed—this is who you heard yelp. Jonas went to get him from Dwayne Ed; probably Dwayne Ed never would have seen you except Jonas was taking care of Derrick. Derrick's the neatest dog you could have." Derrick's massive tail thudded against the bare floor in agreement.

Emily approached Derrick with fingers curled in her outstretched hand, and Derrick laid his head against her hand. Laughing, Emily put both hands on the side of his head and stroked it. Louisa asked the family to come into the parlor and sit, but they declined.

"We just came to thank you for all you did. We want you to know how much we appreciate your giving our lives back to us," began Laurel.

"No, we didn't do anything," started Louisa. "If anything, we were a catalyst. You were all so concerned about looking out for each other, it had to happen sooner or later. It makes more sense that way because you couldn't have all continued to live like you had been. We're just happy it happened while you all can still enjoy each other. Now, what are the plans?"

"First plan is to give you all this stuff for your trip back to Dallas," interjected Phoebe as she handed over her basket. Eddie followed suit with the cooler. "That's a long ride back there, so we decided you needed to have good cooking to accompany you. There's sandwiches and cakes and food in this basket and drinks and water in that cooler."

"No snakes?" asked Louisa.

"Nah, I imagine the snake festival will be winding down. There's waning interest in that kind of thing with all the awareness of ecology anyway. Rattlers are good for keeping the rodents down. Maybe there's a new crusade we can do, huh, kids?" Phoebe signed to Daphne as she spoke the words. "Now, that we've got Mom back, I've got to find something else to focus on."

"So, plans, what're the plans?"

"I think Daphne will live with us and go to the day program at the Easter School. Mom will move in with us, and Eddie will finish high school and then decide his future," Laurel began.

"I'm not going any further than Austin, to the University of Texas. Maybe even Texas Tech. I don't want to leave home now that we can all be a real family. I went and visited those schools while I was gone. Figured it'd give me something to think about besides being accused of murder," Eddie stated.

Louisa and Emily smiled. Louisa said, "A little different than a few days ago, huh?"

Eddie grinned with relief and nodded.

"So, you all are going to live on the ranch or at Phoebe's house?" asked Emily.

"Not in Mom's house," laughed Laurel. "That house couldn't begin to be big enough for four people. Why, Derrick, alone, would take up her living room. No, we're going to the ranch, but we're going to build a house for all of us. That old rattrap that Dwayne Ed lived in is a poor excuse for a house. It isn't fit enough for a den of rattlers. I think when that house is bulldozed, we'll throw a party. We've all got a chance at a new life together, and we're going to make the most of it. A lot of details to take care of, but it should work."

"We'll make it work, Mom," assured Daphne in her flat voice.

With the last hug in the leave taking, Emily admonished, "This time, Laurel, don't lose touch. I want an e-mail or a phone call or something at least once a month."

Laurel in a clinging hug agreed, "I promise. You're truly my best friend, Emily. I promise."

*   *   *   *

Louisa had just slammed the back hatch of the four-wheel shut when Sheriff McIntire screeched up behind the car blocking their exit.

"Louisa, Emily, wait," Sheriff McIntire called as the ladies walked to the front of the car.

"Well, well, the sheriff with the eagle eye. You come to escort us out of the county?" asked Louisa.

The Sheriff grinned. "No, I imagine you ladies, of all the ladies I know, can handle anything you'd come up against. You don't need me anymore.

"No, I want you to meet someone. Can you come back to the car?"

"This isn't some kind of trick, is it?" asked Emily. "You're not going to put us back in jail, are you?"

The Sheriff laughed as Louisa said slyly, "You know, Sheriff, you just missed Laurel. She and the whole family were here."

"I know," he said.

"You following her, now?" asked Emily.

"No. This was easy information to find out. She told me. When we went out to dinner last night." He raised his eyebrows and smiled broadly.

* * * *

As they approached the squad car, a robustly tall man emerged from the front seat.

"Hello, ladies. I wanted to meet you and thank you for saving my life."

"Your life?" Louisa asked.

"Louisa Daniel, Emily Kristich, meet…"

"…Henry Wade," they said in unison. "You're all cleaned up. What happened?"

"Agent Henry Wade," corrected the Sheriff.

"As in the FBI?" asked Emily.

"No, ma'am, as in the ATF."

"You mean you aren't a drunk?"

"No, ma'am, I try to avoid the stuff. This assignment made that a little difficult to do. I've had enough rotgut booze for twenty life times. I'm sticking to mineral water from now on."

"Henry and I joined the army together after high school. We were in the same military police unit for a while. I got out, but he stayed in a little longer and got out after the Gulf war. Then he joined ATF and now works out of the Dallas office. When I heard about Dwayne Ed and his gun running, I contacted him. He got moved out here temporarily, so he could help us out," Bonham explained.

"You mean no one remembered you?"

"Oh, sure, they remembered me. I got hurt in the Gulf and spent time recovering from that. People remembered I got hurt, but we, Bonham and I, spread the word that I got hurt really badly and had to spend much more time recovering than I did. We made it sound like I would never really get back on track. Seemed to embellish the Gulf story so I could go under cover would be a good idea. So, we did. It worked pretty well.

"If you two women hadn't come along at the time you did at that rally, I would be one gone gosling. Hanging around that bar gave me information that I could feed to Bonham here. Whenever he drove me home, he and I talked about what I had heard in the bar. Only I got fed the wrong date for that rally. That was a little too close for my comfort."

"Agent Wade, you wouldn't by any chance be married to Cindy, would you?" asked Louisa.

"None other, and we've got three kids. Now that this is over, I think I'll bring her on out here. I think she might like to see our friends."

"Did you know he was alive after the rally, Sheriff?" asked Emily. "Did you find him that night?"

"You two did such a good job of scattering that crowd, that all I had to do was sit and wait. If I hadn't been in the middle of that noose, I would have laughed out loud watching all those people running and tripping over those sheets. I found a bunch of mesquites and sat in the middle of them waiting for Bonham. Knew he'd have to come around eventually," explained Agent Wade.

Emily shook her head, "You just looked so drunk. Every time we saw you, you looked so different than the way you look now. We never would've guessed."

Henry good naturedly punched Bonham in the arm, "It worked. The plan worked. Just like those plays on the field. We're a team."

Bonham crossed his arms, smiled at Henry and nodded. "A team, what friends should be."

"How's Jonas, Sheriff?" asked Louisa.

"He'll be fine. We'll take care of him and keep his spirits up. He wanted to plead guilty, but Utley advised against it. Utley said he has many, many friends in Gold County."

"And, Mel? What about Aunt Mel?"

"We're sending her case over to the Grand Jury to investigate for fraud. There's not a whole lot that will happen. After all, she and Dwayne Ed are dead. If they were the only ones in on the scam, the case is pretty much dead."

"So, how does Eddie work in all of this?" asked Louisa.

"Eddie's going to be all right. It might be tough for while, but I'll be around to help. Eddie, Laurel, Daphne, Phoebe and I will work things out. I'll look out for them."

"I bet you will. Nothing will escape you, the ever alert sheriff," said Emily.

Bonham tipped his hat, smiled his cocky smile and said, "You got that right. So long, ladies. You gave us hell here in Texas; now go home and do the same in California.

"Oh, and, ladies."

Louisa and Emily, as they climbed into the four-wheel, glanced up at Bonham and Henry.

"Thanks. Thanks from all of us."

"The only truth in this book is that there is a state of Texas. The people, incidents and places scuttle about my head bumping themselves against walls of bone looking for a way out. This book is their exit."

www.ingramcontent.com/pod-product-compliance
Lightning Source LLC
LaVergne TN
LVHW091536060526
838200LV00036B/638